# FORGOTTEN PLACES

BY THE SAME AUTHOR


**NOVELS**

*Bridles Lane (West Country Trilogy Book 1)*
*Hills of Silver (West Country Trilogy Book 2)*
*Wild Light (West Country Trilogy Book 3)*
*The Devil and the Deep Blue Sea*
*One of Us Buried*


**SHORT STORIES**

*Moonshine (West Country Trilogy Prequel)*
*Goldfields: A Ghost Story*
*The Dutchman*
*Afterlife*

# FORGOTTEN

# PLACES

**A NOVEL**

# JOHANNA CRAVEN

ISBN: 978-0994536495

Inspired by true events.

EXTENSIVE
FORESTS

LAUNCESTON

NORFOLK PLAINS

WELL
WOODED

CAMPBELLTOWN
CAMPBELL
TOWN

OYSTER BAY

MACQUARIE
HARBOUR

CLYDE

OATLANDS

BOTHWELL

HAMILTON

RICHMOND

NEW
NORFOLK

NEW
NORFOLK

HIGH
ROCKS

RANGE OF WHITE TOPED MOUNTAINS

HOBART
TOWN

HOBART
TOWN

BRUNI ISLAND

PORT
ARTHUR

VAN DIEMEN'S LAND, 1833

*'Sacred to the genius of torture, Nature concurred with the objects of its separation from the rest of the world to exhibit some notion of a perfect misery. There one lost the aspect and heart of a man'*

Rev. John West
Historian and transportation abolitionist
1842

# PART ONE


## DERWENT VALLEY, VAN DIEMEN'S LAND

### AUSTRALIAN COLONIES

# I

There were ghosts in this forest. Perhaps she was already one of them.

She lay on her back, tangled in a faded tartan cloak. Her skin was pale, almost translucent. Shadows beneath her eyes.

*Yes*, thought Dalton. *Dead*. The forest had done the job for him.

He peered down at her. Long, spidery fingers, veins stark on the backs of her hands. Her hair was a mess of jagged brown curls that barely reached her shoulders; tufty and uneven as though they'd been hacked at with blunt scissors. Some clung to her cheeks and neck. Others sprung from her head like piglets' tails. A blood-flecked hand lay beside her chin.

The first white person he'd seen in almost eleven years.

He saw it then; a faint rise and fall of her chest. He knelt, one hand tight around the legs of the possum he'd pulled from the trap, the other gripping the handle of his knife.

No one could know of this place. Of him. No one could know he hadn't died when he was supposed to: eleven years ago in the heart of this wilderness. Out here, the trees were legs of giants; the ferns knitted together like brambles. Rivers carved the cliffs and the earth fell away without warning.

This was a place of thick darkness, a straining moon. Soupy fog and rain that thundered down the sides of mountains.

No place for a woman in a faded tartan cloak.

Perhaps the woods were shrinking, hacked away by convict axes. Attacked from the east. He'd come from the west. Knew there wasn't an axe in the world that could penetrate the bush of the western highlands.

Dalton put the possum down beside her head. Its glassy pink eyes caught the last threads of daylight.

He had a free hand now. He could shake her, wake her. Food and water and *thank you*. Or he could press the blade into that milky skin beneath her chin and never have his world invaded again.

Grace's eyes flew open. A scream caught in her throat. She scrambled out from beneath the wild creature and the knife hovering above her neck.

She spun around. *Where was Violet?*

"Where are you, angel? Violet! Are you hiding?"

The girl was crouching behind a tree several yards away, the hem of her pinny in her mouth and tears rolling down her cheeks. Grace ran to her. "I'm so sorry, angel. I don't know what happened. I just meant to rest. I—"

Violet grabbed a fistful of Grace's skirts and stared at the man. Stared at his knife.

"Stay away from us." Grace's voice was tiny. Dizziness coursed through her and made the forest twirl. She gripped the tree trunk.

A tall man. Hunched and bearded.

A savage? No. The skin on his bare chest was grimy and tanned, but she could tell it had once been white.

He picked up the dead possum and walked, his bare feet soundless on the faintly worn path.

And he was gone. Grace drew in her breath and tried to slow her racing heart.

The smell of wood smoke began to filter through the bush. And then, cooking meat. Her stomach lurched with hunger. She reached into the pocket of her cloak. A few oats clung to her fingertips. The last of their food.

She gripped Violet's hand and followed the threads of smoke. The man looked up from the fire as they approached. The knife lay across his knees. Blood on the blade now. Fur was scattered beside a chopping block. He had skewered the meat on two thin branches and laid them across smoking coals. Behind him was a crude bark and clay hut. Crooked and box-like. Barely tall enough for a person to stand.

A madman, surely. Who else could live in a place so devoid of humanity?

She ought to run. But they were five days walk from Hobart Town. Miles and mountains from the last settlements. Grace's steps were crooked and her pockets empty.

She swallowed hard. "Perhaps you might help us. We're ever so hungry. And my girl, she's, well, as you can see, she needs a rest and…"

He looked past Violet. Stared at Grace.

"We'll be no bother," she managed. "I swear it."

He backed away from the fire and stood at the edge of the clearing. Grace glanced at the skewered meat. She reached out and carefully lifted a piece from the coals.

The food slid hot down her throat. Her stomach turned over at the forgotten sensation.

When she looked up, the man was gone. She glanced at the hut.

A little piece of inside.

It felt easier to face the forest at night with walls around them, however flimsy they were. Walls offered at least the illusion of security against the spiders and snakes, the devil dogs with razor teeth, the savages who roamed this land like shadows.

She pushed aside the bark door. Inside was dark and windowless. The floor was damp earth, one wall filled with a rough wooden hearth and chimney.

The man sat on a stool beside a crooked table. A rifle leant against the wall behind him.

"Are we to stay here?" Violet asked in a tiny voice.

Grace glanced at the man, searching for some reaction. His face remained unmoved.

"We need to stay here tonight," she said, loudly, clearly. "With you."

He slid back on his stool until his spine was hard against the wall.

Grace ushered Violet into a corner of the hut and laid her cloak across the floor. "Lie down here, angel. Good girl." She glanced at the man, waiting for him to stop them. He stayed motionless, avoiding her eyes. Grace curled up on the floor and wrapped herself around Violet's body. The man leapt up suddenly and grabbed the rifle. He disappeared into the purple dusk.

Grace heard herself breathe loud and fast.

A sudden gunshot echoed across the forest. Birds shrieked. And then stillness as night crept over the sprawling woods.

She closed her eyes and tried to slow her pounding heart. Stay, and death at the hands of this man was a possibility. Leave, and death in the forest became a certainty.

# II

He heard breathing that was not his own. He sat, yanked from his dreams with a thumping heart.

The marines come to hang him.

Greenhill with his blood-slick axe.

But then he remembered.

Her.

Pale morning light pushed beneath the door. She lay on her side, chest rising and falling. He stared at her. More than thirteen years since he'd watched a woman sleep. A part of him longed to reach out and touch her. Instead, he drew the rifle close to his body. A little security. He was as afraid of her as she was him.

He was suddenly conscious of the animal blood on his toes, the mat of hair down his back. Aware of his ragged clothes and the stink of him. He pressed a hand into the wiry expanse of his beard and felt his leathery, dirt-encrusted cheek. Felt the hollows beneath his eyes. He was a terrifying and inhuman sight, surely. Only the most desperate of situations could have led her to ask for his help.

Dalton stood and pulled on a yellowing linen shirt. The woman opened her eyes. She sat, face foggy with sleep, and glanced at the hunk of bread on the table.

"May I?"

He nodded. She snatched the remains of the loaf and tore at it hungrily. Chewed slow and loud, savouring the sensation of food on her tongue.

*Yes, I know. An incredible feeling.*

"Thank you." Her voice was husky. She placed the last chunk on the table, nodding towards the girl. "For Violet." She frowned at him. "You don't speak. Why don't you speak? You know English then? You understand me?"

Dalton turned away.

"There ought to be settlements here. Hamilton. Bothwell. Have we gone in the wrong direction?" She began to pace. Her shawl slipped from her shoulders and tangled around her ankle. She kicked it away and tugged at her hair, making white beads of her knuckles. "Are we at least close to civilisation?" She clenched her jaw at his silence. "Get up and put your boots on, Violet."

She'd come too far west. Walked for days in the wrong direction onto the fringe of near-impenetrable bush. Four days or more to Hamilton and her limbs were twigs. No path, just brutal wet mountains laced with natives' spears.

She'd never make it. He could barely believe she'd gotten this far. Leave this hut and a hunger the likes of which she'd never known would take her over. A hunger that would quickly become madness. Her only hope of survival was to stay in that hut with him.

But he wanted her gone. This life wasn't made to share it with others.

She held out her hand for the girl. "Well," she said, the brassiness in her voice doing little to disguise her fear. "Thank you and all. Can you at least show us in the right direction?"

He pointed northeast and handed her a few strips of smoked meat. She nodded her thanks. Dalton turned away to face the emptiness in his hut. But, once she'd left, he stood in the doorway and watched until her grey skirts had vanished into the settling mist.

Before her, his thoughts were simple.

*Cold. Tired. Hungry. Afraid.*

A life without words, for what words were to be had in this nothingness?

The world Dalton couldn't see had stopped existing. For all he knew, Britain had turned its back on this place, leaving creepers to swallow the huts and gallows. Downpours to wash away the white man's footprints.

The emptiness of the land was beautiful. Never silent, of course; there was always the howl of the wind, the devils' grunts, the patter of rain, of ice against the thatches of his roof. Carolling birds as the sun rose and set. But devoid of words.

If he were to pick up a pencil, would the language he had once known come back? Would he remember the words he had used when he was among the living? Remember that once he had laughed and whispered and shouted the abuse that would see him thrown onto a prison ship?

In the afternoon, he thought to make more bread. Something to keep himself busy after the woman had set his mind rattling.

First, a fire. It had drizzled throughout the day and the undergrowth was damp. He whittled away the wet bark to find the dry hearts of the branches. He set a pile of twigs flickering on last night's ashes, inhaling the scent of wood smoke and damp eucalyptus. He carried the flour into the clearing and poured in the water from the pot he kept beside the woodpile. Stirred it slowly with a stick.

Had he impressed her with all this? The way he could make something from nothing? Bread from crushed seeds and river water. A fire from rain-soaked branches. House from a fallen tree.

Stay out here long enough and the bush begins to give up its secrets. Eat this berry, crush this pod. Dig here, lay a trap there. Instinct, they call it. Like the animals have.

Instinctive animals have no need for language, of course. But as he stirred the dough, words circled through his mind.

*Cold. Tired. Hungry. Afraid.*

He lifted the stick from the pot and ran its pointed end through the dirt, tracing letters beneath the blue gum.

*Greenhill.*

He stared at the word for a long time.

"That your name?" she asked. "Greenhill?"

He wasn't surprised to see her. Just surprised it had taken her so long to come back. How far did she get before she realised they were truly surrounded by nothing? Dalton stood and stamped out the writing. His throat felt dry and tight. Why of all the words for all the things on this earth was it *his* name he'd chosen to scribble first?

"No?" She chewed her thumbnail. "Then what?"

For near on eleven years he'd been a ghost, a dead man. Nameless and invisible. He didn't know if he could go back to being real.

He carved a careful 'A'.

Paused. Should he hide himself? Use another man's name? But perhaps if he gave himself his identity back, he could pull together some other pieces of his life he thought were gone forever.

A dreamless night.

His voice.

Careful letters. *Alexander.*

The woman gave a tentative smile. Those hacked curls danced around her cheeks. Dalton saw a sudden beauty that had not been there when her face was twisted in fear.

She took the stick. "Grace," she said, carving her name in childlike letters below his.

And for a moment they were children in the schoolyard. Lovers carving their names in a tree.

"We've nowhere else to go," she said. "I can't take Violet out into the open again. There ain't nothing out there. Just miles and miles of forest."

Dalton heard a grunt from the back of his throat.

"You've been most kind to us, Alexander. Violet and I are very grateful."

Such a strange thing to hear his name spoken aloud after so much time. How had she found some lingering scrap of *Alexander* within this wild animal? He glanced down at the scribbles.

Alexander and Grace.

Above it, his angry footprints where he had scrubbed out that name.

"Who's Greenhill?" asked Grace.

With a sudden swipe of Dalton's boot, the writing disappeared. He felt a dull ache in his chest. The ache of being Alexander Dalton again.

# III

Colonial Times, Hobart Town
Tuesday 11<sup>th</sup> December 1832

*'Ship News*
*Dec. 7: Arrived the barque* Duckenfield, *from England.'*

"Carry me," said Violet. She clutched a grimy rag doll beneath her chin, its one beady eye peering up at Grace. The stitching of its mouth had come loose and left it with a permanent look of bewilderment.

Grace pulled Violet into her arms, her legs and back aching. Last night's hot supper had brought back little of her strength. Violet wrapped her legs around Grace's hips.

"You're getting too big for this, angel." She walked slowly to the edge of the clearing, drowning under Violet's weight. Alexander disappeared towards the river.

Had she angered him by returning? Those grey eyes were hard to read. She'd eaten the last of his bread. Interrupted his silence. But surely he knew she had no choice. Surely he knew she couldn't take a little girl any further into the forest.

Five days, she and Violet had been out here. Five days since she'd escaped. She'd swallowed half a pot of paint so they'd take her to the hospital wing where the windows were unbolted for ventilation. They'd fed her castor oil and laudanum. Scrawled in her record. She'd made it out the window and over the gate before emptying her stomach on the edge of the Hobart Road.

There was a fogginess to her memories; the details lost in a drug-induced haze. She remembered little but the walking. The crunch of boots on earth. Back to Harris's house in Hobart Town where she'd plucked Violet from her bed. They'd buried deeper into the woods until the lights of the settlements had disappeared. Grace had woken to an otherworldly pink dawn, Violet curled up beside her.

She looked down at the pot of dough Alexander had abandoned. Should she put it to the fire? Did she need to wait for coals? She'd never been much of a cook.

Violet chewed the end of her blonde plait. "I'm thirsty."

Grace set her down and ushered her inside. Took the canteen from the table and handed it to Violet. She dragged a stool across the hut and used it to prop the door open. A rat darted out from beneath the table. Daylight flooded the room, making stars of the dust motes.

A crooked shelf was hammered high on one wall. Along it sat hunks of wood, finely whittled into human forms. Some were whole bodies; lanky legs, sunken chests. Others just smooth wooden busts, their features meticulously detailed. Eyebrows. Lashes. Buttonholes and ribboned bonnets.

Grace stood close, taken aback by their beauty. She reached out and ran her finger over a dimple in a woman's cheek. Her tiny, motionless eyes stared over Grace's shoulder. Beside her sat an old man with deep wrinkles and a crooked smile.

An exquisite talent. How could a man speak in grunts and go about filthy and half-naked, yet whittle such life into chunks of wood? Grace could sense the personalities of the people who lined the shelf. The seductive woman. Grumpy child. Cheeky old man. Such detail carved by those meaty black paws.

And then, at the very back of the shelf: seven wooden men. Each with beards and long, unkempt hair. Wide haunted eyes. Each so real she expected their chests to rise and fall with breath. Their tortured faces stared into her. She saw coldness, desperation. A little of herself.

"Grace," said Violet, making her start. "I want to go home."

Grace's throat tightened. She ran a hand across Violet's downy hair and kissed the side of her head. Her skin was pale and dirty.

"Papa will be mad when we get home so late," said Violet.

Harris would be looking for them, of course. Perhaps lost in the forest was the safest place for them to be.

Violet stared at the carvings and gnawed the edge of her finger. "I don't like the wooden men."

Grace squeezed her tightly to ward off her own sudden chills.

"I want to go home to the blue house. I want to go and see the sideshow again. I don't like it here."

Tears pricked Grace's eyes and she blinked them away. *No, my darling, I don't like it here neither.*

They had stepped onto this foreign soil beneath a blazing, exposed sun. Had sailed out of a wet London summer and watched the sea turn grey, then black, then become green and full of light. As they crossed the equator, seamen dressed as Neptune danced shirtless in the hot evening. And then down they went. Down, down, down to the bottom of the world.

Down to the land where her country sent its most unwanted. To the bottom of this prison colony with its roaring oceans and inland sea, neighboured by the great frozen world of the Antarctic. At the end of the earth, Grace was expecting ice and snow.

But when they stepped off the *Duckenfield* that hazy December afternoon— she and the twins and Harris, gripping hold of each other like they were trying to salvage some sense of family— she breathed the air and thought her lungs would turn to fire.

They were marched off the rocky outcrop of Hunter Island to a lodging house in Market Place, Violet clinging to Grace's hand, her sister, Nora, to their father's. All the migrants wore a slightly vacant expression as though they were trying to remember what bizarre twist of fate had led them to this place.

The wharf was lined with warehouses and taverns spilling dishevelled men onto the street. Half-built boats and whaling pots peeked out of workshops. Red-coated marines lined the docks, rifles across their backs. A Union Jack dangled from a flagpole, lolling in the hot wind. But this was no England. Here, the clouds were high and the sky was a vivid, cornflower blue. Men walked the streets in rolled up shirtsleeves and bare feet. Sunburned foreheads, peeling cheeks. Smells of sea and sweat and the minty fragrance of the great grey-green trees.

Grace squeezed Violet's hand. The motionless earth beneath her feet made her stomach turn. That same awful churning she'd felt as the *Duckenfield* slid out the mouth of the Thames. The hot wind swirled, blowing dust onto her damp cheeks. She swatted at the flies until she grew weary of it and let them settle in clusters on her back.

They queued for two hours outside the lodging house before being herded into a pen of a room with peeling plaster walls. The beds were sagging and covered in stained sheets. Mice scuttled across the floor. Grace wondered if those sent here on His Majesty's pleasure were being treated to the same luxuries as the free settlers.

She didn't sleep that night. Just sat up in bed, hugging her knees. There were no curtains in the lodging house and an orange glow from the street lamps lit the room. Beside her, Harris lay on his back, snoring in a deep, sweaty sleep. Violet and Nora were curled up at his feet in cotton nightgowns; their matching mouths open, matching eyelids fluttering. A fly crawled across Nora's cheek.

On either side of them were two more beds, each filled with people. The room stank of breath and hot bodies. Grace got up and wove through the maze of beds, stepping over drawers stuffed with sleeping babies. Below them, the street was almost empty. A policeman on horseback paced through the dust and a dog pressed its nose beneath a warehouse door. Through the open window, Grace heard the faint clop of hooves. An owl hooting. The sea slapping the docks. And between these frail sounds of life was a great, overwhelming emptiness.

What she would have given for sooty skies and dung-filled streets. For street vendors and Bow Bells and clunks and hollers and shrieks and the filthy all-night-ness of London.

*This will be a great adventure*, Harris had said, striding down the hallway of his house in Covent Garden and shaking the tickets in the air.

Grace had been drawn in by his excitement, the way she was drawn in by everything else about him. There was a foolishness in her she hadn't been able to see until it was illuminated by Hobart Town's orange light. A need to rise above herself, which had sucked her towards Harris like riptide.

Across the room, a bed creaked.

"What's the matter, Gracie?" Harris was leaning up on one elbow, his nightshirt sliding off his shoulder. The waves of his pale brown hair hung about his cheeks.

He climbed out of bed and stood behind her at the window. Wrapped one arm around her middle and traced his fingers down her arm. She shivered and pressed herself against his body, needing the familiarity of him. He pushed aside her long brown plait and kissed her neck.

"Come to bed. You need to sleep. Everything will seem better in the morning."

She closed her eyes at the feel of his lips against her skin. "You're right." She reached behind her and ran her fingers through his salt-hardened hair. "A great adventure."

She felt Harris's lips turn up against her neck. "That's my girl."

She looked out at the vast, foreign sky, glittering with unfamiliar stars. A thin peal of laughter rose from the drunkards by the docks. Grace leaned out the window, straining, straining towards that fragile sound of happiness.

# IV

As the sun drooped towards the horizon, Grace began to wonder if Alexander had left.

*Don't panic*, she told herself. She had the gun, the hut, the fire. Still, she felt a surge of relief when his footsteps crackled up to the clearing. He had hacked off the length of his hair and it lay sleek and jagged against his neck. His skin had been scrubbed free of the film of black filth. A tattered linen shirt clung to his wet shoulders, dark coils of hair escaping out the open neck.

A dead creature dangled from his fist— something rat-like, but larger, with the tiny front paws and pointed snout of a kangaroo. He flopped the furry body onto the chopping block.

"You caught that? Without the gun?"

He slid a knife down the animal's belly.

"You got traps set up out there?"

He nodded without looking at her.

"I was afraid you weren't coming back."

He pulled out a trail of intestines and flung them into the scrub. Grace chewed her thumbnail.

"You're wondering, no doubt, what in hell I'm doing out here with a six-year-old girl."

Alexander didn't take his eyes off the animal. If he truly had been wondering about her, he was damn good at hiding it. Grace watched for some reaction from him. A flicker of the eyes, a movement of his lips beneath that dense black and silver beard.

Nothing.

His expressions hidden, age hidden. Could have been anywhere between twenty-five and fifty.

He smacked the knife into the tree stump and took the head off the animal. His silence made Grace's voice seem louder, garish with its east London vowels, cutting through the slop, slop of his slaughtering.

"It was right foolish of me to come out here, I know it. But I had to run away. It's Violet's father, you see, in Hobart Town. He's treated me awful bad and I was so afraid of what he would do to the girls that I didn't think this through. I suppose I thought we'd come across the northern settlements if we kept walking. Somewhere I could keep Violet safe, then go back for her sister."

In her head, the escape had been the only hard part. She'd spent weeks memorising the attendants' schedules, committing the layout of the compound to her mind's eye. She'd given little thought to what would happen once she'd made it out that window. Surely it would be no more than a day's walk to the next settlement. With no money, she'd have relied on charity when they arrived, but she'd felt certain they'd find someone willing to give a bed to lost women and children.

But what was in her head was much different to the reality. She'd avoided the main road, so she wouldn't be caught. Had no thought it might have been the only road. The lights of the next settlement hadn't appeared when they were supposed to. The earth had risen. The undergrowth thickened and tangled. And the sun had dipped below the horizon leaving she and Violet lost in the dark with nothing but a pocket of stolen oats and flint.

Her first night in Hobart Town, Grace had feared the wildness of this land, but tucked up safe in the settlement, well that was nothing. This unclaimed forest was a place from a dark fairy-tale. A world of ghosts and shadows and nameless creatures beyond the reaches of her imagination. She'd made up names for them to try and keep Violet calm.

"That's just a curly bear. A golden goose. A wriggly worm."

One night became two, then three, four, five. Days of crawling through mud and clambering over the monstrous mossy corpses of fallen trees. Days of torn, bloody hands and aching feet. Hysterical tears and desperate prayers. They spent hours traversing what could barely have been a mile. With each day came the slow dawning of the expanse of this place. As the pile of oats grew smaller and their stomachs shrunk with emptiness, Grace saw that they would die out here. Her own foolishness would bring about Violet's death.

"I don't understand how there can be nothing out here," she told Alexander, pacing in front of the chopping block. "Where I come from you can't walk more than half a day without reaching another village. When I was a girl my sister and me once walked from Stepney to Cheshunt and back to fetch a flour grinder off my aunt. You been to London? Never? What are you, some country dandy? An Irishman? Took us all day to get there, mind. Got chatting with some lad who reckoned he knew our ma, but it turned out he was just trying to get up our skirts.

'Anyway, I'm damn glad me and Violet came across you when we did, what with your fire and your traps and all. We were nearly out of oats and then Lord knows what we would have done." She forced a smile, but he didn't look at her. He just peeled the skin off that creature like he was turning a coat inside out.

Grace pulled her cloak tighter around her shoulders. "This

land, it ain't like nothing I ever seen before. So wild, like even God never been here. You're the first person we've seen in four days. When I was a girl there were eight of us living in one room. Couldn't scratch yourself without getting an elbow in your face. I never imagined there was a place on this earth you could walk for four days and not see another soul." She glanced at Violet, who was sitting in the doorway making her doll dance on her knees. She swallowed hard. "These girls, they mean more to me than you could ever know. I love them like they're my own. I loved their mother too, and I promised her on her death bed I'd do all I could to keep her babies safe." She felt a stabbing in her throat as she thought of Nora back in Hobart with her father and the convict workers. "I couldn't get her sister out. Their father came home before I could get her out of bed. But I'll go back for her. I'll find some place safe for Violet and go back for Nora. I'll go back for her if it kills me."

Still nothing from Alexander. Suddenly she despised him; so cold and silent while she wrenched her heart open in front of that stupid slab of dead rat.

"Nothing then? Not even a nod? A cough?" She wanted suddenly to strike him, tear words from his lips. Her fists flew into his arm, pounding, pounding, trying to shake out an answer. He dropped the knife and grabbed her wrists. Grace struggled against his grip, then gave up, stilled. His grey eyes looked past her.

"I'm sorry," she coughed. "I'm sorry."

His grip tightened, then he released her suddenly, picking up the knife and turning back to the meat. Grace stumbled backwards, her breath short. She held out her hand to Violet.

"Perhaps we should leave you a while. Have a walk or something. Won't we, angel."

And so they walked, she and Violet, hand in hand along the narrow path worn through the scrub. Threads of late afternoon sun shone through the trees. The evening chorus of birds was beginning; a great wall of trills and shrieks and bells. The river roared to their left.

"Not the river," said Violet, her hand tensing in Grace's.

They turned and began to walk in the opposite direction.

"We going home now, Nanny Grace?"

She thought of Harris's vast rolling paddocks in Hobart Town; a place she'd never call home. He had bought the land before they'd left London. For two thousand pounds he'd put his name to fifteen hundred acres of the finest farming land on the edge of the settlement.

"Fifteen hundred acres, Gracie," he'd announced, the day he'd come home with the deeds in his valise. "All mine. Can you imagine?"

Now how could she imagine such a thing? Fifteen hundred acres? The words meant nothing to her. He opened the papers with a flourish.

Fifteen hundred acres. Covent Garden to Whitechapel.

How was it possible that a man who wasn't the king could own so much land? Even the richest men in London had houses jostling their neighbours for space on the street.

That was the allure for Harris, of course, all that property to his name. Heard of it from a friend emigrated to Sydney Town. Fortunes to be made in wool, in wheat, in land ownership. He spoke of it like it was a paradise across the water.

But when they came to that precious land, it was just miles and miles of coarse brown grass and tangled, wiry scrub. The forest pushed onto the western edge of their land; a vast bank of ancient, gnarled tress they were too afraid to venture into.

On the edge of the property, close to the dirt road, Harris strung a sheet of canvas from a tree and hammered three edges into the earth.

Home.

Grace had grown up drinking from the drains in Stepney and had never had such miserable lodgings.

"Well," she said, too brightly, one girl attached to each hand. "There sure is plenty of space." She didn't know what she had been expecting. But it wasn't this.

They spent the first three nights bathed in dust while the girls screeched themselves silly at the depth of the darkness. Grace took them outside to the rolling, black expanse of their father's land. Behind them, the mountain rose solid and lightless. Mosquitoes hummed around their ears.

Grace looked upwards. An eruption of silver light. "Look," she said. "It ain't darkness. Did you ever see so many stars?" No clouds for them to hide behind. No lamps to dim their brilliance. They sat with their necks craned, trying to count the things until she felt the girls go heavy in her arms. On the fourth night they found a snake under Nora's pillow and Grace demanded Harris take them back to the lodging house until his palace had a floor.

She never saw much of that floor, in the end. He had her sent away before the house even had walls.

She'd gotten far too close to him. She saw that with such clarity now.

She was seventeen when she became his wife's lady's maid; the most coveted position in the household that Grace, with no experience, had little right to step into. She didn't know a tiara from a turban, and the only curling tongs she'd ever seen were the ones she'd dug out of the Thames in the mud-larking days of her childhood.

For the mop fair, she borrowed a dress from the woman in the room above them who bragged she'd once been on the stage. It was a ridiculous pink powder puff of a thing with rosette sleeves that made Grace look like a wedding cake. It was inches too long and so tight around the shoulders she could barely lift her arms.

Her mother laughed as she sucked on her pipe. "What you playing at? You think anyone's going to hire you looking like that?" She gave a loud, wet cough. "God made a place for everyone. And I'm sorry to say it, my treasure, but you're stuck down here with your old ma."

Grace said nothing. She'd argue with her mother after she'd proved her wrong. She went into the street and peered at her reflection in a shop window. Crammed her hair beneath a ratty straw bonnet and practiced the smile a man had once told her had made him forget where he was going.

She'd settle for washerwoman, be overjoyed with scullery maid. Anything that might get her out of the leaky lodging house and the bed crawling with her sister's snotty fingers. Anything to prove God had a damn better place in mind for her than this.

She stood among the other job seekers with their pressed aprons and *how do you do, my lady*s. Watched them thrust glowing references into the hands of wealthy employers. She'd be going home to Stepney tonight for certain. Back to stale bread and the sticky-handed monster God had deemed she share a bed with.

But then, there he was, Mr James Harris, the young customs attorney after a lady's maid for his new wife. He had a jawline like a Roman statue and eyes that shone like pebbles in the rain. He wore a dark blue frock coat and a tie of silver silk. Grace flashed her most disorienting smile.

Harris took off his top hat and rubbed his freshly shaved cheek. "You have experience?"

"Oh, yes sir. Of course."

His lips turned up. "Are you lying?"

"Yes sir, I am. Whatever gave it away?"

Harris laughed and looked her up and down. His grin widened as he took in the pink monstrosity of her gown.

Grace's cheeks flushed. Her eyes hardened. "I got no experience, sir, but you'll not find anyone who wants to work as much as I do. And you'll not find anyone who'll learn half as fast as me."

Harris tilted his head. His eyes met hers and something passed between them. "You'll be good for my wife," he said with a gentle smile. "She has a knack of taking life a little too seriously."

Gratitude flooded over her. She curtseyed low. "Thank you, sir. Thank you. You ain't going to regret it."

It wasn't until the first night of her new position, when a plate of mutton was set in front of her, that Grace realised she'd spent the rest of her life hungry. The gnawing in her belly had been such a fixture she'd ceased to notice it. As she felt her stomach press against her bodice for the first time in her life, she vowed she'd never go wanting again.

The Harris's life was filled with silk dresses, red wine and Beethoven. A great three-story terrace house on Maiden Lane with pale blue walls that made Grace think of the sea. Wind chimes in the entrance hall sung when a breeze moved through the house. Though Grace was lacing the gowns instead of wearing them and carrying the wine glasses instead of drinking from them, she was besotted with the luxury of her new home.

The lady of the house, Charlotte, was a great porcelain-doll beauty: fair and fragile, polite and sweet. She moved in willowy whispers of pink and blue silk. Next to her, Grace felt like a mess scraped off the bottom of someone's shoe.

But when the twins claimed their mother's life, Grace took her place indecently quickly.

Harris, lonely, full of brandy. Grace, love-struck at nineteen with no prospects of marriage. He called her beautiful and poured her a drink. Waited until the rest of the staff were asleep and led her upstairs by the hand.

Oh, she kept the promise she'd made to Charlotte and looked after those babies like they were her own. But she was in her husband's bed before the girls were crawling. Kept on as the twins' nurse, her pay bumped up to thirty pounds a year. Enough to buy her silence.

"We shan't tell anyone about us, shall we," Harris whispered, panting into her ear. And she smiling, nodding, unbuttoning. Pretending the secret was to protect the beauty of their love and not a gentleman's reputation. She told herself she pitied him; this generous man, widowed at just twenty-five. But there was far more lust and greed than pity in her. She'd seen James Harris as her step out of poverty since the day he'd plucked her from the mop fair. As his mistress, she saw an even greater chance. Soon she'd be the one in silk dresses, drinking wine from crystal goblets. The shadow of herself stealing from the markets to survive began to fade away.

He bought her silk petticoats that sighed when she walked. Sometimes she'd go without drawers to feel them slither against her skin. When there was no one around, he'd help her practice her letters, taught her to play 'Home, Sweet Home' on the piano. She'd sit beside him on the bench, his shoulder pressing against hers. She'd play with the flattest hands you ever saw, so he'd lift them in his own and curl her fingers over the keys. He sang along in a syrupy voice, pausing patiently when she found the wrong chords.

*Mid pleasures and palaces though we may roam*
*Be it ever so humble, there's no place like home.*

Harris was a gambling man; a frequenter of the whist tables at White's Gentlemen's Club. He prided himself on being a winner; on parading his overflowing pockets in front of his adoring mistress.

A dispute, he said. Came home in morning sunlight with his shirt untucked and his top hat bent. One cheek was red and swollen. The girls, near on five, sat either side of Grace at the breakfast table, kneeling up in their chairs and chasing slivers of egg around their plates. Thank the Lord they barely noticed their father stumbling in like a vagrant.

A dispute. Harris had accused the Earl of Wilton of cheating. Refused to pay the fifty pounds owed. Fist to the jaw.

"Just pay the man, James," said Grace. "Swallow your pride and pay him quick smart. Get him out of your life." She'd never stood up to him before. Never argued, never questioned. But even she knew fifty pounds wasn't worth another thrashing for a man as wealthy as James Harris.

He flung his hat onto the table. He stank of sweat and cigar smoke. Violet cowered in her seat as he strode past.

"It's not about the money," he said. "It's the principle of the thing." The goddamn principle of the thing.

The next night they came to the house; the Earl of Wilton and his footmen. They pushed past Ann at the front door and charged into the parlour. Harris leapt from his armchair. Grace and the girls were reading by the fire. Nora leapt into Grace's lap. Violet hovered at her shoulder, tugging at her shawl. The men shouted all at once, like they were ever going to come to any agreement like that.

One of the earl's men threw a wild punch. Harris ducked, cursed and swung at the man. He called for his valet and footmen. Grace tried to stand. Nora's arms were clamped around her neck, Violet dangling from her back.

"Get the girls out, for God's sake," hissed Harris. "Now!"

The men stumbled towards them, all curses and wild arms. A stray fist flew into the crystal vase on the mantle above their heads. Nora shrieked and down the thing came, crashing onto her sister's head. Grace felt the shards explode against her cheek. Blood poured from a gash on Violet's forehead and ran into her fluttering eyes.

Harris pulled off his cravat and pressed it to Violet's head. "Why didn't you get them out?" he demanded.

Grace felt rage bubble inside her. She left the door open as the doctor stitched closed Violet's tiny forehead. Let Harris hear his daughter scream. She flung the bloodied cravat onto his bed sheets.

*See what you have done. You and your goddamn pride.*

She saw regret behind his eyes.

Harris was an intensely private man. He kept his emotions walled-up behind polished manners and a deep honeyed voice. After the incident with Violet, he said little, but vanished to White's more often than before. *To ease the guilt*, he said, when Grace finally pried an explanation from him. To help him forget how he had failed his daughter.

He came home at midnight and climbed up to Grace's attic room; slid into her bed and pressed himself against her.

He was jittery and restless. He pulled his arms around her tightly. "I don't blame you for what happened to Violet," he breathed. And then, for the first and only time, said: "I love you, Grace."

She held her breath. James Harris had been her path to security. She'd not meant to fall in love with him. And yet love had found her, with an intensity that made her ache. She'd never spoken of it; sure it would never be reciprocated. She was a product of the Stepney slums, he a handsome lawyer of the gentry. She had no right to love him, or to expect love in return.

His declaration hung in the dark. Grace was afraid to speak, as though any words from her might scare his away. Instead she pressed her lips hard against his and breathed in his heady scent of rosewater and brandy.

She woke to an empty bed. Harris stood up from the breakfast table when she arrived downstairs clutching Nora's hand. He looked at her with distant eyes. Eyes that knew he'd made a terrible mistake. Eyes that said: *you are not their mother. You are not my wife.*

He cleared his throat. "The nursery wash-bin needs emptying, Miss Ashwell."

They slid back into their roles as employer and employee with alarming speed. Grace was sure she'd be out of a job soon. She starting asking around. Signed herself up for the next mop fair. Glanced at the job pages of Harris's newspapers.

But then he came home early one day, all serious and glowing about the eyes. He called Grace down from the nursery. She was sure he was about to let her go. Instead, he sat beside her on the sofa and took her hand. In spite of herself, she felt a fluttering in her chest.

And how his eyes lit up when he talked about that place. His Majesty's Australian Colonies. The land and the wheat and the opportunities, all those damn opportunities.

"A prison colony," Grace said, for her cousin had been sent out there for stealing a pair of shoes.

"Not just a prison colony. We've been there forty years or more now. Made a real civilisation of it." Harris filled a glass and brought it to his lips. "New land has come up for sale on the southern island. Van Diemen's Land. They say it's the best farming land in the colony."

"You don't know nothing about farming."

He smiled. "My friend Richard in Sydney Town has told me all about it. He's got himself a fine wheat crop. Thinks I could do the same. Get myself a few convicted men to do the toughest jobs. They say they're good workers. Happy to do anything after they've been spared the rope. I'm sure I've it in me to do this. And the change will do us the world of good."

Grace saw he had his mind made up. Couldn't say a thing to change it. She felt something in her throat clamp up. "I'll miss you then," she said.

Harris gave a gentle laugh. He squeezed her hand. "Gracie," he said. "I want you to come with us."

She lifted the glass from his hand and took a long gulp. "Bloody hell."

Her world went as far as the marshes in Cheshunt. A day's walk. That day, the Earth had seemed to go on forever. Harris's friend in Sydney Town and her thieving cousin, they'd just been shipped around the river bend, hadn't they? It was impossible to imagine the world going further than the snaking brown mire of the Thames.

Harris slid across the sofa so his knee pressed against hers. "It will be a great adventure. In a new world."

Grace managed a brandy-warmed smile.

Harris squeezed her knee. "You know, Gracie, in Hobart Town no one will think to bat an eyelid at you and I. We'll not have to hide any longer. Who we are, where we are from, it won't matter. We can live as husband and wife. Be a real family."

That was the clincher, of course. She saw herself in silks and lacey bonnets, walking on Harris's arm through his forest of wheat. No longer just the nurse. No longer just the mistress. The allure of it was intense. That great open land with all its opportunity.

He leaned in and kissed her, his tongue hot with brandy. "Think on it," he said.

But she didn't need to think.

Until they left London, it was all make-believe. They'd packed up the house, said their farewells, but they'd be back soon, wouldn't they? London was all Grace knew. How could it not be a part of her life?

But then, there they were in the cab to the docks; all their worldly goods packed into wooden trunks. The dome of Saint Paul's grew smaller and smaller until it disappeared into the bank of cloud. Out of the soupy sky, three skeletal masts appeared.

*Duckenfield.*

The weight of it swung at her suddenly. They weren't just going around the river bend. Her neck prickled. She tried to gulp down more air, her lungs straining against her corset.

Harris put a hand over hers. "A great adventure, Gracie. What we need."

Her heart banged against her ribs.

*Turn around. Please. I can't do this.*

She couldn't get the words out. What would he think of her? A coward, that's what. No sense of adventure. No seizing the bloody opportunity. He'd probably throw open the carriage and kick her out without even bothering to slow down. And then she'd be forced to crawl back to Stepney with her tail between her legs while the loves of her life sailed off the edge of the Earth. She couldn't bear to lose them. Couldn't bear to lose her life of pianos and red wine. Without Harris she'd be back at Leadenhall Market, pawning her petticoats and sliding stolen eggs beneath her shawl.

And so she got on that ship. Watched everything she knew fade into a white haze. Harris stood behind her at the gunwale and said: "I'm going to marry you in Hobart Town."

Grace concentrated on counting her breaths to stop herself from collapsing.

On and on Harris bleated about his *great adventure* between those hideous bouts of seasickness. When the ocean grew so big Grace thought it would swallow them whole.

Harris had unrolled the world map ceremoniously across the dining table and traced a finger along their route. A stop in the Canaries, rounding the Cape, across that vast stretch of unbroken sea. Atlantic Ocean. Indian Ocean. Southern Ocean.

Well, all those bloody oceans looked the same when you had your head between your knees coughing your kidneys into a bucket. She never imagined the world could go on so long. Never imagined they could travel so many days and nights and still have nothing around them but sea.

For four months they lived in a cabin smaller than Grace's attic room. Slept in bunks with raised edges that kept the sea from spitting them out in the night. They ate cabbage and pickled fish. Salted meat and suet. At night, Grace lay awake listening to the ship groan. She could hear the coughs and snores of fifty other migrants through the paper-thin bulkheads.

She longed to walk down the Strand and hear the chimes of Saint Mary's. Longed to sit in their parlour in Covent Garden with the girls squeezed onto her lap, books in hand. But with each watery mile, that life grew further away. The blue house drifted to the furthest edge of the world.

A great adventure.


She ought to have known how easy it would be for him to be rid of her. Even in an upside-down world where the land baked at Christmas, a man still wielded the power. A woman could only argue her point so many times before she found herself imprisoned.

Grace and Violet returned tentatively to the hut. Alexander was crouched by the fire, holding two skewered slabs of meat over the coals. The rest of the carcass sat in pieces on the chopping block.

"I'm sorry for my outburst. It's just that... well, I'm afraid."

He looked up.

"I thought it would be easier. Find the northern settlements and earn some money. Make enough to get me and the twins back to London."

Creases appeared in the corners of his eyes. A smile?

"What?" she snapped. "You think I'm mad for trying to protect my girls?"

He turned the meat.

"Well I don't care what you think." She clenched her jaw. She did care. Greatly. She knew what happened when people thought you mad. "I know now it won't be easy. I'm sure there are people looking for us. And I know what the forest is like. But somehow, I'll get us back to England. I swear it. Just you watch." She tilted her head and watched Alexander curiously. "You can speak, can't you? You's just choosing not to. Why? You afraid of what will come out if you open your mouth?"

He lowered his eyes.

Violet was snuffling around in the ferns beside the hut. Grace watched her pull the narrow leaves from the fern fronds and carry them in her pinny. The rag doll was stuffed beneath her arm; eye gazing at the clouds.

"I'm making a bed for Rosie," Violet announced. "A bed of leaves, like ours. Nice and warm cos she don't got no coat."

Grace smiled.

'She *does not have a coat*, Violet,' she imagined Harris sighing. She liked it when a little of the east rolled off the girls' polished West End tongues.

She stood, feeling useless. An intruder. "Perhaps I can do something to help, Alexander? Perhaps I can cook that for you?" She leaned towards him, but he held up a dirt-streaked palm, blocking her way. "Water," she said. "I can collect us some more water. Shall I fill the pot, then? From the river?" She snatched the heavy iron pot from beside the woodpile. Violet looked up from the ferns.

"I'm going to the river to fetch more water, angel," said Grace. "Do you want to come with me?" Violet's forehead crinkled. She crammed her pinny in her mouth, the leaves scattering at her feet.

"She's afraid of the river," Grace told Alexander. "She don't like how fast the water moves. Will you watch her? Just for a moment?"

He paused. Gave a slight nod. Violet's eyes widened.

"I'll not be long, angel. I promise. You stay here."

Violet stared at the swarthy figure hunched over the fire. She picked up her doll and hugged it to her chest.

When Grace returned, lugging the pot up the path, Violet was still watching Alexander like a hawk. She ran up the path and flung her arms around Grace's waist, Rosie tossed face down in the dirt.

Alexander lifted the meat off the fire and held it out to Grace.

"You don't got no plates?"

He scratched his beard, his forehead creasing in thought. He laid the meat back against the coals and wandered into the bush, returning with two small sheets of bark. Grace smiled slightly.

"There's three of us."

He marched back into the forest and returned with a third, smaller piece of bark. Grace laid the meat on the three wooden plates. The largest serving for Alexander. Smallest for Violet.

She looked up and he was watching; eyes right on her. For a second she saw behind them. Saw pity, compassion, the soul of a man. He turned away hurriedly.

# V

Conduct Record of Convicts Arriving in Van Diemen's Land
1804-1830

*Alexander Dalton,* Caledonia *1820*
*May 22nd 1821: Assault and beating his overseer in Oxley.*
*Fifty lashes and gaol gang labour for three months and to be*
*confined at nights.*


He followed her to the river. Several yards behind so he
might stay hidden. She bent to unlace her boots, slide off her
stockings. White knees, stick-thin calves.

She began to unbutton her dress. Dalton realised he was
holding his breath. There was something about the way her
fingers pulled at that row of buttons down her chest that made
him need to watch.

Curiosity, that was all. Just curiosity.

A woman's dress was such a novelty to him. A woman's
fingers. A woman's skin. He'd forgotten these things.

He felt a sudden urge to touch. He tensed his fingers
against the tree he was leaning on. Bark crumbled into his
palm.

She'd been here a week. No, closer to two. Had built
herself a bed where he could hear her breathe in the night. She
had him eating off plates and writing his name. Had left his
fingers tingling where their skin had touched. Fingers he had

thought too hardened to feel any sensation again.

This wasn't meant to happen. He was the only person in the world.

She stood knee-deep in the coppery water; her shift pooling around her like a lily. She pounded her petticoats against the rock with fragile white arms. Her grey dress lay on the bank. She had not chosen to wear such a dress. He felt this instinctively. Someone had given it to her; forced her into it perhaps. She was not a wearer of grey. She was pinks and blues and yellows. *Why the grey dress*, he wondered, listening to the *thwack thwack* of linen against stone. She stepped out of the water, her underclothes clinging to the narrow curves of her legs. What would she do, he wondered, if he came from the trees and put his hand to her face, or her arm, or the protrusion of her hips? Would she believe it if he said:

*I just want to remember? I just want to remember how it feels to be human.*

"What are you doing, angel?" Grace sung suddenly, seeking the girl out over her shoulder. She squeezed the water from her shift and stepped into her dress. She flung her wet petticoats over the mossy branches of a gum tree that arched over the river. Laughter. "You trying to dig your way to China?" She ran into the forest after the girl and Dalton was alone.

Her wet skirts fluttered in the breeze like sail cloth. The mud hadn't all washed out. They were becoming the colour of tea. Had they once been white?

*White petticoats*, he thought, and suddenly there was a girl attached to them. Blonde hair, with freckled skin and firm breasts. Maggie? Sally? Her name was lost to him. All he remembered was the velvety feel of her, his hands exploring every inch of skin.

Her breath against his ear, the soft sigh of muslin when the petticoats dropped to the floor. Yes, once he'd been just like any other man.

Grace's petticoats danced in the wind like there were legs inside them. Dalton stepped closer. Touched. He felt the coarse thread of them; saw the crooked stitching on the hems. Stains that couldn't be washed away. The grey of river muck, rusty bloodstains, great green streaks where the bush had left its mark. He felt hot and disoriented.

"What in hell do you think you're doing?" She yanked the skirts from the tree and bundled them into her arms. "In case you didn't know, it ain't the done thing to go about playing with women's underclothes."

He was vaguely aware what he'd done was wrong. Vaguely aware of these social outlines. He wanted to explain the way the rest of the world dropped away once you left it. Away, with its rules and codes and finely whittled etiquette.

"How long you been there?" she asked icily. "Come to watch, did you?"

*Yes, come to watch.* The pull towards humanity, towards her, was intoxicating. Terrifying.

He had to put an end to it.

Grace ran into the forest with the petticoats in her arms. "Look Violet," he heard her say. "Let's take this branch. We can sweep the floor with it, like we done in Hobart.... This one's a pretty colour. Why don't you put it in your hair? All right, angel, you pick one for me too. Mind the bugs now."

Dalton walked back to the hut and sat at the table. The nose of his rifle stuck out from beneath his sleeping pallet. He stared at it.

Look at her and her helpless predicament. He'd be doing her a favour, putting an end to her hopeless life.

He crawled towards his locker and opened the cartridge box. Five balls. His supplies were getting low. Powder flask;

far too close to empty. He poured powder into the rifle and slid in the ball. Slowly, carefully. He was out of practice.

*Three rounds a minute*, he thought suddenly. Something heaved itself up from deep in his memory. Once, he could fire three rounds a minute. And suddenly he was back in Gibraltar with sunburned cheeks and a rifle across his shoulder, beating rhythmic footsteps in tight-fitting boots.

He'd joined the army out of necessity. What love did a pauper from Kilkenny have for England? His dead mother surely rolled over in her devout Catholic grave, spitting *curse of God on you, Alexander. How can you risk your life for that vagrant King George?*

*Well, sorry Ma, but a man's got to eat.*

He'd been the son of a fleshmonger in Ireland, but as a military private, he was at the very bottom of the pile. He couldn't stand the state of this world where men were ranked like horses.

*Yes, sir. No, sir.* He'd never been much good at yes, sir, no, sir. Eat, sleep, shit when you're told.

"What am I, sir, your fucking dog?"

They had him pegged as a troublemaker from the beginning.

"Do we have a problem, Mr Dalton?"

"Aye, sir. A big problem."

Knocked out the captain's teeth with the butt of his rifle.

From the sun-bleached cliffs of Gibraltar to the battered shores of Van Diemen's Land.

*It is therefore adjudged by this court that you be transported upon the seas...*

The bush had let Dalton forget he was ever a soldier. A fat black chunk of the past he'd managed to bury. But yes, he felt very comfortable with a rifle in his hands.

He heard Grace's voice floating on the wind. "Look Violet,

see that bird? Ain't he a colourful one!"

He imagined putting her in the earth. He'd give her a proper grave, a proper burial. After all, it wasn't really her that was the problem. She'd just gotten in his way. Stepped into a space that was only made for one. Crowded him into the corner of this vast, empty land. And when there was another person about, well then there was that human desire to share. To say *all right then, Grace, you've told me your story. Are you ready for mine?*

Three rounds a minute.

He'd find her a nice spot by the river. Lay her out with her shawl beneath her head like she was just in the deepest of sleeps. Then he'd sit all night in the clearing and listen to the silence. Let himself sink back into a solitary stillness where his memories turned to dust.

He stood. The gun was heavy in his hand. He wished he'd done it the moment he'd found her. Then, she was just a body. Now she was a real woman, with a story behind her. It was harder this way.

Her head and shoulders rose above the green explosion of tree ferns.

He never fired the gun if he could help it. Who knew how far the sound would travel? Who knew who could be listening? Only if the traps were empty and there was no flour and the wild berries were staved off by ice. Or if he'd ceased to be the world's only living inhabitant.

The night she'd arrived, he'd pulled the trigger and sent the bullet into the sky so he'd not be tempted to use it. The echo had coursed through his body. Shaken him to the core.

He'd not gone far enough into the bush. He saw that now. The settlers were pressing themselves up against the edges of the forest. Red-coated marines and overseers with their bullwhips. He ought to have gone deeper, higher, further.

West.

But in the west, the forest rose and darkened. No possums stirred the trees. The birdcalls were few and distant. He'd seen that western bush and it was full of death.

A place man did not survive.

Grace watched him bring the rifle to his shoulder. One eye closed, the other squinting down the barrel. *Must be possums in that tree*, she told herself. Up there in those twisted grey branches.

She knew nothing about this man, she realised. Not a thing. A madman? Murderer? Or just a self-sufficient hunter?

"Violet," she whispered. "I want you to lie on the ground. Be as still as you can."

"Like the Mary statue?"

"That's right, angel, just like the Mary statue."

She sucked in her breath and stood. "Alexander? Are you hunting?"

He didn't move. He stood several yards away, poised liked a soldier in battle.

"Nothing in the traps then?" She glanced upwards. "What will you shoot? A possum?"

He opened his eye. Kept the rifle resting against his shoulder.

"Did you not see Violet and I down there?" She tried to push the tremor from her voice. "Let us get back safe to the hut and then you shoot, all right?" She stepped towards him until she was inches from the barrel. She swallowed hard and looked him in the eye. "You want to kill me, you'll have to do it to my face." She reached out and touched the cold metal.

Pushed it downwards. Alexander jerked the rifle and fired into the scrub where Violet was lying. Grace shrieked and dove towards the girl. Violet lay motionless, her eyes wide, fingers clinging to the ferns. Grace pulled her from the ground and squeezed her to her chest. Her hands trembled violently.

"You animal! Why do you want to hurt her? She's just a little girl!"

Alexander looked towards Grace's feet. She glanced down too. A thick seam of blood was edging towards her boots. She held Violet out in front of her, searching frantically for any injury. Alexander reached down and lifted the carcass of a wallaby from the scrub. He gripped it in his fist and stepped back over the tangled undergrowth. Violet watched wordlessly, clinging to Grace's neck. Blood from the dead animal dripped over the ferns.

"We've nowhere to go," Grace called shakily. "I'd leave you, but we ain't got nowhere else to go." Tears threatened to spill down her cheeks. "I'm begging you. Please don't hurt my girl."

Alexander looked over his shoulder and met her eyes. She looked back into them. The cinder grey of storm clouds. His cheeks and chin were covered in so much woolly black hair she could see little skin. But deep into those eyes she saw. There was loss in them and suffering and shame.

He walked back towards the hut, the wallaby carcass in his fist and the rifle bumping against his thigh. Grace kept her eyes on him until he disappeared. She and Violet clung to one another.

"Are you all right, angel?" she asked finally, her voice husky.

"I don't like him," Violet whispered. "I don't like the bear man."

Grace carried her to the edge of the clearing, afraid to

venture too deep into the forest, afraid to be close to Alexander. She heard him skin the wallaby. Smelled the meat smoking on the fire.

Night fell quickly; cold and solid. Violet lay in Grace's arms, blinking wearily. A blanket of clouds had drifted over the moon. Grace shivered. Early May. The edge of winter in this upside-down land.

She stroked Violet's hair. It was greasy and tangled beneath her fingers.

*My little angel. I'm sorry for all I've done to you.*

She kissed her forehead at the place the vase had struck her, feeling the dent of the scar beneath her lips.

"Nanny Grace?" Violet's voice was thick with sleep. "Do you remember the sideshow? By the river?"

"Yes, angel."

"What was your favourite thing?"

"My favourite thing?" She hesitated. Truly, she remembered little of the sideshow. The Palace of Curiosities had come to London the day after the earl had sent the vase crashing onto Violet's head. Grace remembered little but her blinding fury at Harris, her need to get the girls out of the house. She had vague memories of the twins in fur-trimmed coats, their mittened hands in hers. A trail of coloured flags, hairy men and tattooed women. The details were blurred by anger. And then, her own guilt: Violet complaining her head ached and Grace knowing she ought to have been home in bed.

That night, Harris had ranted and screamed, all red-cheeked and brandy breath.

"What were you doing taking her out, Grace? What in hell were you thinking?"

"My favourite thing was the mermaid lady," said Violet. "I liked her long hair."

Grace was glad she remembered the sideshow fondly.

"Perhaps when we go back to London we can visit her again."

Violet fell asleep, limp and heavy in Grace's lap. She wrapped the girl in her cloak and lay her on the mossy ground. She rolled her tired shoulders, stretched her neck. Violet was too big, too heavy. Grace couldn't carry her much longer.

She could hear Alexander clattering about in his wooden chest.

The hut was too small for three of them. Shelter for three, food for three. A much different sum than food and shelter for one. They were a burden to be shot at like wild dogs. But where could they go? She'd be locked up if she went back to Hobart Town. And heaven only knew how many more days until the forest cleared and showed the next settlement.

She'd wait out here until Alexander slept. Give him a little of his solitude back.

With each crackle of the undergrowth, her heart sped. The darkness was terrifying. She kept her eyes on the few flimsy stars, trying to drink in their light.

It must have been close to midnight when Alexander strode from the hut, his boots missing Violet's head by an inch.

"Christ! Be careful!"

Violet woke at Grace's screeching and crawled into her lap. She watched Alexander with distrusting eyes. He stared at the patch of earth where the girl had been sleeping.

Grace swallowed hard. "I'm sure it ain't easy for you to be sharing your home. And, truly, I appreciate all you done for us. Soon as I figure out what to do we'll be gone. I promise."

He held out two pieces of smoked meat.

"We ain't hungry."

Alexander nodded towards the hut. Beneath the door Grace could see the fire's orange glow.

"You want us to come in?"

He nodded.

Grace held Violet to her chest. "Did you mean to shoot us?"

Alexander gestured to the hut again. Grace hesitated. A throaty grunt echoed from the trees beyond the woodpile. She stood slowly, Violet's feet dangling down past her waist. Followed Alexander inside. The rifle leant against the wall.

She paused in the doorway. "Tell me you ain't going to shoot us in the night. Tell me I can trust you. Just one word. Please."

He opened the chamber of the rifle and pulled out the ball. He had reloaded while she had been outside, Grace realised sickly. He pressed the bullet into her palm.

She managed a faint smile. "Thank you." Hesitantly, she laid Violet onto their sleeping pallet and curled up beside her. "I'll not say a word," she promised. "Quiet as a mouse, I swear it."

Her hand around the bullet, she closed her eyes and tried to push her breathing into the same sleepy rhythm as Violet's. She heard Alexander poke the fire.

A shallow trust, but what choice did she have? Take away that shallow trust and she was completely alone.

# VI

Standing Orders from Lt-Gov. William Sorrell to Lt John
Cutherbertson, commandant of Macquarie Harbour
Saturday 8th December 1821

*'You will consider that the active, unremitting employment of
every individual in very hard labour is the grand and main
design of your settlement. They must dread the very idea of
being sent there ... You must find work and labour, even if it
consists of opening cavities and filling them up again ...
Prisoners on trial declared they would rather suffer death than
be sent back to Macquarie Harbour. It is this feeling I am most
anxious to be kept alive.'*

"Violet?" Grace burst outside, tugging on an ankle boot.
Dalton watched from where he sat on the tree stump, cannikin
of tea in hand.

"Violet? Where are you, angel?" She circled the hut.
"When I woke this morning she weren't in her bed. Have you
seen her?"

Dalton shook his head.

"You didn't think to wake me when you saw she weren't
here?" Urgency rose in her voice. "Where is she?" She strode
around the tiny hut again as if she could possibly have missed
her the last time.

"Violet!"

The calls turned to shrieks. Dalton looked down at the mud and the trails of prints leading out of the hut.

Grace's footprints. His footprints. No little girl's footprints.

Grace's eyes followed his to the trails of prints. She grabbed his collar and shook. Tea slopped across his trousers.

"You carried her! You took her!" She shoved him hard. "What have you done with her? I never should have trusted you!"

He let her punch and shriek, her arms, skirts, hair, all wild and flying.

She ran into the bush. "Violet!"

The shouting grew distant.

Dalton followed. Didn't know why. He wanted his silence back, but curse of God on her, his legs wanted to follow. They walked, then ran towards *Violet, Violet.*

When he caught up to her, her eyes had overflowed with messy tears. "She wanted to go back to Hobart. She thought her father would be angry at us for being late home. I'm so afraid she tried to find her way back." A deep, gasping breath. "She's just a baby. She ain't going to last a minute out there on her own."

Her suspicion of him gone.

Did she truly believe he hadn't carried her out of the hut and cut her throat? Of course, it was easier to convince herself he was just an irresponsible bastard who'd turned a blind eye as a girl lost herself in the wilderness. The alternative was to believe she was alone with a madman who had her child's blood on his hands. He'd have chosen to believe the easier option too, if he hadn't seen what men were capable of. Now choosing the easier option was just naivety.

They searched the entire day, following the river as it narrowed and swelled. Grace beat the brush with a long stick, scouring the land for any sign, any clue. Dalton followed wearily, sure they'd not find a thing.

"She's afraid of the river," Grace kept saying. "She wouldn't have come this way." But she kept along the edge of the water, thrashing at the reeds, calling her name.

When the light turned orange, Dalton stopped walking and pointed towards the hut. His stomach growled. No point them spending the night out there.

Grace's tears had stopped several hours ago, but at the suggestion of turning back, another great sob welled up from her chest. "She's gone, Alexander, just gone."

Yes, gone like a ghost. Left no trace; not a bootlace, or a button, or a thread of hair. But nor had she left a drop of blood, or scrabbled finger marks, or any cause for Grace to lose hope that she'd stumble back to them, disoriented, hungry and stained with tears.

Dalton pointed again.

"No. I can't give up on her."

He began to walk. What, did she think he was going to do the chivalrous thing and follow her to the end of the earth?

"Alexander," she said. "Please."

He kept on towards the hut, knowing how quickly the light would disappear.

Grace called his name. She ran towards him, staying close to his heels.

Her shoulders sank when they arrived back at the hut to find it empty. She paced, tugged at her hair. Dalton lit a fire in the hearth, though he was still hot from all the walking.

"I got to go back out," Grace kept saying. But it was dark by then and he was sure she knew it was no use. She chewed fingernails. Alternated between heaving, messy sobs and single, silent tears.

Dalton lifted a small stump of wood from the pile beside the hearth and sat on his stool. He began to carve. Grace stopped pacing. Dalton could feel her eyes on the knife; on its rapid back-and-forth *scrape, scrape, scrape*. Shavings settled at his feet. He began to forget himself in the monotony. He imagined the features on the wood as though they were already there. The determined eyes, narrow nose. Bird's nest of curls.

Then Grace said loudly: "We ought to be out there looking for Violet. Instead, you're sitting here carving dolls."

He put down the knife. Looked up at her. That's what she wanted, wasn't it? Some attention?

She gnawed the side of her thumb. "Your chimney. It's made of wood."

*Yes, pine.*

"A wooden chimney? That's the most ridiculous thing I ever heard."

He tore a hunk off the loaf of bread on the table, flicked away the ants and held it out to her. She shook her head. He gestured again, insistent.

"No," she said sharply. "How could I eat?"

Dalton tore the bread in half and chewed slowly on his piece. He placed Grace's share on the table.

"She must be so hungry. She'll not sleep out there without me. What will she do? It's so late. Must be eight or nine at least. Not that that means anything to you, I'm sure. Have you any idea what day it is? Do you even know the year?"

Stay out here long enough and she'd realise the hours and days were meaningless. Just names. A way of measuring the immeasurable.

He had kept track for a while; counting the days after they ran from Macquarie Harbour.

Escaped on a Friday.

Reached the river on a Monday.

He had left the other men on a Sunday.

After that there seemed to be little point counting.

He had walked alone through land that twisted into caves and mountains. His stomach was empty, his legs like lead. His heart was weary and hopeless. Each night, he had closed his eyes and waited for the end. A big part of him wanted to die. What was there to live for when he'd been thrown from society like a rabid dog? But the part of him that wanted to live was stronger. It kept him walking, kept him seeking out the lights of those mythical eastern settlements. Kept him placing unknown berries and roots on his tongue, gambling with his life for a meagre supper. A slab of kangaroo meat stolen from a native camp. The discovery of the purple berries. And each morning, another rising sun. Another reprieve. His body refused to give up. Dalton felt he'd been cheated out of death when he found the cattle duffers.

Delirious with hunger, he stumbled into the camp of a cattle-raiding ring on the Fat Doe River. They poured water down his throat and stuffed his mouth with salted pork until he could sit up and look at them. Six men; bolters and crooked emancipists who'd not lost the taste for crime. They took one look at Dalton's convict slops and decided he was the perfect man to join them.

Livestock plucked from the settlements, driven down the coast and sold in New Norfolk and Hobart Town. In their plans they saw riches; the wealth they had been denied in England. Dalton saw a ticket back to Macquarie Harbour.

So this is how a man makes his own world:

While the duffers are plucking cows from the paddocks, he takes other things from the farmhouses. A rifle and cartridge box, powder flask, knife and saw. An axe, rope for the traps.

He uses his own resources. While the men are snoring, he wraps up their boiler and cups in the shirt they gave him. He raids a farmer's shed in the middle of a thunderstorm. No-one will see him and even if they could, would they bother braving the rain for a hammer and a tin of nails?

Dalton left the duffers' camp in the middle of the night, stolen goods in a pack over his shoulder. He walked in the fragile light of the moon. The bush became a labyrinth of purple and green. The beginning of his own world.

So no, he couldn't have told Grace what day it was. The sun and stars kept time for him, beyond the restraints of ticking clocks and calendars. The colour of the sky and the changing winds told him of each year's passing. Eleven summers. Eleven autumns. Made this a cold night in the year eighteen hundred and thirty-three. The eleventh winter was on its way. Sit a little closer to the fire.

Grace rubbed her eyes. "She got Rosie with her at least. Her doll. I didn't find it nowhere. Least she got Rosie." She pushed her tears away with her palm. "What is it you're making?"

Dalton held it out to her. He had barely begun; one edge of the branch still rugged and dark, the other smoothed down to its soft white flesh. He'd begun to whittle her narrow chin, her long, graceful neck.

Could she tell it was her? Soon he'd have her sitting on the shelf with the others. He'd put her at the front, beside the farmer from Oxley who had given him a pair of boots in exchange for digging a ditch.

Carving was the one piece of his old life he'd allowed himself to keep. He'd not let himself think of the things he didn't have. They'd just stopped existing. Sugar. Tea. Whisky. *Good morning.* Over the years, his mind had stilled and, before long, it was enough to spend his days hunting, stripping bark, making flour. Watching the light change and the land swell and wither with the passing seasons.

But, over time, familiar faces had begun to appear from amongst his woodpile. The commandant of Macquarie Harbour with his dead slug smile and *fifty lashes*. That bastard of an overseer at Dalton's first convict post in Oxley. And there at the back were Pearce and Bodenham and the others. He'd carved them years ago in the hope that giving them some form might drive them from his mind. All seven of them, in the order Pearce had claimed they had died. Bodenham first, then Mather, the weak fuck. Greenhill with madness in his wooden eyes.

Grace stared into the glowing remnants of the fire. She felt the carved faces watching her. Judging.

*How could you lose her?*

"I got to go back to Hobart Town," she said. "Bring a search party."

Alexander's breathing was deep and even with sleep. He didn't stir.

Five days to Hobart Town. Five days back, if she could ever find the hut again.

Ten days at least, then she'd be thrown back into New Norfolk for her troubles. Violet couldn't last out there for ten days. She had to stay here and find her herself.

She stepped outside and pulled her cloak tight against the cold. She couldn't just stand still and hope. But where to even start? Perhaps if she were Violet's mother, she'd have been able to find her. Perhaps if she were Violet's mother she'd never have lost her to begin with.

She'd had her chance to be a mother. Life had stirred inside her before the twins were a year old. There was a woman, Harris had said, in Seven Dials, who could take care such things discreetly. Grace had left the blue house in tears and walked all the way to the lodging house in Stepney. She sat on a stool and cried while her mother puffed on her pipe. The house smelled of tobacco and piss and her childhood.

"And here I was thinking you had a few brains in that skull of yours." Her mother gave a loud, wet cough.

Grace had been bringing her mother a crown each week since she'd begun working for Harris. She knew it went mostly on booze and not the coal she'd intended it for. Grace always left Stepney with a quiet satisfaction that she'd crawled her way out. That she'd have walked the shit off her boots by the time she'd returned to Covent Garden. But now, as she sat opposite her mother and stared through the rag-patched window, she saw how easily her charmed life could topple.

"I love him," she said. And, in spite of herself, she loved the unborn child they'd created. Couldn't bear the thought of losing it at the hands of some witch in Seven Dials.

Her mother snorted. "You love him. You think that matters one scrap? He's a gentleman. You ain't ever going to be nothing to him but a good time."

Grace cried harder. She knew these things happened all too often; the man of the house making a stitch with the help. For all she wanted to believe things were different, she knew a girl who'd crawled out of these shit-infested slums would never be clean enough for a man like James Harris.

Her mother leant forward and grabbed Grace's chin in her hand.

"Stop that weeping. You want to end up on the streets with some snotty-nosed chavy hanging off your hip?"

Grace shook her head.

"Course you don't. So if your Mr Harris says he'll take care of it, you let him take care of it. Plenty more than most girls in your position could hope for. Don't know how lucky you are."

She returned to the blue house after midnight. Harris was pacing across the parlour, shirt untucked and waistcoat unbuttoned.

"Gracie," he said, "I was afraid you'd left."

The next day he sent her off with a pouch of silver to take away the shame.

The second time, six months later, the pennyroyal potion hadn't worked. Harris's woman had taken to Grace with a bowie knife and the resulting torrent of blood ensured she never need worry about bastard children again.

Losing her phantom babies was a dull ache compared to the desperate pain of Violet. She longed for that little voice singing along to her lullabies, the sticky hands at her skirts. Of course, she had no choice but to think of Violet safe in a bed of moss like a fairy. Couldn't let herself consider the alternative.

Violet had left no footprints. Had Alexander truly carried her out? Or had the previous night's sprinkling of rain been enough to wash away any trace of her? How desperately she wanted to trust him. But perhaps Violet was safer out there than she was in the hut with him. A gnawing fear sat in her stomach. Only two sets of footprints. The thought circled through her mind until she was convinced he was about to bury her beside Violet.

She ought to run. But what if she was wrong? What if Violet found her way back to the hut and Grace wasn't there? As much as she knew Alexander wanted his silence back, she had to stay.

She sat on the tree stump, shivering in the drizzle. Moonlight spilled across the tree ferns. She squinted, trying to make out shapes in the dark. The more her eyes strained, the more the shadows blurred and shifted. A moving branch? A native? Perhaps nothing at all.

She heard rustling in the bushes. Saw a flash of glowing

eyes. Two devils pushed through the scrub. Grace drew her knees to her chest, balancing on the stump. They came closer, drawn to the smell of meat. She ran into the hut and curled up on her side. Beside her, Alexander lay with his coat pulled to his waist. In the dim glow of the fire, she saw the interwoven trails of the cat splayed across his back. The white whip scars stood out against his brown skin the way a dewy spider web glowed in the sun. She tried to count the lashes, but they ran together, curled, meshed. She had an odd urge to touch them. Instead, she stared into the mess of it until the first hint of sun slid beneath the door.

# VII

Confession of Alexander Pearce
As recounted to Lieutenant John Cutherbertson, commandant
of Macquarie Harbour
1824

*'I was working with a gang at Kelly's Basin, under Overseer*
*Loggins. On the 20th September 1822 ... we made up our*
*minds to seize a boat and proceed to Hobart Town.'*

He found the bones poking from the mud. A skull, backbone, a few other scattered pieces. They were aged and yellow.

Human.

He'd kept her away from the cliffs the previous day, knowing she'd want to search them. He sure as hell didn't want to climb down there.

But by the second morning, Grace had found them herself. She must have gone looking again at dawn, because when she shook Dalton's shoulder to wake him, the light in the hut was still grey and pale. He rolled over. Grace's eyes were shadowy from sleeplessness, her skin blotchy with tears.

"We need to go down the cliff. What if she's fallen?"

Dalton stood wearily. He'd not slept much either. Had found himself worrying she would run into the darkness and try to find the girl.

He laced his boots and took a chunk of bread from the table. Turned to offer some to Grace, but she had already sprinted away.

He caught up with her on the edge of the escarpment. She knelt, peering over the edge into the hazy valley. Beneath her, the cliff fell away in columns like the pipes of a church organ. Dalton pointed west. Further around the ridge, the rocks opened out into an incline. Steep, but climbable. He turned up the collar of his coat as they walked. The back of his neck, having been covered in hair for the best part of a decade, was feeling the chill.

Grace tucked her skirts up and began to climb. She moved quickly, streams of pebbles shooting out beneath her boots. Twice, she lost her footing and cried out. Perhaps she'd fall. Dalton hoped it would be a swift death. Skull against rock. Not a broken ankle or something that would have him shooting her like a lame horse.

He reached the bottom first and began to beat his way through the web of creepers. The bush was wetter down here. Water trickled beneath his collar and soaked through the holes in his boots. He could hear the dull thunder of a waterfall.

And there, poking out of the ferns were the bones.

Dalton picked up the skull. Turned it over. A gaping hole at the back.

A fall down the escarpment?

Axe to the head?

*Flit flit* said a bird above his head.

"Alexander? Where are you?"

He dropped the skull and kicked the bones into the undergrowth.

"What have you found?" Her eyes were wide with fear.

He shook his head.

*Nothing at all.*

They walked along the base of the cliff. One end to the other, until their path was blocked by a great curtain of water. No Violet.

Grace's steps were crooked with weariness. He'd not seen her eat in days, Dalton realised. She turned her eyes to the steep, mossy slope and sank to the ground, skirts pooling around her like tar.

"I got to rest a moment."

Dalton pulled a handful of berries from a bush and handed them to her.

"To eat?"

He nodded.

"Not poisonous?"

He took one, swallowed. Grace placed one cautiously on her tongue. She winced with the bitterness and flung the rest onto the ground.

Dalton plucked them from the scrub and held them out to her. Food. A gift.

*Don't you know what happens when it runs out?*

He stood with his hand outstretched, the berries like flecks of blood on his palm. Finally, Grace took them, crammed them into her mouth and swallowed.

"Now can we go?"

He nodded.

Up she went, her long fingers curling around the rocks. Sometimes she would pause and look back over her shoulder at him. Dalton would point: *this way, that way,* and up they went like this until they both collapsed at the top of the escarpment.

Grace stumbled back to the hut and fell asleep at once, her skirts still tucked up and one bootlace undone.

Dalton paced back and forth across the clearing, thoughts banging against his head.

Bones in the gully.

The skeleton of a black? No.

Once he had heard their songs drifting through the bush and followed the sound for half a mile. He peered out from behind a tree and watched them shroud a dead man's bones in a hollow log. Their chants and sung prayers reverberated inside him. Human life at one with the wilderness. If the blacks could survive out here, so could he.

That burial was a thing of beauty, of respect. They'd never leave a man to rot at the bottom of a cliff. That was the domain of the Macquarie Harbour bolters.

Eleven years this September since they had run from the harbour. The timing, the decomposition was right. The place? After the first death, Dalton had run north. Perhaps the others had continued this way, southeast past the lakes and into the valley. That gaping hole at the back of the skull, well that was Greenhill all over.

Could be anyone.

But there was no one else out here.

In eleven years he'd seen no one but a few blacks.

Likelihood of it being one of those seven men? High.

So what? Whoever it was was dead. It mattered little if Dalton had known him or not.

His thoughts knocked together until he wanted to cry out.

He didn't want the bones near his hut. He'd done his best to forget those men. Forget what the worst of humans were capable of. How could he do it with a beaten skull lying at the bottom of the cliff?

Next he knew he was standing in the gully with the axe in his hand. He swung the blunt end into the skull. Bone splinters shot into the sky. He swung at the arms, the rib cage. And then with the blade, hacking at the legs, the spine. With each swing, he felt anger rise within him.

There was a beauty to being the only person in the world. When there was no one to judge, a man stopped judging himself. When there was no one judging a man's past, the past ceased to be. A man could kill another and learn to forget it, as long as there was no one there to hold him accountable. What do the trees and the birds know? What do they remember?

*A beauty, wouldn't you agree? You see now what you took from me when you thundered into my life?*

He swung again, again. Finally, he dropped the axe. He had reduced the skeleton to a pile of brown fragments. Could be bark now, or dried leaves. It would wash away with the next rain.

It had been many years since he'd thought of the world he'd left behind. Grace had brought a little of it with her. Started his thoughts churning again. Forced him to remember that once there had been an alternative to living like an animal. Forced him to remember what he'd done to end up here. His thoughts were forming with increasing complexity. Now there was no longer just *cold, tired, hungry, afraid*. Now there were stories, histories, guilt and self-loathing. A reminder of his own dark capabilities. He hated her for it.

He swung the axe. *Thunk* into that tree trunk. Into that mud bank. Into that burrow.

Anger at her, at himself. Why hadn't he been able to pull the trigger? In that second, as her chatter had stopped and she'd stared at the rifle, he had felt himself drowning in the silence. Found himself longing for another word from her. More garbled instructions to the girl. He hated the way she'd crawled beneath his skin.

His world had begun to feel small and empty, inhabited by dead men's bones.

With each swing of the axe, he imagined he was able to silence her. Her endless babble and burnt bread and her little vanishing Violet.

Animal rage. He welcomed the familiarity of it. Nothing of the past weeks had been familiar. He charged up the escarpment, wild sprays of rock flying from his boots. Beads of animal blood dripped from the axe blade. He scrambled over the top of the cliff and ran towards the hut. *One swing of the axe*, he thought. All it would take. He thought of her sprawled across her sleeping pallet, passed out with exhaustion and grief. She'd never even see him coming. Never have a chance to be afraid.

She opened her eyes as the axe arced above his head. She scrambled from the sleeping pallet, her scream sticking in her throat. He swung the blade into the table and felt the vibration charge through his body. He released the handle and kicked the table leg. Grace pressed her back against the wall. She glanced at the rifle leaning beside the door. She would need to pass him to reach it. Dalton yanked the axe from the table and hurled it into the clearing. It left a cavernous slash in the wooden surface. He hated himself for not being able to do it. Hated himself for considering doing it. He was afraid of how much he'd remember if she stayed, shaking his mind from its decade-long hibernation.

He upended the flour pot over the table and traced a finger through the mess, carving letters in the scattered black seeds.

*Leave.*

Grace kept her back pressed to the wall. Dalton smacked the table hard.

"I can't leave. What if Violet finds her way back? Why do you want me to go? Why now? I thought we was all right." He grabbed a fistful of her shawl and yanked her towards him. He felt heat rising from her body. Her face was inches from his. There were details that hadn't been there before. Faint pores, freckles. A fleck of wattle clinging to an eyebrow. Tiny white scar on her chin.

His lips quivered.

"What?" She leant forward.

*Leave. Go before I hurt you.*

He heard the words in his head. Felt them rising in his throat. He exhaled loudly, hoping the words might escape on his breath. Grace pressed a hand against his fist. His skin tingled beneath hers.

"Tell me, Alexander. Whatever it is. Just say it."

Dalton let go of her shawl and shoved her away. He swept his hand over the table, scattering the flour. The roof creaked and rustled.

"I can't leave," coughed Grace. "Not without Violet. If you want me gone, you'd best kill me too."

# VIII

Colonial Times
Thursday 29<sup>th</sup> October, 1863

*'It is ... very generally acknowledged that the New Norfolk Asylum stands pre-eminent throughout the colonies for ... the admirable mode of its management.'*

The rain began. Grace went out to search in the grey dawn, the hood of her cloak pulled over her head. She shoved her way through banks of dripping ferns and trunks running with silver water.

*Violet, Violet.*

But each call was answered only by the patter and drizzle of the downpour. She heard hopelessness creep into her voice.

By the third day, the forest was a great expanse of mud, the land beyond the river near inaccessible. Grace paced the clearing until her boots and cloak were soaked through, calling out into the shimmering mist. Finally, Alexander pushed open the door and took her wrist. Led her back inside the hut and gestured to the fire.

When, on the fourth day, the rain finally eased, she carried their dirty clothes and cooking pots to the river. The sky had cleared to a fierce blue. The water roared as rapids charged towards the falls.

She crouched in the mud at the river's edge and beat Alexander's shirt against the rocks.

Was she trying to prove herself indispensable, she wondered? Show him he couldn't survive without her? Prevent him from swinging the axe again?

She looked up edgily. He was stripping sheets of bark from the blue gums with his whittling knife; a replacement for the curling, wet wood of the door. Snowflakes of gold wattle clung to his chest.

Grace turned away and scrubbed the grimy sleeves, laying the wet shirt over a log to dry. She stopped suddenly.

A swirl of blonde hair in the river.

Her stomach plunged. She leapt into the water, her feet sliding through the pebbles on the floor of the river. She dove towards the swirling mass.

Not blonde hair, she realised sickly, but a thatch of yellow reeds. She grabbed them anyway. Fell to her knees in the water and lay her cheek against them. She felt their dampness, cold like the skin of the dead. A sob welled up from her stomach.

Her teeth began to knock together, arms trembling with cold. And suddenly she was back at the asylum in New Norfolk, strapped to a chair beneath streams of freezing water.

*Be a good girl now. You'll feel much better after this, I promise.*

The river snatched her. She clutched at the reeds, but they snapped in her fists. She was pulled along, down, under. White water, brown water. Leaves and branches and sharp twigs. She tried to stand, but her feet tangled in her skirts. Ahead, a low branch stretched across the water. She clutched at it desperately and managed to lift her head and shoulders out of the rapids.

She was following Violet's path. She knew it. Could sense her flying, terrified through the swells. Could sense the water closing in over her little head.

Grace felt an arm around her waist. Alexander pulled her tight against his body. She could feel his heart thumping.

"Is this where you brought her? She was here. I can feel it." Her legs flailed, tangled in her petticoats. "Let go of me. I can walk."

He kept his arm tight around her waist and dragged her upstream. And then a dip in the floor of the river. Alexander stumbled, losing his grip on her. Water rushed over Grace's head. She saw her then, little Violet, blonde hair floating around her face like a halo. Grace opened her mouth in a silent scream and the river rushed down her throat. And suddenly she was dragged through the surface, coughing, gulping air, more air, feeling herself go limp in Alexander's arms.

He hauled her onto the bank. Water streamed from her dress.

"She's here," she sobbed. "I saw her. I saw Violet." Her throat seized with tears. Alexander picked up his greatcoat from the riverbank and slid it over Grace's shoulders.

"She's in the water." She moved to stand, but he pushed her back to the bank with such force she didn't dare argue. He stepped into the water. The river hissed around his knees.

"There." Grace pointed to the place where the branch hung low. "That's where I saw her."

Alexander dived beneath the surface. Grace held her breath. She could see his hazy shadow moving along the bottom of the river. She felt dizzy with fear, terrified that he both would and wouldn't find her.

He resurfaced empty-handed, his hair slick. He dived under again, again. Grace held her breath in the same rhythm as he; filling her lungs to bursting as he plunged beneath the surface.

Each time he came up with nothing and each time she let herself breathe. Eventually, he waded out of the river and shook his head.

*I'm sorry*, said his eyes.

Grace wondered: *sorry for which part?*

He shook the water from his hair like a dog, picked up the clothes and pots and tucked the bark sheets beneath his arm. He began to walk, dripping, back to the hut. Grace followed slowly, his coat around her shoulders. Violet's watery face flickered through her mind.

It was all too easy to see things in this forest. Things that weren't there. She grappled with the image of that little face as the memory threatened to lose its sharpness. By the time she reached the hut she was unsure whether Violet had ever been there at all.

She sat by the fire with the coat around her, watching steam rise from the wet petticoats that clung to her legs. They'd drunk cups of wattle tea, cooked a possum they'd caught in one of the traps. Grace had sat her share on the floor and stared at it until Alexander had picked it up and swallowed it in one mouthful. He sat at the table, knife in hand and a hunk of wood in his lap.

"She's gone, isn't she."

Alexander met her eyes.

"I can't bear to think how Nora will cope. The two of them were so close. How is she to go from being a sister her whole life to being an only child?" She smiled slightly. "They were so different, you know. Violet's the shy one. Nora's always doing the talking for the two of them. She's a bossy little thing. A real chatterbox. Suppose she picked that up from me, right, Alexander?" She pressed her chin to her knees. "They were so different, but looked so alike. Both even got a freckle in the same place near their nose. It's awful hard to tell them apart when they got their bonnets on."

Alexander ran his palm over the chunk of wood in his lap. A tiny version of Grace watched them from the shelf now, beside a man with weathered cheeks.

"Will you carve Violet?" she asked.

Alexander raised his eyebrows. Shook his head.

"Please."

He sat for a moment with the knife motionless in his hand. Then he began to carve.

Selective absence of speech. An intriguing project for Doctor Barnes at New Norfolk, Grace was sure.

There were fifteen women on the ward in the asylum. Forty or more men on the other side of the compound. Convicts and free settlers thrown in together, labelled insane. The cell to Grace's left belonged to Molly Finton, who'd been plucked screaming from the Cascades Female Factory. On the right, a woman transported for life who'd slit her wrists in grief for the husband and son in England lost to her forever.

New Norfolk Insane Asylum. Twenty miles from Hobart so those on the outside could forget.

The building was a few years old at most, built by the government when the streets of Hobart Town became a gauntlet of madmen. A government asylum for government men and women. But always willing to take the money of a free settler with a troublesome mistress he wished to dispose of.


While Harris had watched his convict workers lay the foundation stones of his house, Grace had tried to make a game of it for the girls; tried to make their miserable tent liveable.

*The palace,* they called it. And the flap of canvas sheltering their convict workers: *the summer house.* Tree branches became brooms, their fire pit, a marble hearth. They hung great swaths of blue gum across their sleeping pallets so they could pretend they had bed curtains.

Yes, yes, they were just playing house. All a game.

"Why not go into town?" said Harris, like the fool hadn't seen the whores plying the docks or the bloodied backs of the men tied to the triangle. Grace had been at the wharf with the girls one day when a ship arrived full of female convicts; dirty, sorry creatures with bare feet and swollen bellies. Wrists and ankles bleeding from their shackles. Violet and Nora pressed themselves against Grace and peered at the women from behind her skirts. They watched silently as the prisoners were herded into a wagon bound for the Female Factory. Grace imagined she was the one in leg irons. Seven years' transportation for theft of an egg.

Slowly, slowly, the house grew up around them. And with it, the tension that had begun to build in London.

*Mrs Harris* they'd called her on the voyage. Who was there to argue? They were heading to a colony without parents or pasts. A few well-spoken lies could make a man and woman husband and wife.

But fifteen thousand miles of sea had not changed James Harris. He was the same starchy man in Hobart Town he had been in London. His promise of marriage withered and vanished. He found the whist tables in Wapping before their first fortnight was through. Came home bragging about his winnings. And when the owner of the neighbouring farm came to introduce himself, Harris was deliberate in keeping him out of the hut. God forbid anyone lay eyes on his rough-spoken, frazzle-haired mistress.

She'd let herself believe things would be different. That here in Hobart Town she'd no longer be a source of embarrassment. That *I love you, Grace* might become more than just a drunken mistake.

Van Diemen's Land, it turned out, was populated by half of London. Hobart Town was full of familiar faces. There was Harris's school friend William Bell, who ran the apothecary on Collins Street. The Allens from Islington who'd bought land out in New Town. Bloody Archie Tyler who they'd run into their first week in town. He may have been digging a ditch in leg irons, but it didn't stop him grabbing his crotch and yelling: "over here, Grace Ashwell, I'd know them tits anywhere."

And then there were the Wintermans; clients of Harris's from London. When they'd crossed paths leaving church one morning, Harris had turned white.

Mr Winterman clapped him on the back.

*James, my boy, small world, blah blah blah.*

His wife peered over her fan at Grace and the girls who were fidgeting in the heat. Violet had been moaning for weeks. Desperate to go home.

*The blue house.*

*The river.*

*The sideshow.*

Grace tugged her hand to make her stand up straight. "Stop your bleating this second." She hurried towards Harris, pulling the girls behind her. Waited to be introduced.

*My wife, Grace…*

"I'm dreadfully sorry, James," said Mr Winterman. "You've had a rough time of things haven't you. You'll let us know if you need anything."

Harris smiled thinly. "Very kind of you, but we're managing just fine."

Violet erupted into an epic tantrum; arms and bonnet flying. Harris grabbed Nora's hand, leaving Grace struggling with the screeching Violet. He nodded hurriedly to the Wintermans and marched back to their waiting carriage.

"He's dreadfully sorry?" Grace climbed into the seat opposite him and hauled Violet onto her lap. "Sorry about what?"

"Nothing."

"Sorry about what, James?"

Harris looked out the window, avoiding her glance.

"He's dreadfully sorry you're stuck with a woman like me? Dreadfully sorry you couldn't find no one better to come out here with you?"

Harris sighed. "Of course not. It doesn't mean anything. Just an old mess at work, that's all."

"You're lying."

He glanced at Nora, who was making handprints on the window. "Let's not have this conversation now."

When the girls were asleep, Grace stormed up to the table where Harris was reading by candlelight. She slammed the book closed. "You're ashamed of me."

"That's ridiculous."

"You didn't even introduce me to those people. Couldn't wait to get me away from them. How am I supposed to take that? You think I don't know shame when I see it?"

"Keep your voice down," he hissed. "The workers will hear you." He stood and marched across the single, dirty room of their new home. Reaching the other end of the tent, where the girls were curled up on their sleeping pallet, he turned, striding back and shoving Grace out of the way. He'd never lived in a place so small, she realised.

"You can't walk away from me here," she said with a bitter smile. "Fancy that. You carted us out here for all the bloody space, but look where we've ended up. Crammed together like pigs in a sty." She picked his top hat up off the table and flung it across the tent. It thudded against the wall and dropped onto their sleeping pallet. What was he trying to prove, dressing up like some cursed dandy in a place like this? His silk waistcoats were dulled with dust, shirts stained with sweat. She glared at him. "Your daughters hate it too."

Harris rubbed his eyes. "Grace, please…"

"It's true. You heard how much Violet's been whining. She hates it here. You just ask her."

"Grace, stop it." His voice began to rise. "Now!"

Violet sat up in bed and began to cry. "Nanny Grace?"

She forced a smile. "It's all right, angel. Everything's all right."

Harris sighed noisily. Violet cried harder.

"Look at her!" Grace gestured wildly. "Look how miserable she is! Tell Papa, Violet. Tell him what you told me. Tell him how you want to go home. Tell him how you want to see the sideshow again."

Harris whirled around. A sudden flash of white-hot pain as his palm struck her face. Grace stumbled backwards, blood blooming inside her mouth where her teeth had dug into her cheek. She glared fiercely. She had grown up dodging her father's fists, and when he'd died, she had sworn she'd never take such a thing again.

"Good Lord, Grace, I'm sorry. This tent and that damn couple and this blasted mess with Violet… It's just more than I can take."

Violet's sobs turned to shrieks. Harris swore under his breath and marched towards the girls' bed. He clenched his fist. Grace's heart leapt into her throat. She lurched at him suddenly and yanked his arm back.

"Don't you dare! You lay a hand on those girls and I'll break your damn neck!"

Harris turned, his cheeks flushed. He looked back at the girls, chest rising and falling with rapid breath. Violet's shrieks became terrified murmurs. Harris rubbed his eyes.

"I'm not—" he began. "I—" He reached for Grace's arm.

She shoved him away. Her cheek throbbed and she tasted blood. "Don't you touch me! Don't you even bloody look at me, you bastard!"

"How dare you speak to me this way?"

"I'll speak to you however the hell I like! I ain't your wife, as I know you're so damn happy about!"

His eyes flashed and Grace wondered if he was about to strike her again. She planted her hands on her hips, daring him. Harris glowered for a moment, then gave up and sank back into his chair. "To hell with you, Grace. Can't you see all I've done has been for your own good?"

"My own good? You lay a hand on me and tell me it's for my own good?" She'd not spend her life with a violent man. Wouldn't let the twins be raised by one. Wouldn't let them grow up as she had.

She crammed into the girls' bed and stroked Violet's hair until her tears stopped. Flies pattered against the inside wall of the tent. She could smell the salty remains of the pork she'd cooked for supper. Cicadas shrieked in the paddocks.

What a mistake she'd made by coming here. Believing Harris would give her the life of security she craved. She vowed then and there she'd see London again.

Harris's sleeping mat rustled. "Come on, Gracie. Come back over here. Please."

The thought of lying next to his hot body made her stomach turn.

"Come on. I've told you again and again how sorry I am. It won't happen again, I swear."

Grace snorted. She'd heard the same line from her father more times than she could remember. She'd stood for it then because it was all she had known how to do. But she was a woman now. She had the girls to protect. She would give her life to make sure they never knew the pain of their father's fists.

"I know things have been hard for you," said Harris. "Believe me, they've not been easy for me either. But we need to do this together."

"Together?" Grace spat. "You couldn't wait to hide me away from those toffs."

"I'm sorry. I wasn't expecting to see them."

"I thought we'd left our old life behind. But you'll always be ashamed of me, won't you." She rolled over and curled around Violet's body. "You needn't worry no more. I'll make sure everyone in this colony knows you're just a beard splitter who docked with his children's nurse. And who uses his fists when things don't go his way."

Harris sat up suddenly. "Grace. Please—"

She laughed coldly. "Don't worry. I'm sure such a scandal will make you well popular around the gambling tables."

Two days later, Harris rode into town and returned with a carriage. The girls ran out excitedly to meet him.

"We're going for a trip." His smile was forced.

Grace folded her arms. "We'll stay here if it's all the same to you."

"No!" whined Nora, grabbing Harris's hand. "I don't want to stay! I want to go in the carriage!"

Grace gritted her teeth. She was thankful Nora had slept through the whole ordeal, but her adoration of her father felt like a betrayal.

"You must come," said Harris. "I insist. It will do us all good to get out for the day."

Violet gripped Grace's arm and peered warily at Harris.

"Come on!" sighed Nora. "We have to go! Tell her, Papa!"

Harris smiled stiffly. "You heard the girl."

Grace sighed and climbed into the carriage. She sat with Violet on her lap while Nora scrambled across the bench and knelt with her head pressed against the glass. The carriage snaked through a chain of brown potato-sack hills.

"Where are we going?" Grace asked finally.

"New Norfolk," said Harris. "The next town to the north."

They rolled into a sleepy settlement, cottages dotting patchwork fields. Purple mountains rose in the haze behind the town. Men reclined shirtless on the riverbank.

The coach turned off the main road. It rolled towards a long sandstone building that rose from the sun-bleached plains.

Grace stiffened. "James." Her voice was throaty. "Where are we going?"

He avoided her eyes. "I'm sorry, Grace. This is for the best."

The carriage pulled into the gates and came to a stop beside the long verandah.

"Stay here," Harris told the girls sharply. He took Grace's arm and pulled her from the bench.

"James? What in hell is this?" She gripped the door of the carriage, but he took her by the waist and pulled her down the carriage steps. "A hospital?" The realisation squeezed her chest. "A *madhouse*?" She felt suddenly hot and breathless. Harris tightened his grip and led her up the gravel path towards the entrance.

"Please don't make a scene," he whispered.

"Don't make a scene?" Anger flared inside her. She glared at their convict worker, Samuel, who was driving the carriage. "Are you just going to sit by and watch while he does this? Help me!"

Harris jabbed a finger at his convict. "Stay where you are. This is none of your business."

Grace thrashed against his arms. "Why are you doing this? Because I won't whore myself to you any longer?"

"You know things can't go on the way they have. It's not fair on any of us."

"Then let me go! Give me my earnings and let me go back to England."

A man in glasses and a shiny brown frockcoat came out the front door, trailed by a woman in a nurse's apron.

"Good afternoon, Mr Harris." The man smoothed his moustache. He nodded at Grace. "Mrs Harris."

"It's Miss Ashwell," she spat. "He don't have no power to put me in here!"

"Her things are in the carriage," said Harris. Grace whirled around to see Samuel hauling her trunk from the back of the coach. When in hell had they packed her things?

Harris stepped close. "You're to stay here with Doctor Barnes a while." His voice was thin and controlled. "It's important you remember the way of things."

"The way of things? You think you can bring me here and turn me into a woman who'll just sit by and let you treat her as you please? Don't know what in hell I were thinking coming to this place with you!"

The doctor rubbed his chin. "You were right to bring her here, Mr Harris. She is quite hysterical."

Grace stared at Harris with glacial eyes. "You're trying to turn me into Charlotte."

His eyes hardened. He stepped back and pursed his lips. "Take her," he told the doctor, his voice stiff and empty of emotion. "Goodbye, Grace."

A cell the size of a cupboard. Force-fed castor oil to purge the madness from her body. Tied in a freezing bath to ease her sadness.

*Your husband has your best interests at heart.*

Once a week, Doctor Barnes would take her to his office, sit her in the leather armchair opposite his desk and speak in a honeyed voice Grace assumed was supposed to be calming.

"Tell me about London," he would say, puffing on his pipe.

*Tell me about London, Miss Ashwell.* Or: *let's start at the beginning.* In her four months of incarceration, they never seemed to get past the beginning.

"You were a nurse to Mr Harris's twin daughters."

"I was more than their nurse. I was the only mother those girls ever known. Was I just to stand there and watch when he became violent? You think I'd let the bastard put a finger on them?"

Barnes made a noise from deep in his throat. In a fleeting moment of optimism, Grace imagined him unlocking the door to her cell.

*Forgive me, Miss Ashwell, we've made a terrible mistake.*

"All right." She sighed. "I ain't stupid. What is it that Harris wants? Does he want me out of the way so he can hunt down another hedge whore at the gambling halls? Or does he want me in his fancy new house as a well-behaved little wife? Come on Barnes! You're taking his money! He must have told you what he's after. Why don't you just tell me and then I at least know what I need to do to get out of here. Then we can put an end to this stupid game."

"I can't do that."

"Of course you can't. Because then he'd stop paying you. You know as good as I do that Harris and I ain't married. He's got no right to put me in here." Her voice began to rise. "But you don't care, do you. Sixty pounds per year in your pocket. That's the sum, ain't it? It's nothing to Harris. Spare coin!"

Barnes took off his grimy glasses and wiped them with an enormous handkerchief. "Calm down, Miss Ashwell, or there'll be consequences."

"Shove your consequences! You expect me to be calm when Harris has me locked up like a criminal?" She sat back in her chair defeatedly. "The men with the money always have the power, don't they. The rest of us can just bloody well curl up and die."

That afternoon, an attendant led Grace into a room covered in murky white tiles. In the centre, a chair sat beneath a series of narrow pipes. Doctor Barnes stood with his back pressed against the wall. He smiled warmly.

"You'll feel much better after this, I promise you. Much calmer."

Grace stood shivering in her shift. Her heart sped. Nausea tightened her stomach. She tried to imagine which part of this might possibly make her feel calmer.

The attendant sat her on the chair and buckled straps around her waist and chest. Fastened her wrists to the arms of the chair. Fear shot through her.

"Let me up. I'll be calm, I swear it."

Doctor Barnes said nothing. Grace squeezed her eyes closed and tried to will herself away. The whir and groan of the pipes began from somewhere deep within the building. The sound moved through the walls and up above Grace's head.

And then the water. A thin, icy stream. Her hands clenched around the arms of the chair, shocked at the coldness and the intensity of the pressure.

*Just water*, she told herself. How could such a thing hurt her? But down it poured, stealing her breath, freezing and relentless, like chiselled shards of ice. Against her head, the water felt like needles, then nails, knives. She tried to move, but the straps kept her pinned to the chair.

She gritted her teeth. She wouldn't cry. Wouldn't scream. Wouldn't give them any reason to think her hysterical or weak.

Behind her eyes she saw a great expanse of stars. The room was washed away into blackness.

Molly Finton was playing the game the other way around. Weighed up life as a convict at the Female Factory and a life at New Norfolk asylum. Decided she could play the part of a lunatic.

"Sometimes you got to choose the lesser of two evils, you know." She looked at Grace across the sewing table. Spoke in a hushed tone so the attendants couldn't hear. "You know what I'm talking about, don't you, girl. You got more wits about you than the rest of the rabble in here put together. You don't belong in this place any more than I do."

"You think this were my own doing?" Grace snorted, pushing a needle through the chemise she was hemming. "No sir. Just got mixed up with a man who thought he could put a hand to me and his girls. When I didn't sit down and take it he threw me in here."

"Fucking men," said Molly. She leant across the table. Molly was twenty-five like Grace, but her skin was as leathery and wrinkled as an old woman's. "The bastards at the factory put me in solitary for a whole week. Left me in the dark and fed me nought but bread and water. When I come out, I pretended I was seeing ghosts. Started screaming in the night and keeping all the girls awake. When I waked up all the babies in the nursery one night they had enough and threw me in here."

"You got out of the factory," Grace said. "Do you have to keep up the act so good?" She'd been yanked from sleep many a night by Molly's howling. Hated being dragged from the bliss of unconsciousness.

"Got to keep it up, don't I? Or they'll think I come good and send me back to the factory."

Grace heard London in Molly's words and was hit with a bolt of homesickness. She'd kept away from Molly at first, the way she'd kept away from all the others. She wanted Doctor Barnes to see her apart from all the dribblers and shriekers and think, *well that Grace don't belong in here, do she?* But then Molly asked her for the cotton across the sewing table one day and Grace's loneliness got the better of her.

It turned out Molly Finton had grown up in the slums of Whitechapel, a mile from the room where Grace's family had lived. At seventeen, Grace had gone west to the mop fair and Harris's grand blue palace. Molly, east, into a world of pickpocketing in Rotherhithe where she found an undercover policeman and seven years' transportation.

Grace knew Molly's fate could easily have been hers. A step to the left instead of the right and she'd have been hauled out to this place on a convict ship. But what did it matter now? She and Molly; free settler and convict, and here they were side by side at the sewing table. Here they were with matching grey dresses and matching shorn hair, a matching wild anger that simmered beneath their skin.

"Sometimes I think you truly are mad," Grace told Molly. "Choosing the hell of this place."

"See this." Molly leant forward so Grace could see the thick brown scar on her neck. "At the factory they had me six weeks in an iron collar. Trussed up like a dog." She tossed her head indignantly.

"What d'you do? How come they put you in solitary?" But Molly wasn't answering. She just ran a hand through her unevenly cropped hair.

How fitting it was they'd hacked at Grace's hair here, her pride and joy. Curls she'd been growing to her waist since she was a girl. Harris had loved to wrap them around his fists and pull her into him. She'd never plaited her hair when she was in bed with him; just let it loose all over his pillow. Once, his hands in her hair was the best feeling in the world.

When she sat in that chair at New Norfolk there was a cold satisfaction to watching those curls pile up at her feet.

"This will cool your mind," the attendant told her as the scissors squeaked around her ears. But her short hair made Grace hot with anger.

*Look what you've lost, James Harris. Look what you'll never have again.*


Grace lay on her side and pulled Alexander's greatcoat around her. Sometimes she wondered if this hut was real at all. What if she'd passed out beneath the water pipes with shackles at her wrists and this strange silent man was nothing but a dream? She shuffled closer to the flames. No, the heat was too real for this to be a water-induced fantasy.

She watched the silver blade dart across the wood, tiny in Alexander's hand. A frown of concentration creased his forehead. Wood shavings clung to his bare feet.

He placed the figure of Violet by Grace's head. Its wooden eyes were level with hers. She squinted. The cheeks were too round. The hair too short. Eyes too close together. It had none of the personality of the other carvings. This was cold, empty.

"That ain't Violet. It don't look nothing like her."

Alexander's lips twitched. He flung it into the fire. They sat watching as the flames closed in around the carefully whittled face.

# IX

Mist hung over the bush. Dalton could smell rain in the air. He sat on the tree stump and opened the chamber of the rifle. Electricity gathered in the sky.

He tied a piece of cloth to a bootlace and fed it into the gun for cleaning. He pulled slowly, carefully. When he was a young man he had loved the feel of a weapon in his hands. It gave him a sense of power. That ability to control life and death. His captain could holler at him all he wanted, but if he pulled the trigger the bastard would die.

Dalton had trained at Gibraltar among men who'd fought in Spain, across America. Men who'd been at Waterloo. They'd speak of their adventures while they puffed on pipes and watched the sun sink into the water. Great men, great soldiers. Dalton, he had a great anger in him. The great anger of the poor and oppressed. The great anger of the Irish.

The sky tore open. Globes of water pelted into the mud of the clearing. Dalton lifted his face and felt rain explode against his skin. He was dimly aware the soaked rifle would be useless for days, but he didn't care. He couldn't leave the energy of the storm. He shrugged off his coat and shirt. Tiny rivers ran down his chest. He opened his mouth and tasted the water. So clean and cold. Christ, he felt alive. The bush smelled fresh and clean, as though the storm was washing away the terrors that had taken place among these trees.

Grace ran out of the hut and laid the pot and cups on the chopping block to catch the water. She was barefoot in her shift and cloak, her dress hanging from a tree branch after being washed that morning. There was a routine to her cleaning, Dalton had noticed. One session she would wash her dress, the next her petticoats, then her shift and stockings. She'd come to him with nothing but the clothes on her back, but did her best to stay clean. There were always clothes hanging up at the hut now, flapping in the trees in fine weather, or thrown over the chairs where they cast shadows that made him jump in the night.

Her decency made him behave less like the rabid dog he'd become out here on his own. With Grace about, he kept himself washed, dug a hole to relieve himself in, drank from a cannikin instead of burning his lips on the boiler. With Grace, he ate at the table like a human being, instead of gnawing at bones while he paced through the bush.

She pulled her dress from the tree branch. Dalton grabbed her wrist.

*Stay.*

She had to experience this storm. Had to see the thickness of this sky, the great forks of gold lightening. She glanced down in surprise at the hand he had clamped over her wrist. Unlaced her cloak and tossed it and her dress inside. She lifted her head and smiled, but her eyes didn't reach him. A private smile. What was she thinking? It was the first time he had seen her smile since the girl had disappeared. Her first acceptance there could be life after Violet.

Thunder rolled across the sky and a flock of blood red birds shot screeching from the trees.

Dalton watched the water run over Grace's eyelids and cheeks, through her hair. The skin on her upper arms was the colour of milk, a contrast to the tan on her wrists and hands. A contrast to his own leathery brown skin.

He moved towards her, but she turned away. She lifted the

pieces of the gun and carried them inside.

Rain had made its way down the chimney and soaked the ashes. No fire tonight. Their wet feet and the seeping rain were turning the floor to mud. They ate hunks of bread and drank the rainwater, sitting opposite each other at the table. Around them: the smell of soaked linen, wool, and the clean mint fragrance of the wet bush. Rain pattered rhythmically in the doorway. Rivulets of water drizzled onto the shelf and bathed the carved faces.

Grace in her petticoats, Dalton bare-chested. He was dimly aware he ought to have been cold, but felt lit up inside. He breathed deeply, enjoying the coarseness of the bread on his tongue.

"You got two stools," said Grace. "Why? Were you expecting me all along?"

Why two stools? He had wondered that as he had hammered together the second so many years ago. Maybe a part of him *was* expecting her.

She wrapped her fist around the handle of the knife they had used to cut the bread. Something tightened in Dalton's chest. He stood. His stool toppled and thumped against the dirt floor.

"Sit." Grace clutched the knife.

He reached down and lifted the stool upright. Sat.

She stood over him, droplets of rain falling from the ends of her hair. The bare skin on her neck and arms glistened. She slid the blade of the knife beneath Dalton's chin and used it to tilt his face upwards. His eyes to hers. When was the last time someone had looked at him so closely? He couldn't turn away.

She held his chin between her thumb and forefinger. Human contact. A precious thing.

Could she begin to imagine the coldness, the sense of

isolation that comes over you when you go eleven years without touching another soul? When the only life you ever feel is an animal thrashing in your hands before you break its neck?

She pushed the knife into the wiry hair beneath his chin. Dalton held his breath. What was she doing? That blade, it was far too close to his throat. Was she after retribution for Violet? For the first time in years, he felt a flicker of panic at the thought of death. He couldn't die now. He'd only just come back to life.

She slid the blade across his cheek. Whorls of black hair fluttered to the ground. Dalton saw it had become flecked in grey. He was beginning to grow old. What a gift. To sprout a grey hair had seemed so unachievable when he was waist deep in water hauling pines at Kelly's Basin. He was sure he'd be dead by twenty-five.

The blade moved over his chin. Dalton sat motionless, heart thumping, entranced by the touch of Grace's hands on his face and the wet, white skin at the top of her shift.

He watched the hair fall from his cheeks. What would he hide behind now? Did he want to hide any longer? He was afraid of what Grace might see.

He flinched at the thought and the blade caught on his skin. A flash of pain. Grace pushed her finger against the cut. A bead of blood hung on her fingertip.

Dalton touched his cheek. The skin felt silky, raw, like a gum that had just lost a tooth. The remains of his beard were scattered around his bare feet.

Grace smiled faintly. Wet hair clung to her cheeks and a thick, ropey strand had worked its way into the corner of her mouth. Dalton thought of reaching out and lifting it off her skin. He played that simple action out in his head.

His finger curling around her hair. His skin to her skin. A gentle pull. And she would say *thank you, Alexander.*

*You're welcome,* he would reply.

But when he raised his hand, her smile disappeared and the strand of hair came free. Her eyes fell to their sleeping pallets, which were soaked in black mud.

"Oh," she said. "Alexander..."

He wanted her hands against his cheeks again. There was so much life in her. He wanted to feel it. And so he said: "You missed a little."

Grace stared at him. The knife teetered in her fist.

Dalton was surprised by the pitch of his voice. Didn't sound like him. And that odd vibration in his throat, he'd forgotten that.

Eleven years since he'd last used his voice.

*Go n-éirí leat, mo chairde.* Coughed out to Kennerly and Brown, as they crawled their way back to Macquarie Harbour.

*Good luck to you, my friends.*

Grace kept staring, her mouth opening and closing around unformed words, as though he'd passed his voicelessness onto her. Suddenly he wanted his silence back. She'd ask questions, expect answers.

He stumbled out into the orange dusk. He paced across the clearing with his hands behind his head. The rain was cold against his cheeks and reminded him of their nakedness.

"You missed a little," he repeated, listening to the words slide off his tongue. His voice sounded tiny against the slapping rain. And then he tried: "Greenhill."

For those men were pushing hard inside his head, begging for attention. She could never know of them.

He came back inside. Grace was scooping the pieces of the sleeping pallets from the floor. The hem of her shift was covered in threads of brown fern, her toes black with mud. Dalton sat at the table and said: "Grace."

"Grace," he said again, as though testing his voice.

"Yes?" she said. "Yes, Alexander?"

She thought: *I see you now. You ain't no old man.*

Thirty-five, perhaps. She saw the sharp angle of his jaw, the wideness of his cheeks. His eyes seemed bigger, darker, dominating a face that still held the last flush and smoothness of youth.

His hand went again to his chin, feeling, feeling, reminding himself of what was there. He used his wet shirt to wipe away the stray bristles. Rain slapped into the mud outside the door. He pulled the shirt on and it clung to his chest. Grace's heart beat hard, desperate for answers, yet afraid to hear them. Her thumbnail went to her mouth.

"Don't know where we going to sleep tonight. The sleeping pallets all fell to bits. All this rain we had lately. Maybe we can take turns sleeping on the table. Won't be much comfortable but be drier at least. I suppose you're used to this. Where do you sleep when it gets so wet?"

Alexander's eyes fell to the mess of leaves and grass she'd strewn around the hut. Somehow she'd managed to make more of a mess than before.

She sucked in her breath. "Why you out here? You hiding?"

Nothing.

"You're a government man."

He nodded.

"No, speak to me."

So he said: "Yes."

"What d'you do?"

"Struck my army captain."

Grace reached tensely for her cloak and hooked it around her shoulders. She sat at the table and folded her icy feet beneath her. "Well," she said finally. "You done your time then?"

He shook his head.

*Oh. I see. So we hide.*

"How long you been out here? You got any idea?"

He answered in a rusty Irish lilt. "Eleven years."

She'd misheard, surely. "You been out here alone for eleven years? I don't believe you. You would never have survived." But as she spoke, she began to see the possibility of it. Water from the river. Berries from the trees. Meat from the traps.

She began to see a possibility for herself. A life in which she might never be forced back beneath the water pipes at the New Norfolk asylum. A life free of James Harris. If Alexander could escape and survive, then she could too. Yes, she believed him. She believed him because she had to.

"No-one has ever found you? Before me and Violet?"

Alexander shook his head. He pulled on his coat and climbed onto the table. When Grace thought she'd get no more from him, he mumbled: "No-one goes searching for a dead man." His voice was thin and hollow. Told her to ask no more.

# X

Conduct Record of Convicts Arriving in Van Diemen's Land
1804-1830

*Alexander Dalton,* Caledonia *1820*
*July 6th 1822: Wilful and corrupt perjury. One hundred lashes
and remainder of sentence to Macquarie Harbour.*

As hard as Dalton tried, there were fragments of the past
that refused to be forgotten. A human brain, he'd come to
realise, needed madness to truly forget. And so, with another
living person in his life, the story had begun to slip out.

Prologue.

Convicted for assault at Gibraltar Court Martial. Fourteen
years' transportation.

Grace had thought nothing of it, surely. In Hobart Town
this was every second man.

Fourteen years. At twenty-three, it was almost two-thirds of
his life. But then there were the stories of those lucky bastards
who'd made their fortune in this new land. Cast off their leg
irons for early pardons and ended up rolling in gold. He'd be
one of those men, he'd told himself. Turn up back in Kilkenny
and buy the whole bloody town a drink.

If he'd stayed with his first overseer in Oxley, perhaps he'd
have made it through his sentence. Managed a ticket of leave.

But he saw the stain of authority in that overseer and took

him down with his fists.

He was sent to Hobart Town to work in the chain gangs, carve this new colony with his bare hands. A miserable existence to be sure, but in Hobart, the convicts still felt part of the world. A working week. Church on Sundays. They had coins in their pockets, rum in their bellies. Friends to laugh with and women to ogle. Yes, their ankles were scarred from the shackles, but they walked the streets with felons who'd been pardoned and rewarded with land. For the convicts of Van Diemen's Land, Hobart Town brought a speck of hope that they could salvage something from their lives.

But then: an Englishman shuffling along in front of Dalton in the chain gang. A staunch royalist with a hatred for the Irish.

Michael Flannagan, with a mouth like a fucking moocher.

Dalton's ticket to the great green hell of Macquarie Harbour.

While they stood waiting for the chains to be locked, Matthew Brown whispered to Dalton that he was going to rob a man and buy his way off Van Diemen's Land.

"You'll swing for it," said Dalton.

"Aye, perhaps I'll swing. But then I'll be in God's kingdom instead of this Englishman's hell."

"I saw it all," said Dalton, when the police came searching for the thief. "I saw Michael Flannagan rob that man. Said he planned to buy his way off Van Diemen's Land."

They said all men had a chance of making it in this new land. Said even the Irish could rise above the lowliness of their birth. But when forced to choose between the guilt of the English and the Irish, it was always the bog-jumper who would swing.

Flannagan watched with a grin as Matthew Brown was led to the scaffold. Dalton to Macquarie Harbour with a flayed back and a certainty that any God he may have known did not exist in this backwater of the planet.

Dalton knew his lies, like all his crimes, had been foolish. He had never set out to live the life of a criminal. He'd just been cursed with a need to see his own perverted sense of justice done. Cursed with an anger that took away all sense and reason. Even back when he was marching in the King's colours, he felt he belonged somewhere far from civilised men.

Hell's Gates, they called the wild swells at the mouth of Macquarie Harbour. And when the ship bucked its way through the whirlpooling sea, Dalton felt the devil at his shoulder. He'd spent five weeks at sea without a hammock or coat, curled up on the ballast with thirty other men. The ship ploughed through winds that howled between the rigging and somehow managed to penetrate the hold. Days passed where they seemed to make no progress, the ship plunging left to right, up and down, but never forwards towards their destination.

Macquarie Harbour, for reoffenders. The most secure of all the colonies' penal settlements. At Sarah Island Penitentiary, the pounding heart of the harbour, great purple swells heaved themselves out of the Southern Ocean and made whirlpools of the cove. The rocks were bald and glistening, the bush thick as castle walls. Rivers poisoned with salt and decay. A prison perfected by nature.

When Dalton stepped onto Sarah Island and felt sleet sting his cheeks, any speck of hope he'd had in Hobart Town was gone. His new world was grey and brown, coloured only by rust-streaked rocks that rose jagged from the water. On one side, a chain of mountains. On the other, a screaming ocean.

This was it, Dalton realised. This was where he belonged; living on an island even God had forgotten, among people who were slowly turning wild.

Most of the prisoners were normal men when they arrived

on Sarah Island. There was some rage in them, some bad decisions, but they were able to laugh a little, tell a good story from home.

From Bill Kennerly, a poteen still that could blow your very eyes out.

From Tom Bodenham, a girl with tits the size of melons.

John Mather was a married man with three sons in Edinburgh. He relayed their entire lives to the men while they hacked away at the pines.

But the stories didn't last long. Hauling logs back to the boats like they were oxen sucked away the chatter.

One morning Dalton swam out to the boats with Pearce. Shivering beneath sheets of rain, they waited to be rowed to the logging station. Pearce turned his eyes to the grey sea.

"*Cad atá cearr leat*, Pearce?" What are you thinking?

"Leave him be, Dalton," said Greenhill. "He's due a flogging for breaking his axe. Don't feel like hearing your blathering, do he?"

Pearce's silence fell over the rest. Their thoughts turned from women and grog to escape or death. Suddenly that was all there was.

Escape or death.

Dalton had not been at the harbour two months and he knew his sentence would kill him. In a way, it already had.

Eyes would meet across bowls of porridge and in each man's glance was a dream of leaving Van Diemen's Land for a paradise across the water. They'd cursed at the rest of the world before they came to Macquarie Harbour. The poverty in London, politics in Ireland, tyrannical leaders in Gibraltar. But suddenly those places were heaven.

"The boat," said Greenhill, "gets left unattended." And then he was too careful to say more. The men's eyes went back to their porridge. Hands in bowls, bread chewed with open mouths.

*Look at us.*

Turning into animals long before they escaped.

*Is it really any wonder we did what we did?*

A drizzly day at Kelly's Basin. Eight desperate men waist-deep in water, arms aching from hauling pines. The boat unattended outside the coal miners' hut.

They eyed each other silently.

A chance.

Greenhill motioned for them to wade ashore. He used his axe to crack open the miners' chest. Sacks of pots, boilers, flint. Bread and flour. Salted meat.

"Take it all," said Greenhill. He emptied the boiler over the fire to prevent the miners making a signal. Smoke hissed and plumed. Dalton slung a sack over his shoulder. The food was heavy in his arms. He felt a burst of optimism he'd not experienced in years. A boat would get him off Sarah Island, past Hobart Town. Hell, if he rowed far enough, a boat would get him back to Ireland.

A rustle in the trees.

"Go!" Greenhill shouted. "Hurry!" Eight men leapt into the boat, water cascading over the gunwale. Bodenham grabbed one oar, Pearce the other. The boat crawled along the rocky coast; Sarah Island disappearing behind a wall of trees.

Columns of smoke began to spiral up along the waterline. The miners had built new signal fires, alerting the settlement of escapees. Dalton began to laugh. They were playing with death and it made him feel dazzlingly alive.

Greenhill grabbed Dalton's slops and wrenched them hard around his neck. "Shut your fucking mouth, flogger. You want them to hear us?"

Dalton swung furiously, but Bill Kennerly grabbed his arm before he could make contact. Greenhill stumbled and the boat seesawed wildly. Dalton glanced over his shoulder. A cutter was approaching from the harbour. Marines. Dogs. Rifles.

"Leave the boat," Greenhill said suddenly. He grabbed the oar from Bodenham and began to pull furiously towards the shore.

"You lost your mind?" spat Kennerly.

"We can't out-row them. I ain't letting the bastards put a rope around my neck."

"Where do you plan to go? There's nothing out there."

Greenhill pointed to the tallest of the purple mountains that cut into the horizon. "That there is Table Mountain. Other side is Hobart Town."

Dalton stood and felt the boat pitch. Five weeks at sea between the town and Macquarie Harbour. Surely Greenhill was mistaken. "He's wrong," he said.

Kennerly nodded.

But Greenhill and Pearce had thrown down the oars and were splashing their way to shore. Dalton swung the pack from the boat and followed Greenhill into the bush. Behind him, Kennerly's aging legs slipped in the ankle-deep mud. Dalton grabbed his arm and pulled him to his feet.

"Madness," hissed Kennerly. "You hear me, Alexander? This is madness."

As far as Dalton could tell, no one came after them. No one wasted their time. This was wilderness in which few could survive. Certainly not eight foreigners for whom the land was an unreadable maze.

Leave the fools to fight the forest and the darkness that lay within themselves.

# XI

She started making plans. The other girl. Nora.

Christ Almighty. He'd forgotten there was another one.

He woke to find her beating the dust from her cloak with a stick. Her petticoats were laid out in the clearing, drying in the bright morning sun. The boiler and canteen had been filled and a fire was crackling in the pit. Two loaves of bread lay baking in the coals.

There was something about the way she carried herself that morning. Her shoulders had straightened. Her head was up. There was a newness about her.

"I made a decision," she said. "I got to go back to Hobart Town for Nora."

Dalton raised his eyebrows. *Back?*

"I can't stay here forever. I'll go mad." She slapped the stick rhythmically against her cloak. "This forest does things to your mind, don't it. The way the light gets trapped, it makes you imagine things that ain't there. I imagined three or four times now I seen Violet coming out of the trees. But there's never anyone there." She stopped beating. "Don't know how you done it, Alexander. Lived out here so long. Don't know how you ain't barking at your own shadow."

He saw it then; what life would be like without her. Empty. Silent. Full of death instead of life. Just him, the bush and memories of dead men.

"You can't go," he said.

She raised her eyebrows. "I thought you'd be glad to be rid

of me."

Did she not remember the walls of trees and the freezing rain and the earth that sinks and rises with each step? Did she not remember the hunger? The pain in every muscle of her body? He had to admire her optimism, he supposed. Thinking she could flit across this savage island like she was crossing the street. But he couldn't let her go.

She didn't look at him. Perhaps she could see the foolishness of her plan. Perhaps she was afraid his eyes would reflect it back at her.

His voice was husky. "Where will you take her?"

She hesitated. "I'll try again for the northern settlements. I know now I came too far west. I'll not make the same mistake." She swallowed hard. "I know you're thinking I'm mad to try again. But you don't know her father. He's become a violent man. I can't bear to imagine how he's treating Nora without Violet and me there." She traced the stick through the mud, her confidence gone. "I tried to get them both out. I tried so hard. Violet, she weren't sleeping. She hated Hobart Town. When I came to get them, she was already awake. Had her pinny on quick smart. But I couldn't get Nora out of bed. Harris came back from the gambling houses early. Me and Violet had to run or none of us would have got away."

Dalton sat on the tree stump and poked at the fire. "Is that really what happened, Grace? You just left one of your precious girls behind?"

Her blue eyes flashed. "You wasn't there, Alexander! You don't know!" She bent the stick between her hands. It snapped loudly and she hurled the pieces into the scrub. "He threw me into New Norfolk. Do you know what that is? Do you? No? An asylum for the insane. He told them I was mad. And for what? For daring to stand up to him when he became violent! For not standing by and letting a man treat me however he wishes!"

Dalton said nothing. He was too out of practice with conversation to think of anything that might calm her.

"You can't imagine the things they done to me in that place. The cells and the water pipes and the oil forced down my throat til I was sick. I know how lucky I was to have gotten out without being caught. If Harris had found me in the house that night he would have thrown me straight back in. The colony thinks us married, so he has ultimate power over me. Any man can have his wife committed if he got enough money. I tried to tell them the truth at New Norfolk but the bastard just told them it was part of my affliction. I saw the true side of him when we came to this place. I got to go back and get Nora away from him."

She'd be lost in an hour. Dead in a week.

"You don't even have any oats left," said Dalton.

"You'll give me food and water won't you? And I've thought it through. This river leads to the Derwent, don't it? I can follow it back to Hobart Town."

His chest began to shake with humourless laughter.

"You think this funny?"

"The Derwent will lead you straight into New Norfolk. You want to be thrown back in the asylum? Although if you ask me, if you think you can get back to England with a pocket of bread, the madhouse is where you belong."

Grace glared at him. "I didn't ask you, did I?" She folded her arms. "I preferred you when you were silent."

Dalton batted the two charred loaves out of the fire. How many times did he have to tell her not to put it on the flames?

She kicked furiously at one of the burned loaves. There was such desperation in her eyes, he thought she'd charge back to Hobart then and there. He held her shoulders.

"They'll catch you if you follow the river. And if they get

you back in the madhouse, they'll never let you out."

She shrugged out of his grip and charged down the path towards the river.

*Don't be like that, now. I gave you a chance to leave. You ought to have taken it.*

He was sure somewhere deep inside, she always knew the girl wasn't coming back.

# XII

Hobart Town Gazette
Friday 6<sup>th</sup> August 1824

*'Pearce is desirous to state that this party, which consisted of himself, Matthew Travers, Robert Greenhill, Bill Kennerly, Alexander Dalton, John Mather and two more named Bodenham and Brown, escaped from Macquarie Harbour ... taking with them provisions which afforded each man about two ounces of food per day, for a week.*
*Afterwards they lived eight or nine days on the tops of tea-tree and peppermint, which they boiled in tin pots to extract the juice. Having ascended a hill, in sight of Macquarie Harbour, they struck a light and made two fires. Kennerly, Brown and Dalton placed themselves at one fire, the rest of the party at the other; those three separated, privately, from the party on account of Greenhill having already said that lots must be cast for someone to be put to death.'*

She walked to the river.
*Violet? Are you there, angel?*
How could she stop hoping for a miracle?
A bird chirruped above her head. She sat on the riverbank.
Another five days walk through the mountains. Her stomach turned at the thought. It would be different this time,

she told herself. Easier. She'd have food and water. No one chasing her.

No one to carry.

She felt an awful sense that she was abandoning Violet. Leaving her lost in this wild land, so far from everything she knew.

A flicker of white in the river. Grace stood. A piece of leather. Not Violet's. Her heart lurched with sadness. She'd take anything; a torn piece of dress, a thread of hair. Any clue, any fragment of Violet. Any meagre reminder that she'd once been here.

The belt had snagged itself on a rock. Grace picked up a thin branch and lay on her front to pull it from the water. It swung, dripping, on the end of the stick like a resigned, weary fish. She ran her fingertips along the stiff leather. An ammunition belt? She'd never seen Alexander wear this. Perhaps he wasn't as hidden as he believed. He would be furious if he knew another person had been here. She had seen that anger. The enormous gash down the middle of the table was a constant reminder. Still, it was best he knew. She rolled up the belt and carried it in her fist.

When she arrived back at the hut, Alexander had laid strips of smoked meat on the table. Steam was rising from the boiler.

"You're going back?" he asked.

She nodded.

"When?"

"I'll leave in the morning."

"And you'll not change your mind."

"No."

"Eat then. You'll need strength." He poured the boiling water into two cannikins filled with wattle seeds. Passed one to Grace. She wrapped a hand around it, the other clinging to the belt in her lap. Alexander sat opposite her.

"And you?" she said finally. "You'll stay here forever? Die alone in your hut and vanish into the earth?"

He nodded at the strips of meat. "Eat. I'll not let you go if you've nothing in your stomach."

She bit off a mouthful of meat. It was tough and tasteless. She washed it down with a mouthful of tea. "You don't wish for a little more from your life than to grow old and die out in the wilderness?"

"That's more than I could have hoped for. Once, I thought I'd die out here as a young man."

"Well," said Grace, "I think you want more, but you'll not admit it. Just surviving ain't enough for a person. They got to have a purpose."

"Perhaps surviving is my purpose. Perhaps we don't all have great dreams of revenge."

"Revenge?"

"That's why you want the other girl, aye? To take revenge against her father for throwing you in the madhouse?"

Grace stared into her tea. "No," she said finally. But she felt an ache of truth to Alexander's words. She squeezed the damp belt, desperate to change the subject. "At the river, I…" She put down her cup. A faint blurriness on the edge of her vision. She blinked hard.

"You what? Are you well, Grace?"

"I don't feel right." A sharp pain seized her stomach. Sweat prickled her face. She threw down the belt, rushed outside and vomited in the clearing. Alexander followed, holding out the canteen. She pushed it away, gasping. "What d'you give me? What was in that tea?"

"Nothing. It was the same tea you've been drinking since you came to me. You must have eaten some bad meat."

"We've been eating the same meat. Why ain't you sick?"

"I've been out here longer. My body's used to it."

"You poisoned me." Another violent pain in her stomach. She dropped to her knees in the kaleidoscope sunlight.

"Drink some water." Alexander knelt beside her and pressed the canteen to her lips. Water drizzled down her throat. She coughed it back up, along with what was left inside her. Her heart raced.

"What d'you give me? Am I going to die?"

"Of course not. It's a little bad meat, is all." His voice was distorted and distant.

"This ain't bad meat." She tried to stand, but her legs gave way beneath her. Trees swung in front of her eyes. Alexander carried her into the hut and laid her on his sleeping pallet. The heat of the fire was unbearable. She felt his fingers at the buttons down her chest. She thrashed her arms. "No! Stop! Get away from me!" She tried to force away the heaviness in her eyelids.

Alexander placed his hands on her cheeks. "Grace, calm down now. You messed up your dress. I just want to clean it for you."

The softness of his voice, his lilting accent made her muscles heavy again. She dropped her arms and felt him open the buttons of her dress, sliding her out of it. She shivered in her shift, though her skin was damp with sweat and her cheeks burned.

"I got to go. Nora…"

"Not today," Alexander said gently. "Not today."

Grace felt her cloak being laid over her body. A damp cloth against her face. The chalky smell of the fire, the hiss of his breathing. In and out. In and out.

Pink gill mushrooms.

*You ought to have been more careful, Grace. We live in a vicious land, where nature is against us and the men are animals.*

He knew of those mushrooms and the way they messed with your body as well as your head. He'd swallowed some early on, gambling with his survival on the edge of starvation. Had spent the afternoon curled up beside the river, puking out his insides and dreaming he was chained at the legs to a string of men.

Where were they taking her? Back to the asylum? Her eyelids were fluttering as she rolled about, pulling the sleeping pallet to shreds, groaning, clutching her stomach.

*Yes, I know. I'm sorry. The pain will pass.*

In a moment of lucidity, she opened her eyes and said: "I know you put something in my tea, Alexander. Why?"

She could have come up with a thousand reasons if she'd tried hard enough. Let her mind wander and think of how he did it to save her from Harris, from New Norfolk, the bush. Or did it out of jealousy, or love, as if he were capable of such things, any more than a dog that wags its tail and slobbers over the hand that feeds it.

"Why kill me?" she said.

Oh no, she had it so wrong. He didn't do it to rid himself of her; he did it so he'd never lose her. So he'd never be alone again.

She tossed and groaned and wretched into the pot he had placed beside her bed. Then she fell still, lying on her back with her cloak tangled around her legs.

Dalton dampened the cloth and ran it over her face. He slid it down her neck and across her white shoulders. One, two, three buttons at the top of her shift. He undid them carefully and drew the cloth over her chest. He rested his palm between her breasts, feeling her heart beat beneath his hand. Feeling her rib cage rise and fall. Feeling her life flood into him.

As night closed in, he crawled across the hut and threw a log on the fire. He noticed something white lying beneath the table. A bandoleer. He had worn one himself many times. His heart quickened.

"Grace," he hissed, shaking her shoulder. "Where did you find this?"

She rolled onto her side, mumbled a stream of rubbish and batted him away. The belt was damp. Had she found it in the river? The rivers flowed downstream to Hobart Town. This could not have come from the settlements. The bastards must have been here. Searching. For which one of them?

He stepped into the clearing and squinted in the dark for any signs of life. The bush was still. He could hear the river hissing in the distance. Could hear his own breath.

He took a step, then froze as twigs crackled beneath his boots. The noise seemed to radiate across the forest. He felt a pang of deep loneliness. He peered through the door at Grace, but she was asleep on her side; her flushed face lit by the fire.

Was there someone out there to see their light? To see the glow of silver smoke? Dalton pushed aside the bed of leaves on the floor of the clearing and dug up a handful of earth. He hurried inside and tossed it on the fire.

Blackness. Silence. The kind of stillness that falls over a place touched by death. From deep in his memories, Dalton heard Pearce's mournful lilt, singing to break the silence. So real he could swear the men were sitting in his clearing.

*Ma'am dear, I remember*
*When the summer time was past and gone*
*When coming through the meadow,*
*Sure she swore I was the only one*

*That ever she could love*

The saddest, most desolate sound he ever heard. A lone man's voice in the middle of an empty world.

Dalton wrapped himself around Grace's limp body. He let the blackness engulf him.

On the edge of sleep, he saw them. Seven men in convict slops, their faces as strained and desperate as they had been the last time Dalton had seen them. Hovering in his hut where the fireplace should have been. He scrabbled into sitting, yanked back to consciousness. His breath was hard and fast. He fumbled in the darkness for the flint and lit the end of a log. Had he been dreaming?

He felt watched. He stood and whirled around in the flickering light, half expecting to see a little girl with plaits and a dirty pinny. But no. There was a heaviness here that did not come from a ghost girl.

*A dream. Just a dream.* A memory crawled from the wilds of his subconscious.

His ma, she'd believed in these fantasy tales, God rest her soul. Fairies and ghosts and otherworlds. But not Dalton. He didn't believe in anything anymore.

Suddenly he wanted to be anywhere but this forest. Tie him to the triangle. Throw him in chains into the stinking hold of the *Caledonia.* Anywhere but here, where the past hung so thick in the air.

For eleven years, he'd managed to block out the things that had gone on in this forest. But Grace was right. There was something about this place. The threads of gold light, the cavernous shadows, they trapped memories. Imprinted whispers and screams in the atmosphere.

His hut felt unfamiliar. The table he had carved with his

own hand was suddenly strange, deformed. That sound? What in hell was that sound? And the grotesque shadows made by the firelight; how had he never noticed those before?

He blew out the flame and curled up close to Grace.

*You wouldn't leave me, would you? Not alone with these men.*

*But oh the false and cruel one,*
*For all that, she's left me*
*Here alone for to die.*

# XIII

Hobart Town Gazette
Friday 6<sup>th</sup> August 1824

*'Pearce does not know, personally, what became of Kennerly, Brown and Dalton. He heard that Kennerly and Brown reached Macquarie Harbour, where they soon died, and that Dalton perished on his return to that settlement.'*

It was two days before Grace managed to crawl from her sleeping pallet. The sky was vast and colourless, the bush dripping. Winter had descended on them while she was curled up with her fevered thoughts. Her eyes were cloudy and her back ached from days on the sleeping pallet. When she stepped onto the wet undergrowth, her feet turned to ice. Alexander was staring into the fire, the flames hissing and spluttering. He stood when he saw her and hurried to her side.

Grace pulled her cloak around her tightly. "I need to wash. What have you done with my clothes?"

"I packed them away for you. In the locker." He hurried inside and returned with a bundle of grey and white in his arms. "I'm glad you're well. I was lonely without you. Stay here by the fire. I'll bring you some water."

"No. I can walk." She snatched her clothes and set off towards the river, her feet sinking into the damp earth.

Alexander reached for her elbow.

"I don't have the strength to leave," she said bitterly, "if that's what you're worried about. Go away. I don't want you near me."

She walked to the river on unsteady legs. Untied her cloak and placed it on a mossy log with her dress and petticoats. She stepped carefully into the shallows and splashed her face, her arms, trying to wash away the grime of sickness. She plunged her head into the icy brown water and felt awake, alive again. From now on she would make her own tea, cook her own food. And when her strength returned, she would go for Nora.

She'd become a game to Alexander.

*Leave now. No, stay forever.*

Was Violet part of the game too?

She hurriedly pushed away such thoughts. How could she bear to think them when she was stranded alone in the forest with him?

A loud crackle from the woods.

"I told you to leave me alone." Grace climbed from the river and stepped into her dress, glancing edgily over her shoulder. She pulled on her shawl and cloak. Glimpsed a shock of red through the trees. A tall, broad shouldered marine pushed his way towards her. Grace stumbled backwards. The soldier held a hand out in front of him, as though she was a wild animal he was trying to tame.

"Miss Ashwell? I'll not hurt you. Everything's all right. Just come with me."

Grace turned and ran, her bare feet slipping on the muddy undergrowth. She heard the soldier calling out. A second voice.

Their footsteps grew closer. The mud beneath her feet gave way and she slipped into the shallows of the river. She scrambled out desperately, wet skirts tangling around her legs. A rough hand grabbed her wrist.

"Let go of me!" She made a wild swing for the man's face, but he forced her to the ground. She thrashed beneath his arms, shrieking and cursing.

"Calm down," the soldier grunted. "We're not here to hurt you."

And a second pair of hands was on her, pinning her ankles to the ground. She kicked hard.

"Get off me!" she shrieked. "You ain't taking me back to that hell! I ain't no lunatic!"

A sudden crack and the first man fell sideways, the stock of Alexander's rifle flying into the side of his head. Before the second marine could react, Alexander had pulled the trigger. A man trained to fight. The soldier fell across Grace's legs. She scrambled out breathlessly from beneath the bloodied body.

The two men lay on their backs amongst the undergrowth. One stared into the white sky, blood gushing from the side of his head and running into the river. The second looked to Grace with fluttering eyes. A dark stain crept across his middle. Blood was blooming from his mouth. Grace pulled off her shawl and pressed it hard against the bullet wound below the man's ribs.

"What are you doing?" Alexander emptied the balls from the dead marine's cartridge box and shoved them in his coat pocket. He picked up their guns.

"He's still alive."

He yanked Grace to her feet. "Get up. He'll be dead in a minute."

She looked up. The man she saw terrified her. His eyes were dark and soulless. His stubbled jaw was clenched and splattered with blood.

For weeks she had tried to convince herself Alexander was incapable of murder. Convince herself of his innocence. But in the glassy eyes of the soldiers, she felt herself take a step closer to the most dreaded of possibilities: that he had the blood of her little girl on his hands.

"You wanted them to take you back?" he puffed. "Is that what you wanted?"

She shook her head stiffly, afraid of the dark in his eyes.

He charged back to the hut. Grace followed hesitantly.

"There may be others." He threw open the lid of the wooden chest, pulled out the cartridge box and powder. He snatched the boiler and canteen from the table and wrapped them in a shirt. Into the bundle he crammed the last of their bread and smoked meat, along with his whittling knife. He tied the sleeves into a square package. "Get your boots."

Grace grabbed her shoes and stockings, too afraid to argue. She pulled them over her muddy feet and tied the laces with shaking fingers. Alexander shoved one of the rifles into her hands.

"Take this. You might need it."

She shook her head. He cursed under his breath and grabbed the axe from the chest. "Then at least take this." He thrust it towards her. The stained blade stopped inches from her hands.

She wrapped her shaking fist around the handle. "What are we doing?"

Alexander slung the package over his shoulder. He tucked his rifle beneath his arm and marched back out to where the soldiers lay. "We have to bury the bodies."

Choose to believe him or not, but before those soldiers, Dalton had never shot another man.

He'd spent two years marching up and down the training base, but they never saw him fit to be placed in the line of fire. He was buzzing with the feel of it. But the echo of the gunshot had shaken him. How far had the sound travelled? How many ears had heard?

The ground was wet and soft at the foot of the mossy pine tree. Dalton used his hands, tearing through the knots of ferns and roots. Grace dug with the boiler. The marines' blood was on them both; on wrists and hands and clothes. Dalton had laid them face down so the bastards couldn't look at them.

Grace didn't speak. Just knelt down and dug. Now Dalton had gotten his voice back, he couldn't bear this stillness where there ought to have been words.

Finally she said icily: "Is it deep enough?"

"No. More." It was deep enough, yes. But he didn't know where they went from here. They couldn't go back to the hut. It wouldn't be long before more soldiers came looking for the missing. They'd come for him. For them. So for now, he'd just keep digging.

A few minutes more and Grace flung down the pot. She threw her bloodstained shawl into the hole. "Just do it, for God's sake. I can't bear the sight of them lying there no more. Bury them and be done with it."

Dalton dragged the bodies by the legs and rolled them into the muddy graves.

Grace chewed her thumbnail. "Ought we say something?"

He kicked a spray of dirt over the bodies. "Say what?"

"I don't know. A prayer perhaps."

He snorted. Grabbed the pot and began to bury them. Pack the earth tight or they'd be sniffed out by the tigers.

"I never saw a man killed before," said Grace. The fingers in her mouth were shaking.

They stood on the damp soil of the graves. "We can't go back to the hut," said Dalton. "There'll be more of them."

Grace shook her head. "I want to stay."

"They'll find you if you stay. They'll find you and they'll find the blood on the track and what do you think they'll do then?" Anger flared inside him. "Eleven years I've been out here and not a peep from the authorities. Then you turn up and bring half the fucking cavalry with you! They were out here looking for their little escaped lunatic!"

"I ain't a lunatic!" she hissed.

"Then I did you a favour."

Grace wrapped her arms around herself. "I ain't going anywhere with you. So if you're planning to kill me, you'd best do it now."

Dalton snorted. Such paranoia. Perhaps he should have tried to calm her, reassure her. But he was hot and wild with anger. "If I were to kill you, don't you think I would have done it when I killed Violet? That's what you think, aye? That I tossed her in the river and let her float back to Hobart Town?"

At the mention of Violet's name, deep sobs began to well up inside her. She curled into a ball beside the graves, hugging her knees, burying her eyes in her muddy skirts. Dalton felt full of resentment. He knew those marines had been sent to look for her. Sent by Harris and the New Norfolk police.

*Find her. She's in danger.*

And the only men who had ever come looking for him were the ones who wanted his back flayed and his neck broken.

"Here's how it is, Grace. I can't go back to the hut. I can't take the chance now the marines are in the area. So you either come with me into the bush, or you go back to the hut alone. They'll find you there and they'll take you back to your Mr Harris. They all think you're mad. Remember, he threw you in the asylum because you dared stand up to him." He picked up the pack. "So unless you want to go back there, you're just going to have to trust me."

Grace's jaw tightened as she stood. "Where will we go?"

"We'll head northeast. Without the traps we'll struggle to find food this time of year. We'll have to get closer to the settlements. Steal from the farms, or the drovers on the Hobart road."

"Settlements?" A flicker of light in her voice.

They'd need to build a new shelter. With what? His blunt axe could cut little but bark and vine, his saw was long rusted. The ropes of his traps were fraying and his boots worn through.

"We can make Bothwell or Hamilton in four days," he said. "Get supplies from the farms. And then build somewhere new to live where the law won't find us." He thought of his hut with its thatched roof and crooked bark door. Six months of cutting, hauling and hammering. That patch of earth was his world.

He began to walk, away from his world. Clouds hung grey and low, an Irish sky. He shoved the rifle into the pack and took the axe from Grace, using it to hack away the tangled branches in front of them. Beating a path towards civilisation. Not an easy path, he was sure of it. There were mountains this way. Roaring rivers, glassy lakes. He told himself he'd follow the stars, like Greenhill had done.

But look where Greenhill had led them.

In the falling shadows, he imagined them; Greenhill at the front, whispering with Travers and Pearce. Kennerly and Brown hunched together, plotting their escape. Mather and Bodenham in the middle; doomed men.

Dalton was alert to every crackle and hiss, every popping twig. The bush itself was breathing. He saw this dark forest for what it was; a great living entity that kept secrets and took lives. How insignificant man became when pitted against it. These woods had the power to turn men against each other. To send cohorts running in the night with bloodstained axes. And yet, there was a savage beauty to this place Dalton was sure existed nowhere else on Earth.

They walked for two hours or more without a word. When Grace said: "Slow down, Alexander," it made his heart bound into his throat.

She started to sing. Keeping herself calm, he supposed. He wanted to tell her to stop— *what if there are soldiers about to hear you?*— but the sound of her voice made those dead men disappear. He glanced over his shoulder at her. Her head was drooped, her singing flat and tired.

*Here, give me your hand. Lean on me a little.*

But he couldn't dig out the words.

"We can't make a fire," said Alexander. "In case someone should see the smoke."

They'd made it into the foothills on the fringe of the mountains. The ground had risen and the temperature plunged. Thick dark was falling over the forest. Grace's breath made a silver cloud. She stumbled over a log and fell forward.

"Stop," said Alexander. And like that, down he sat, right in the middle of the path they'd beaten. No shelter but the thick canopy of trees. No warmth. No light. At least she'd managed a fire on those dreadful first nights with Violet.

She sat several feet from him, needing her distance. But he shuffled closer to her, his hand brushing the edge of her skirt.

"Your dress," he said. "It's soaked."

She hugged her knees. "The soldiers chased me through the river."

Alexander paused, breathing heavily. "I'll light the fire," he said finally.

"No. No one can find us. I ain't going back to the asylum. I'd rather freeze."

He took off his coat and slid it over her shoulders. She buttoned it over the top of her cloak, pushing her chin against its coarseness. Heat from Alexander's body infused the rough wool.

He untied the pack and broke an end off the stale loaf of bread. Grace struggled to swallow. The thing was too tough and tasted of charcoal. When she reached out to put it back in the pack, she realised she couldn't see her hand in front of her. The darkness was absolute. She tried to slow her breathing.

*It's just darkness. That's all. Just darkness.*

"We'll take turns keeping guard," said Alexander. "Listening for them."

Grace cradled her knees. She was far too agitated to sleep. Far too cold. Far too afraid. Her legs were wet and achy, her eyes stinging from old, dry tears. She wanted nothing to do with Alexander. But nor could she bear to be alone. She sat close enough that she could hear his breathing. A little assurance the forest had not taken him the way it had taken Violet.

A horrid, throaty scream echoed across the bush. Alexander moved suddenly, clattering the pots at his feet.

"It's just the devils," said Grace, swallowing hard. "You know that. You've heard it a thousand times."

He rustled the ground. Mumbled in Irish.

"What? What did you say?" She heard him leap to his feet. Footsteps passed back and forth as he paced like a dog in a thunderstorm. "The soldiers ain't here, Alexander. No one's followed us." She lay back and closed her eyes. Tried to convince herself there would be light around her when she opened them. Convince herself the darkness was a choice.

"What are you doing, Grace? Don't go to sleep. Please don't go to sleep."

"I ain't going to sleep."

"Leave!" he yelled suddenly.

"Who's there?" She leapt up. "The marines?"

Alexander's voice dropped. "Get the hell out of my head." His words disappeared into the night, leaving only the hiss of the bush. An owl struck up with a pale coo.

Grace touched his wrist. His skin was hot, despite the bitter cold. "Alexander, tell me what happened out here."

"You don't need to know."

"Yes I do. You're scaring me. I need to know what's in your head."

He stood beside her, silent for a long time. Finally, he said: "We escaped from Macquarie Harbour. Eight of us. Me and Pearce and Greenhill and some others."

"No one escapes Macquarie Harbour."

"Well, we did. We were fools. But we had to try. The place was hell. We laboured like animals. Lived in wet clothes, shared our beds with rats. So crammed together we had to sleep on our sides. I had twelve more years til I was a free man. I'd never have made it. I'd have taken my own life." He sighed heavily. "We stole a boat. Greenhill was a sailor. Said he'd get us off Van Diemen's Land. But the marines came after us. We had to run into the bush instead.

'Greenhill, he got us lost. Took us round in circles. Into the heart of the island."

Grace saw them then, in her mind's eye. Eight convicted men. She and Alexander were walking in their shadows. She waited for him to continue, but no more words came. "And then?" she said finally.

"There was no food. No shelter. Men died. Bodenham first, then the rest. It's like you said, no one escapes Macquarie Harbour."

"Except you."

"Aye, well. Guess I was the lucky one."

*The lucky one.* She'd always believed a person made their own luck.

Seven dead men and one survivor?

In her mind's eye, she saw the rifle arc through the air. Saw the marines crumple. Was it possible these bolters had fallen at Alexander's hand too?

She couldn't bear to be near him. She walked with arms out in front of her, feeling her way like a blind man along the narrow path they had beaten. Without sight, her other senses were heightened. The screaming devil, the sigh of the wind. Wet leaves grazed her cheek.

The ground dipped suddenly and she stumbled on her skirt. The earth felt unsteady. The blackness turned everything on its head. She looked upwards. Where were the stars? The moon? Suddenly being alone was more terrifying than the possibilities of what Alexander may have done.

"Where are you?" she called, panic rising.

"I'm here."

She heard him shuffle towards her.

"You asked," he said. "You wanted to know."

"What happened to the other men? How did they die?"

"I told you. There was no food. You think the land here is harsh? It's nothing compared to what's in the west."

Grace could hear the bush move. She imagined it closing in around her, circling, entrapping. "Why did it spare you?"

"I found a native camp. Found the berries. Found a ring of

cattle duffers who fed me til I was strong again." He paused. "You doubt me."

There were soldiers about. Her best chance was to go back to the hut and try and get herself found. Holler until those men pushed through the trees. They'd take her back to Harris and New Norfolk. But she couldn't stay here in this restless forest with a man who left a trail of death behind him.

She began to walk again. Quicker this time. The ground was slippery and uneven. She pushed through wiry branches and felt them whip back in her face. Her shoulders bumped against tree trunks.

"Grace?"

She began to run, ploughing through the mud and ferns like she was knee deep in snow. She'd lost the path. She hunched low and kept running; pulling her skirts up over her thighs. A sharp branch stabbed her cheek. She reeled backwards with the shock of it, thudded against a tree trunk and fell to her knees. Pain shot through her shoulder.

She heard the strike of flint, saw a flicker of light. Alexander came towards her, holding a flaming branch out in front of him.

"You can't leave," he said. "I have the food and the water and the gun." He lowered the branch so it was close to her cheek. "If you leave, you'll die."

Grace squinted in the hot light.

Alexander pressed the cuff of his shirt against the cut beneath her eye. He took her arm and helped her stand. "I know you don't want to be near me," he said. "But it'll get near freezing tonight. If we don't stay close we'll likely not survive."

Grace could hear his teeth knocking together. She took off his coat and pushed it back into his hands. He dropped the branch and stamped out the flame. The darkness seemed thicker than before. If such a thing were possible.

His hand tightly around her wrist, Alexander led her back to the path, navigating the dark forest like he was following their scent. Grace's foot slammed into the boiler and she knew they had returned to their camp.

She curled up on her side, cradling her aching shoulder. Alexander wrapped his arm over her, then his leg, encircling them both in his coat. His breath ruffled her hair.

Grace tensed, both repulsed by and craving his nearness. "Where?" she said. "Where did they die?"

"Forget them. Stop talking about them." His voice was taut.

She squeezed her eyes closed and tried to sleep away the darkness. "You can't forget them. So why should I?"

# PART TWO

# HAMILTON

# XIV

Bathurst Free Press and Mining Journal
Wednesday 28th January 1857
Derived from the Hobart Town Gazette, 1824

*'Constant moisture from heavy rains renders travelling unpleasant in such a region under any circumstances. If, with a good commissariat and all available comforts, Sir John Franklin's overland expedition to the harbour from the capital proved so laborious and trying that several men never recovered from the hardships and sufferings they then endured, we may readily imagine the wretched prospect before the eight wanderers in the pine woods.'*

In the morning she wouldn't look at him. She kept her eyes down, as though he was a wild animal she didn't want to provoke.

They were up with the blue dawn. The winter night had seemed endless as Dalton lay shivering at her side. With the first hint of light, he'd unbuttoned the coat wrapped around them. Grace was on her feet first. Eager to get moving or eager to get away from him?

East, they walked, into the rising sun. Dalton hacked a path through the trees, sending twigs and leaves flying. He looked over his shoulder. Grace was cradling the gun. Yesterday she wouldn't touch the thing. With her other hand she held her skirts bunched above her knees. The tears of yesterday had dried and hardened inside her. A stripe of dried blood along one cheek.

The ground rose in a chain of mossy mountains. Dalton had been this way before. He had traipsed west from the Fat Doe River with all his worldly goods on his back, over the mountain range to disappear into memory. The last time, the days had been long and warm. Now there was ice in the air and their breath made clouds.

Settlements to the northeast. He hoped the map in his head was accurate. They had bread and smoked meat for a week at most. There were few animals in these mountains. And many days in this cold would kill them.

Clatter, clatter of the pots on his back. The rhythmic crunch of their footsteps. And the invisible presence of dead men.

Dalton hated this new silence. He reached into the pack and handed Grace a sliver of smoked meat, hoping for *thank you*. She glanced at his hand; still stained with the blood of the marines. Waited for him to eat his share before swallowing hers.

When she finally spoke, what she said was: "Did you kill Violet?"

Dalton didn't answer. He wanted her to trust him, though he knew he'd given her little reason. What would she have done had he said: *yes, Grace, I killed her?* What choice did she have but to keep walking beside him?

When the ground became too steep, they crawled on hands and knees. Mud squelched between their fingers. Dalton's ears and nose stung with cold, but his back was damp with sweat.

She didn't speak of Violet again. Made up her own mind, he supposed.

The earth rose and fell. Dalton tossed the pack and axe onto a rocky ledge and hauled himself up. He reached a hand towards Grace.

"Pass me the gun. Let me help you."

She stood beneath the ledge, hesitating. He understood. That rifle was a little security for her. Reluctantly, she passed it to him. He took her hand and helped her up the cliff, her boots scrabbling against the slippery rock. She pulled away quickly.

Dalton said: "Your tea, Grace. I put poison mushrooms in it." He said: "I didn't want you to try and get back to Hobart Town alone. You would've died. That's why I did such a thing."

She started to laugh, a sound like threads of ice. "The tea. Believe me, Alexander, I ain't thinking about the bloody tea no more."

She didn't look at him. Just step, step, step, like she was trying to walk everything away.

On the third night, the air dropped below freezing. Leaves hardened with ice. With each breath of wind, the trees tinkled like bells. Before the sun had disappeared, Dalton had looked back at where they'd come from. He could still see the fat brown trail of the Derwent River.

He scratched together some bark and fern fronds to cover them against the cold. Built a fire that hissed and spat before succumbing to the wind. He shuffled across the rock and pulled Grace into him, feeling her shiver hard against his chest.

They woke to clouds closing in around the mountains. Banks of mist blew towards them from above and below, leaving them suspended in a great sea of white. Beads of rain exploded against Dalton's cheeks. He began to walk in the direction he hoped was east. The fog made flecks of gold and black dance in front of his eyes.

The rain grew heavier. Tiny rivers rushed through the crevices in the rock. The trees thinned and the ground became slippery like sheets of black marble.

"Why were you at Macquarie Harbour?" asked Grace.

He told her every bit so the silence might not return. The tale of Matthew Brown and Flannagan and how he'd tried to frame the Englishman for robbery. Told tall stories with his hand upon the bible.

"Oh," said Grace. "So you're a liar then too."

Dalton felt the rock give way to sodden earth. He waded through the sludge without speaking. Mud clung to his ankles, his shins, his knees. Behind him, he could hear Grace's heavy breathing, her murmurs of exertion.

When the earth grew solid again, he sat and watched her edge her way out of the mud. "Would you rather I'd let them take you back to the madhouse?"

She sat a distance away and hugged her knees. "I just never seen a man act so vicious before."

"I did it for you."

She met his eyes for the first time in days. A cautious, sideways glance.

"Do you want me to leave you?" he asked finally.

She squinted through the rain to the carpet of treetops, unbroken but for the copper threads where the rivers pushed into each other.

She shivered. "It's like you said, ain't it. Got to stay together or we'll die."

There were always parts of a man a woman tried to ignore. With Harris, it was the way he chewed his meat so damn loud. The way he'd change the subject when Grace tried to talk about her life in Stepney. To make any relationship function, there had to be a certain amount of ignorance.

And so it was with Alexander. With each step, she pushed those murdered marines further and further from her mind. Pushed out the dead bolters and the nightmares of Macquarie Harbour until they were nothing but the stuff of legends.

The land itself made it hard to block out the horror. Grace stood upon on a ridge and breathed air that smelled of mint and honey. Looked out over her toes at a beautiful green and purple land, haunting in its isolation.

But beneath the ridge was the darkness. Trees swallowed the sunlight in one mouthful, and those brutal settlements came to life. Down there, where branches blocked out the light and the tiger dogs tore at their prey, was where the crack of the whip still echoed. Where the men with bloodied backs had vanished into the bush. Where the last cries of the dying hung on the wind. It took every inch of Grace's willpower to keep those stories silent.

But that man who had given her shelter, who had saved her from drowning, well he wasn't capable of killing his seven comrades, now was he? And he sure as hell wasn't capable of killing a little girl. Ah yes, there was a great simplicity to ignorance. A great comfort. A great skill to choose to forget.

On the fourth night, she dared to ask: "Are we lost?" They lay on the rock, wrapped in their damp coats. After a day and night, the rain had stopped, leaving a vast, wet forest. Alexander had crouched over the kindling for an hour, whittling waterlogged bark and attacking the flint. The sparks had refused to take.

"Lost? No, we're not lost. The stars, they show me the way."

Grace curled into a ball, her clothing stiff with mud and ice. Her shivering was violent, uncontrollable. She rolled onto her back and stared at the glittering sky. She could see colours behind the blackness, whirlpools of purple and blue. Its beauty was breathtaking. "How?" she asked.

Alexander pointed upwards. "The five bright ones, they call it the Southern Cross. You see? Now draw a line through that cross in your mind. Imagine it extending out four times the length of those stars. Drop that line down to the horizon. There's south."

"You making this up?"

He gave a short chuckle. "No, I'm not making it up." He paused. "Greenhill said that's the way they do it here. There's no polestar, so they use the cross."

Grace hugged herself. "I don't think this Greenhill were the best of navigators, Alexander."

She gazed up at the cross until she saw that line pointing to the south. Until the sky wasn't so damn foreign. Until the stars began to light the way.

*And that moon*, she thought, *that's the moon that makes the Thames rise and fall. We might be sitting on the edge of the Antarctic, but that's the moon that shone through my window in the blue house.*

She watched the sky until the clouds blew in. Until she could see no stars, just a shower of white crystals that fluttered down and blanketed the earth. She slid her arms beneath Alexander's coat, searching for body heat. Her stiff fingers clutched at his chest, clung to the sparse curls of hair. He unbuttoned the coat and pulled it over their heads.

She woke to sunlight glowing red through the threadbare fabric. She sat and squinted in the white light. Not piss-stained,

London slush, but brilliant sheets of clear ice that lit up the landscape. The whiteness changed everything. Which way had they come? Which way to the settlements? To think was too exhausting. All she wanted was to lie back down and sleep until the cold went away.

Alexander turned in a slow circle, taking in the glittering landscape. "We're close to the settled districts." His voice sounded far away. "I came this way before." He reached into the snow-spattered pack and broke the smoked meat in two. Handed her the larger piece.

Grace sat with the food in her fist, unable to find the energy to lift it to her mouth. Melting ice dripped from her hair and ran down the back of her neck. She stared into the cloud-streaked valley. Everything she knew felt so far away, like she was trapped in a dream she couldn't wake from.

"Grace? Why aren't you eating?"

She looked up at Alexander. His face was blurred, unfocused. She blinked hard. He dropped to his knees and gripped her shoulder. Held the meat to her lips. "Eat. Come on now." Panic in his voice.

"I got to rest some more."

"No. No more resting. Get up." He pulled her to her feet with sudden urgency. She stumbled into him. "We're almost out of the mountains. Won't be so cold." He slid his arm around her waist. "Keep walking. Just got to keep walking."

# XV

At the foot of the mountains, the land opened out into a maze of rivers and creeks. When last here, eleven years ago, Dalton had managed to wade across them, the water barely at his hips. But now they were crawling through a long, wet winter. The roar of the rivers was ever present.

Grace's steps were dizzy and crooked. He had to get her out of her wet clothes and into some warmth. Where he would find such a thing, he had no clue, but the thought of it kept him moving, one arm around her waist, the other clutching the weapons, pots clattering on his back. He felt an undercurrent of terror at the approaching settlements. Towns held police and soldiers and people who could put a rope around his neck. But the thought of losing Grace terrified him more than the gallows. And so he kept walking. Dry clothes and warmth.

The river lay before them, dappled with faint rain. Dalton paced with his hands behind his head. The water looked to be two hundred yards wide or more. His body ached with cold and exhaustion. He'd not swum in years. But what choice did he have?

He pulled off his coat and shirt. "Take off your cloak," he told Grace. "And your dress."

She squinted up at him from the bank. He unhooked her cloak, then fumbled with the buttons down her chest, his fingers frozen and ineffective. He rolled their clothing into a tight bundle and tied it to the pack. He grabbed Grace's chin and she opened her eyes begrudgingly.

"The water's deep," he told her. "You got to hold tight to me, you understand?" He tugged her to her feet and stepped into the water. He pulled her onto his back with one hand, the other holding the pack above his head. Water swelled around his chest. "The settlements," he said. "They're on the other side of this river."

"And then what?"

*And then what?*

He'd planned to wait on the edge of the village until night, sneak onto the farms and gather what they needed to build a new hut. But Grace wouldn't survive another a night in the open. "We'll make a fire," he said. "Get ourselves warm."

Another step and the ground dropped away, leaving his legs flailing. He kicked hard. Grace's arms tightened around his neck.

He stumbled out of the water and carried her onto the grass beside the river. He pulled her out of her wet shift and slipped the damp dress over her head. Covered her with the cloak and greatcoat. He hurried into the bush, searching for anything that would burn. Hacked away at some branches until he'd managed a pile of kindling. He pulled the flint from the pack and poked and puffed at the fire until tiny flames began to lick the wood. Grace opened her eyes.

"That's it," he said. "Lie close now." He held his hands to the fire and felt the heat bring life back to his fingers. He fumbled in the pack for the boiler and filled it from the river. Sat it on the flames until a thin thread of steam began to rise. Lifting Grace's head, he poured the warm water into her mouth. A thin drizzle trickled down her throat, the rest pooling on the leaves beneath her cheek.

She looked at him with vague, glassy eyes. "Where's Violet?"

Dalton stood. "Violet's not here."

"Where is she?"

"I don't know." He paced, shivering hard. She urgently needed dry clothes. Blankets. They both did. They couldn't have been more than a mile or two from the first settlement. He sucked in his breath and crouched at Grace's side. Her breathing was shallow, eyelids fluttering on the edge of consciousness. He pressed his fingers to her neck. A faint pulse. He tucked his coat tightly over her and left the rifle at her side.

The land was vivid green between patches of snow. From a distance, Dalton could make out tiny forms dotting the plains. Cattle, he realised as he drew closer. Kangaroos lolloped on the fringe of the pasture, drinking from the creek. At the back of the paddock was a farmhouse. Smoke poured from the chimney.

Civilisation.

Dalton felt suddenly lightheaded. He grabbed a fistful of the wire fence. Sickness rose in his throat. In the neighbouring paddock, two men were turning the earth with shovels. He fought the urge to leave. Logic told him he was well-hidden by time. If the cattle duffers were to be believed, the reports of Alexander Pearce had convinced the world Dalton was dead. But his fear was stronger than logic. He pictured men lined up on the edge of the settlement, rifles raised, awaiting his return. A scaffold in the town square. Bodenham himself, defaced and dead, yet somehow resurrected.

*Look what he did to me*.

Dalton doubled over and vomited at the corner of the fence. Then he kept walking.

"Can I have a blanket?" he practiced. "I need a blanket."

*Can I have a blanket?* He repeated it under his breath,

forcing his footsteps to keep pace with his rhythmic words.

*I need a blanket.*

On the other side of the paddocks was a smaller cottage. Uneven wattle and daub walls with a thatched roof that reminded him of his hut. He stumbled through the long grass towards the house. A washing line stood in front of the cottage, yellowing underclothes fluttering like sailcloth. Dalton pulled off the wooden pegs and bundled the petticoats beneath his arm. He opened the door and stepped inside. A range stood against one wall, table in the centre. A simmering pot, spitting fire. Smells of cooking meat, pipe smoke and misplaced earth. A sideboard sat opposite the fire, cluttered with rusty cannikins, rolls of twine and a half-drunk bottle of whisky. At the back sat a woven Irish belt. Dalton had not seen one since his father was alive. Never seen one outside of Ireland.

He stepped close and ran his fingers across the red and blue weaving, over the delicate tassels on the ends. For a fleeting moment, the years fell away. He was a boy on his father's lap, letting the tassels slide through pudgy fingers. Watching features emerge on the carving in his father's hands.

"What the bloody hell do you want?" A woman appeared in the doorway, a shovel raised above her head, poised to strike. She looked about Dalton's age, her wide shoulders jarring with a narrow, bird-like face. Pale strands of hair peeked out from beneath a mop cap. She looked up and down at Dalton's mud-caked clothes.

"*Blaincéad,*" he said.

"You'll not find any blankets in there." The woman lowered the shovel. "What d'you need a blanket for? And what in hell are you doing with my underclothes?"

His heart was racing. "My... A woman... She's all cold and wet... Dying..."

"I see. Where is she?"

"I made a fire…"

"You left her out there?"

Dalton nodded.

"Christ. There's no accounting for stupidity, is there. Bring her here."

He paused. "I just need a blanket."

"You're not taking my blankets out there. They'll get ruined. If there's truly a woman needing help, you go and get her. Otherwise you bugger off out of my house and leave my things alone."

Dalton nodded finally. "I'll get her."

The woman folded her arms. "Leave my petticoats on the table."

He rocked Grace's shoulder. "There's a woman. Told me to bring you to her house. She's got dry clothes for you."

Grace lifted her head. "A house?"

"Aye. You got to get yourself warm and dry. Come on now." He took her hand and helped her climb shakily to her feet.

"You went to a house?"

Dalton threw a handful of dirt on the burning embers.

"You said you was going to steal from the settlements."

"Aye. Well." He tied the pack around the axe and gun and slung them over one shoulder. "You need dry clothes, don't you." He wrapped an arm around her waist. "Hear that? That's a boo hoo bird. Only lives where the people do."

"A boo hoo bird? No it ain't."

"Aye, it is. Listen. *Boo hoo.*"

"You're making that up," said Grace. But he saw a smile on the edge of her lips.

"You're not bringing that gun in here." The woman marched out the front door and took Grace's arm. "Give her to me. You want to come in, you get rid of that first."

Grace looked sideways at Dalton. He let his arm fall from around her waist and trudged out across the plains.

He used the boiler to dig a hole beneath a tree and threw in the gun and axe. Tore a strip of fabric from his fraying shirt and knotted it around a branch as a marker.

He let himself back into the house. Voices came muffled from one of the rooms. He followed the sound. The woman stepped from the bedroom and closed the door.

"Grace," said Dalton.

"That her name? I got her out of those wet clothes and into bed."

"Is she going to die?" Dalton asked in Irish.

"Wouldn't think so. But I'm not God, am I."

He tried to step past her into the bedroom, but she blocked his way.

"Leave her. She needs to rest." She marched into the next room and brought out a shirt and pair of brown corduroy trousers. "Here.They belong to my Jack." She nodded to her bedroom. "Get yourself out of those wet things. I don't fancy disposing of you if you freeze to death in my kitchen."

Dalton changed, then carried his wet clothes out to the living area. The clean shirt hung loose on his shoulders, the trousers cinched at the waist with a length of rope. The woman pulled a mug from its hanger above the hearth and filled it with broth from the pot. She handed it to him.

"I got some of this into her. You best have some too."

Dalton nodded his thanks.

Nothing felt real. Not the heady smell of wood smoke, or the hot, salty broth sliding down his throat. Not the noisy breathing of the stranger in front of him. All an illusion, surely.

He sat inches from the blaze. He'd forgotten such heat existed. Illusion or not, he craved the warmth against his skin.

"What's your name?" she asked.

Dalton tugged his shirt towards his neck to cover his scarred shoulders. "Don't think you ought to know that."

She snorted. "Look at you, all precious with your secrets. A bolter then. I'd have done the same if I could have managed it." She threw another log on the fire. "I'm Annie. She your wife?"

Dalton shook his head.

"Didn't think so." She hooked a finger around the rim of his mug and pulled it towards her to check its congealing contents. "The soup is rubbish, aye?" She pulled the whisky bottle from the sideboard and filled two cannikins. Handed one to Dalton. "This is far better."

He smiled faintly and brought the cup to his lips. The smell was overpowering. The whisky slid hot down his throat, warming his belly. Hell, he'd missed this above all things. He took another long drink and felt his thoughts knock together. *Out of practice*, he told himself wryly.

Annie watched him curiously. "Where you from then?" Dalton said nothing.

She sighed. "Look. I'm not asking questions I don't want to hear the answer to. Don't want to know what in hell the two of you were doing in the mountains. Just saw you looking at my belt earlier. I'm wondering where home is."

"Kilkenny," he said finally.

"My da was from Kilkenny. Went to visit when I was a girl. Were a beautiful old church with a tower that reached to the sky."

Dalton smiled crookedly.

"You remember it, aye? Windows made of glass a thousand colours. Feels like another lifetime, those windows. Might as well be too, with all the chance we got of seeing it again." She smiled faintly. "It's nought but a fairy land now, is Ireland. Somewhere we're best off forgetting."

Dalton nodded. He wished Grace could see home in the same way. A distant memory. Unobtainable.

Annie reached onto the sideboard for the belt. She tossed it to Dalton. "Take it. I've another."

He ran his fingers across its rough stitching. "Thank you." His chest tightened with an unexpected rush of emotion. He stood abruptly. "I need to see Grace." His legs felt weak with whisky.

"She's sleeping."

"I'll not wake her."

The belt in his fist, he let himself into the bedroom. Grace lay on a narrow mattress beneath a mountain of grey blankets. A fat curl lay across her cheek. He pressed his fingers to the side of her face. Her skin was warming; not that deathly cold it had been in the mountains. Her breath tickled his thumb. Life. The relief that washed through him was so intense, it brought a murmur from his throat.

He sat on the edge of the bed. Grace shifted in her sleep. She reached an arm out of the blankets and felt for him, as she had done those cold nights in the mountains. Her eyes fluttered open. She clutched a fistful of his shirt and weakly tugged him forward.

"I dreamt I was watching the sun set over the Tower." She smiled sleepily. "If you stand on the hill at just the right time, the walls turn gold. I'll show you one day." She closed her eyes against the sunlight. "What you going to show me, then?"

"Grace," said Dalton. "Can I lie beside you?"

She mumbled sleepily and shuffled across the mattress. He slid beneath the blankets and laid his head against hers, her curls tickling his nose.

Once, before Van Diemen's Land, he imagined he'd live the life of a normal man. Wife, children. Lying here with his body pressed against Grace's, he saw a flicker of what could have been. It was as though he'd managed to catch hold of a thread of the life that had passed him by. The life stolen from him by his own bad choices. There was no normalcy for a man like him. No wife or children. No one holding him in the dark. This was the best he could hope for. A few stolen moments of intimacy with a woman too delirious to fight, while he waited for the world to hunt him down. He wrapped his arm around Grace's chest. Warmth. She would live. He closed his heavy eyes. Today those stolen moments were enough.

When he opened his eyes again, it was dark. Grace lay on her side, breathing deeply. What had woken him? A creak of the floor. Voices. Dalton peered through the darkness, hot and disoriented.

*The night is for the dead*, his ma used to say. *Off to bed with you and leave the house for the spirits.*

His hand tensed around Grace's shoulder until reality returned to him. Tonight he slept among the living.

# XVI

Grace woke to a room filled with pale grey light. Alexander lay beside her, his breaths long and slow.

She'd come close to dying, she knew. Would be frozen on top of the mountains if it weren't for him. How to reconcile that with the man who had aimed the rifle at her and Violet? The man who had killed two marines with a single bullet.

In sleep, there was a vulnerability to him, a childishness. Lying with the blankets pulled to his neck, he looked an ordinary man. Had he left a family behind? Grace knew nothing of his life before this place. Had he loved, been loved? Had children of his own? Who had he been before Van Diemen's Land had turned him wild? Strange it had taken a night in civilisation for her to consider such things.

She climbed out of bed. She felt drained and heavy, but more alert than she had in days. Clean flannel petticoats and a blue woollen dress were draped over the end of the bed. Grace had vague recollections of the woman in the mop cap bringing them to her. She searched her blurred memories for the woman's name. Annie?

She washed, buttoned herself into the clean dress and walked slowly into the kitchen. She stopped abruptly. A tall man stood at the table, pouring a mug of tea. His skin was the colour of caramel, his face with the wide, flat features of the blacks. Grace stepped backwards, her spine pressing hard against the wall.

He looked up and smiled wryly. "A black man with a tea

cup in his hand. Whatever is the world coming to?"

"I'm sorry," Grace spluttered. "I didn't mean no offense. I … Where's Annie?"

He nodded to the garden. Poured a second mug of tea and placed it on the table. "Here. You're still down on your strength, I imagine."

She nodded her thanks and picked up the cup, eying him curiously.

Annie shouldered open the door and tossed a handful of carrots on the table. She kicked off her muddy boots and wiped her hands on her apron. "I see you met my Jack," she said, pouring herself a mug of tea. "How are you feeling?"

"Better," said Grace. "Much better. Thank you. For everything."

Annie shrugged. "We help each other as we can out here. Still finding our way, aren't we. And Lord knows Jack and me have seen our share of trouble."

"What kind of trouble?"

She gave a humourless laugh. "Irishwoman and a man with black blood in him? You think the rest of the village likes having us around? No sir." She gulped down her tea. "Dogs, the lot of them."

Grace waited for Annie to continue, but she just reached for a knife and began to hack the tops off the muddy carrots.

"Well," said Grace. "Dogs or not, I got to find work. I got to earn some money to get back to Hobart Town. You know of anyone hiring?"

"You ought to head up to the Porters'," said Jack. "I heard they just had three of their lags got freed."

Annie snorted. "Bill Porter's the worst of the lot." She attacked the carrots without looking up.

"Course he is. But she needs money. And Porter's got money." Jack motioned to Grace. "I'll show you which is their house. You can see it from here."

She followed him into the paddock at the front of the cottage. The morning was misty and grey, the sun a perfect circle behind the cloud. Jack pointed to a hill behind the village. A sprawling white house sat on the slope.

"Up there. Bill Porter's. He's a bastard of a man, but he's desperate for workers."

Grace nodded. "What did they do to you, then?"

Jack ran a hand through his thick black hair. "Killed our cattle, dug up the crops. Did their best to drive us out."

"But you stayed."

"Where else were we to go? This place is all we got." He smiled to himself. "They underestimated Annie's stubbornness. Takes more than a few dead cows to force that woman from her home."

Grace looked back towards the mountains. Snow glittered on the peaks. "I'm lucky you were here."

Jack followed her gaze. "Men went up there during the black wars. Tried to flush out the natives. There were plenty didn't make it back." He smiled wryly. "Bloody fools come out from the cities. Never seen a mountain in their lives. They think they can take on this land and come out on top."

Grace wrapped her arms around herself, hearing her own foolishness in Jack's words. She shivered. "Alexander, he sees things out there. Ghosts, like. At first I thought it was just his imagination. But there's something about this place, ain't there. It's like the land... remembers." She laughed humourlessly. "You must think me a complete fool."

Jack dug his hands into his pockets. "My ma, she always said the land is alive. It has a spirit. A soul. Perhaps that's what you felt." He began to walk back towards the cottage. Annie was back in the vegetable garden with a shovel in her hand. "Perhaps if the rest of these colonists could feel it they might respect the place a little more." He touched Grace's shoulder. "You're no fool. I promise you."

She smiled faintly. Suddenly Jack's arm was ripped away.

"Get your hands off her," Alexander hissed. Jack whirled around and shoved him hard against his chest. Annie threw down her shovel and charged out of the garden.

"Alexander!" cried Grace. "What in hell?"

He paced in a circle, his hands behind his head. "Get your things," he told her.

Annie hurled out a torrent of bitter Irish. Alexander glared at her.

Grace's eyes darted between them. "What did you say to him?"

Annie planted her hands on her hips and snorted. "Said he's a mad bastard. Ought to have let him freeze."

Grace shoved Dalton into the bedroom. "What the bloody hell's the matter with you?" she cried. "He weren't doing nothing but helping me! And why've you got that filthy shirt on again? You stink like a dead goat." She watched with cold eyes as he pulled off the old shirt and slipped the fresh one over his head. "What's this about then?" she demanded. "You want me all to yourself? Christ Almighty."

Dalton marched into the kitchen to fetch his damp clothes. She chased him through the house.

"You can't go about behaving like this! You're in the real world now! And these people have been nothing but good to us!"

Dalton shoved his dirty trousers into the pack and charged

back into the bedroom. The walls of the house seemed to have closed in on him in the night. He'd never meant to stay this long.

"Get your things," he said again.

Grace shook her head. "I ain't going back into the forest."

"Of course you are."

"No. You were right about me going back to Hobart Town. I can't take Nora with no place to go. I'm going to Mr Porter's at the top of the hill. He's looking for help. I got to earn some money so I can make a decent life for the two of us. And then I'll go back for her."

Dalton's insides felt hollow. For a strange, fleeting moment, he saw his isolation for what it had been: a desperate attempt not to face his own shame. A self-imposed purgatory as he waited out the rest of his sorry life. "What will you tell them?" he mumbled.

"I'll tell them the truth. I'm a free settler who fled a violent master in Hobart Town. They don't need to know nothing about New Norfolk."

"They'll take you for a bolter."

"Me? A bolter?" She laughed, then swallowed it abruptly. "They've no proof."

"They don't need proof! This place is corrupt as hell! There are police running around who are lags themselves! Men who'll do anything for that ticket of leave. They'll lock you up for being a bolter until you can prove otherwise. That's the way things work here, Grace. Guilty until proven innocent."

She chewed her thumbnail. She looked different in her blue striped skirts. Young and clean. Her hair was pinned neatly at the base of her neck. He could smell soap.

So this was Grace in the real world.

"I got to do this for Nora. I got to take that risk. Besides, many more nights rolling in the mud, I truly will become mad. I'm going over there soon as I packed my things."

"You can't. You need to rest. You're not well enough to go looking for work."

She smiled out the corner of her mouth. "But I'm well enough to go back into the forest with you, is that right? I'm fine. Just a little tired. I got to do this, Alexander. You know I do."

She gathered her muddy clothes from the end of the bed and folded them neatly. Dalton searched for an argument that might keep her from going. But he saw the determination in her. Determined, he supposed, to move on from the loss of Violet and do something right for the other girl. Determined to shake off the title of *lunatic* she'd been shackled with in Hobart. He felt ill.

Grace turned to him. "Tell me," she said suddenly, "about your life in Ireland."

"What?"

"Who is waiting for you? A wife? A child? I'm sorry, I don't know why I never thought to ask before."

Dalton let out his breath and looked away.

"There was a woman in New Norfolk what saw ghosts," Grace said after a moment. "One night she couldn't bear it no more and hung herself with her bed sheets."

Dalton clenched his teeth. "Why are you telling me this?"

"Because I can see such a thing happening to you. I can see your memories driving you to your death. You're a human being. It ain't right for you to be so alone. No one here knows who you are. You said yourself, the world thinks Alexander Dalton is dead."

"Then why shatter their illusions?"

"I worry for you," said Grace.

"Why?"

She laughed a little. "What you mean, why?"

"Why should you care?"

"Because I can see a decent man in you."

"Is that what you were thinking when we were burying those soldiers?"

"Well. It's like you said, ain't it." She straightened the bedclothes. "You did that for me."

Dalton pulled the blanket from her hands. "I buried the gun behind Annie's house. Marked it with a strip of my shirt so we could find it. We'll dig it up and shoot a couple of kangaroos. Or those cows we passed. And they've got a garden full of carrots. We can take those too."

Grace glared at him. "How dare you even think it after all they've done for us!" She sighed. "Go if you must. I understand." She ran a finger along one of the thick white scars that snaked over to his collarbone. He shivered. She pulled at the lacing of the shirt, closing the linen over the scars and tying it tightly at his neck. She placed her hands on his shoulders and looked into his eyes.

"You saved my life," she said. "Thank you." The front door slammed and she pulled away.

Grace trudged out of the cottage and crossed the rickety bridge into town. She couldn't bear to think what would become of Alexander. More silence, more loneliness. A life lived in the shadow of the dead.

In spite of herself, she'd come to care for him, perhaps more deeply than he deserved. She knew he'd be forever in her thoughts as he hid, waiting out the rest of his life. She felt an ache in her chest. Isolation wasn't what he truly wanted, she was sure. He'd not buried his human need for companionship so deeply.

The Hamilton settlement was little more than a couple of streets, narrow alleys shooting off like fine veins. The roads were thick with muck, but the clean smell of the bush pervaded the stench of civilisation. Grace walked the length of the high street towards the house on the hill. Sandstone cottages were nestled together between bakers and butchers, an apothecary and a looming two-storey inn. Here; a grand private house. There; a crooked shack with drunken men spilling onto the street. A woman passed with a rickety baby carriage. Two men rode horses down the middle of the road, scattering a flock of disoriented chickens.

The place was a speck on London, but after months in the forest, it seemed bustling. Grace drank in the buzz of humanity. She felt alive. Motivated. Like she might begin to rise above the grief that darkened her days. She had to do right by Nora now. Find work. Get them out of this filthy colony.

The Porters' was a grand two-storey house like the one Harris had been building in Hobart Town. Grace stood at the edge of the property, her fingers tensing around the fence.

*They'll take you for a bolter.*

She'd laughed at the thought until she realised that was exactly what she was.

She strode up to the front door and knocked loudly, trying to conjure up her courage. She was shown inside by an old woman in a food-stained apron and instructed to wait in the hall.

She paced in a nervous circle, listening to an ornate wall clock tick away the seconds. Back where she belonged, she realised. Grovelling to the upper class so she might scratch together a living.

*God made a place for everyone…*

But when the woman returned to lead her into the drawing room, the couple waiting were without the frock coats and finery of the gentry. The man of the house was slouched in an armchair, the sleeves of his linen shirt rolled above his elbows, stockinged feet stretched out in front of him. He was a broad-shouldered man with flat features and a balding head. His wife perched on the edge of the couch, wearing an apron and dark woollen dress, mud streaked along the hem. A younger man with a patchy blond beard and pocked cheeks hovered behind them. Working class people, Grace realised. And yet here they were in this grand house with workers of their own. An upside-down colony, for certain, where society's rules were twisted and bent. And Harris had still been ashamed of her.

She managed a curtsey. "Heard you had your convicts freed and was after some new workers."

Porter sat his teacup on the side table. "Where've you come from?"

"London. I mean, Hobart Town. Had to leave. My master was trouble."

"Your master were trouble, or you were trouble?"

Grace chewed her lip.

"I suppose you ain't got no references then."

"No, sir."

"And nothing to prove you ain't a runaway."

She was silent.

Porter cracked his toes. "You got no references, you got no nothing. I ought to have the police check you out. See if the Female Factory's missing any curly haired Londoners."

Grace's heart sped. "I'm a free settler, sir, I swear it. *Duckenfield,* 1832. London to Hobart Town. Me and Mr Harris and the girls and—"

Porter folded his arms.

"I'll work for half rates," she spluttered. "Give me a trial. Please. One week. I'll be the best worker you ever saw, just you wait. Be twice as good as them lags just got freed."

Porter looked to his wife, who shrugged nonchalantly. "One week trial," he said. "Without no pay. Then we'll see. Agreed?"

"Yes sir." Grace dropped a hurried curtsey. "Thank you ever so much."

Dalton had stood on the edge of the farmland and watched until her silhouetted figure had disappeared.

He dug up the weapons, and trudged towards the mountains. Shot a kangaroo and carried the carcass into the woods. He'd go back to the farms when night fell. Steal what he needed to build a new hut.

He skinned the animal, drained its blood into the river and watched the water turn pink.

What would he need? Ammunition. Powder cartridge. Saw. Boots.

He'd made the same plan by the cattle duffers' fire. Back then, he had craved solitude, stillness. But now, it was the stillness that got to him first. The prattle of the birds. The endless sigh of the river. Sounds so embedded in the landscape, they turned into silence as the night wore on.

Wordlessness had been his sanctuary. Out here, where there was no one to speak, the story of Tom Bodenham's murder could never be told. It was the thing Dalton feared more than death: someone looking him in the eye and knowing the crimes he had committed in order to survive.

Whilst he had sat around the fire with the cattle duffers, he'd heard that that madman, Pearce, had made it to Hobart Town. Told their horror story to anyone who would listen. Pearce was sent back to Macquarie Harbour and their story was plastered across the newspapers. Eight names, a hideous crime. The people of Van Diemen's Land urged to keep a watchful eye for the missing convicts. Six of the men, Dalton was sure were dead. Just himself and Pearce left.

Tales from Dalton's own life were relayed back to him by the cattle duffers. Tales of the bolters from Macquarie Harbour who had done the inhuman. Tales of their gruesome deaths. Of his own death. A strange thing to hear, of course.

Greenhill had killed him. Or was it Pearce?

He had run away and died of exhaustion in the forests outside the harbour.

They all still lived and roamed as bushrangers.

That was the thing when a story got passed around. The truth got lost in no time at all. Make it up, tell your own tale. The bloodier, the better.

As he heard these conflicting stories, beer-fuelled gossip told with glowing eyes, it crossed Dalton's mind to say: *dead? Me?* just to see the looks on the duffers' faces. But of course, then he'd have to face the shame of the crime. So he kept silent. Silence was easy.

He lay beside the fire, listening to the duffers argue the truth of Alexander Dalton and the other missing men. He never wanted to hear those stories again. Never wanted to hear his name spoken as part of such an inhuman horror. Let Alexander Dalton die. Let him live the lonely life of a nameless man.

But he could do this no longer; this *cold, tired, hungry, afraid.* Pretending he could forget his sins by retreating into silence. He hadn't forgotten, had he? Hadn't forgotten Greenhill's flying axe and the sight of Bodenham's mutilated body. The sickness that had lasted long after his stomach was empty.

Perhaps Grace was right. Perhaps the way to make the past fade was to build a new life. Perhaps he truly could do more than hide in the woods and wait for death to find him.

The door to the Porters' kitchen was unlocked. Coals glowed behind the fire screen. Dalton walked into the parlour. A sofa faced the tiled fireplace. Heavy blue curtains, porcelain lamps. A calendar hung on the mantle.

*Well, look at that now.* The month of August, 1833.

Beside it sat a pair of bronze candleholders and a hideous marble bust of the king. A velvet armchair. Felt like a horse's flank when he rubbed his hands across it.

Upstairs, the hallway was thick with the oily scent of extinguished lamps, the darkness filled with snores and coughs. Three closed doors on either side on the hallway. Where was Grace?

He eased open the first door. Inside, he could make out the shape of a double bed with a couple sleeping inside. In the next room, three beds were laid out like army cots. The children snuffled and sighed in their sleep. All this life around him. Dalton felt dizzy, like he'd overdosed on a drug.

The floor creaked. He froze, not daring to take a step until the silence had thickened. Finally, he turned the handle of a narrow door that opened onto a timber staircase. He felt his way downstairs. The servants' quarters, he was sure of it.

Inside the first room, a single bed and washstand were crammed into narrow confines. And there she was, asleep on her back, the fingers of one hand curled beside her cheek.

He crept to her bedside and shook her shoulder, clamping a hand over her mouth to muffle her gasp. Her eyes widened. His nose was inches from hers. "The castle."

"What in hell?" she hissed.

"You asked me what I'd show you. I'll show you Kilkenny Castle. Six hundred years old and right on the river."

She scrambled out from beneath him. "Leave! This second! You got any idea what will happen if someone catches you here?"

"I had to see you. To tell you about the castle."

She threw her dress on over her shift. Shoved him from the bedroom and out into the yard. A pink dawn was pushing against the bottom of the sky.

"You're a bloody madman, Alexander. Get out of here. If I lose this job because of you, I'll never forgive you."

He grabbed her arm impulsively and squeezed.

"Let go. You're hurting me."

"London, Grace. You want to go back to London, we'll go. We'll get away from this place. This forest. This goddamn prison."

"London?" she repeated. "You want to come to London with me? You think I want my Nora around a man who sneaks into women's bedrooms at night?"

*Nora.* There'd been no Nora in the London of Dalton's mind. Just he and Grace.

"There's no one," he told her, "in Ireland. No wife or child waiting for me." His grip on her arm tightened. "There's just you in all the world."

Her eyes caught his for a second. She swallowed hard. "Let go of me like I asked. Please."

Dalton heard fear in her voice. He let his hand fall. "This house is a goldmine. There are candleholders on the mantle that'll see us to London."

Grace closed her eyes. "I want you to go. And I don't want to see you again."

He frowned. "Grace—"

"This, Alexander... Breaking in here like this, threatening Jack... it ain't right. Can't you see that? It frightens me. You frighten me. Now please, just leave. The family will be up soon and I got to lay the fires." She gathered an armful of wood from the pile beside the door. Dalton grabbed at her and the logs thudded to the porch. Her eyes flashed as she bent to collect them. The door creaked.

"Is there a problem, Miss Ashwell?" A balding man stood over her, arms folded against his thick stomach. He wore a muddy greatcoat over his nightshirt.

She stood. "I beg your pardon, sir. I—"

The master looked Dalton up and down. "Who the hell are you?"

Dalton opened his mouth. He looked at Grace, her eyes unforgiving.

She'd turn him in. Now they were out of the bush, she had no need to trust him. They'd haul him down to the police station and Alexander Dalton would be brought back to life just long enough to be led to the scaffold.

"My friend here's come to see you about some work," she announced brassily. "He heard you's looking for help on the farm. He's saving to get to London. I told him how you were so good as to give me a chance and he said he'd be willing to work for half wages too."

Dalton clenched his jaw. He realized he wasn't breathing.

"Told him to come see you first thing in the morning. Didn't think he'd take it quite so literally, coming at this hour. Must be his enthusiasm."

The master scratched his beard. "Half wages? This true?"

Dalton thought of running. His legs would crumble beneath him, he was sure of it. "Aye," he mumbled.

The master looked him up and down. "What's your name?"

Dalton scrabbled through his memories. "Brown," he said.

"Matthew Brown."

Porter nodded. "Wait here. I want a word with my son about this first." He strode inside, letting the door slam.

Grace gathered the firewood and shot Dalton a glare. "Where are the weapons?"

"In the paddock."

"Bury them," she said. "And stay away from me. Come to me in the night like that again and I'll tell Porter who you really are."

# XVII

Conduct Record of Convicts Arriving in Van Diemen's Land
1804-1830

*Alexander Dalton,* Caledonia *1820*
*December 12th 1820: Drunk and disorderly.*
*Fourteen days labour for the government in his own time.*

It turned out the great man of the house, Bill Porter, was
hauled out from England in 1803. One of the first government
men to do his time in the desolate hell of Van Diemen's Land.
But the authorities, they just loved old Porter. No black marks
on his conduct record. Life sentence whittled down to a pardon
within five years. Five fucking years.

At his ma's insistence, Bill's son Edward took Dalton out
to show him the farm and spent the whole time rabbiting on
about how his da was a petty thief come good.

"And now look," he said, waving an arm at the acres of
land. "All this is ours. A gift from the lieutenant governor
himself."

Dalton saw what he could have had if he'd kept his fists to
himself. Bill Porter, he realised, got all this by bowing down to
the authorities. By licking his overseer's arse and doing what
he was told.

Edward was nineteen or twenty, with the flaccid shoulders
of a farmer who liked to dish out his work to other men. Too

much blond hair on his head and not enough on his chin. Spoke with the wide vowels of the currency lads and lasses. Brown skin that had never known the bitterness of a European winter.

At dusk, the workers were herded into the kitchen where the cook had laid out a spread of food Dalton had not seen since he was a convict worker in Oxley.

Mutton and vegetables, gravy, measures of watered down rum. Of course, in Oxley he was eating stale bread while the smell of mutton drifted beneath the door. He couldn't remember the last time such a meal was cooked for him.

There were five of them around that table. The elderly cook and the children's governess; an older woman with hair so thin and pale her scalp showed through. The stable-hand; his muscular arms bursting out of rolled-up shirtsleeves. And there was Grace, dishing out polite smiles, trying to hide her excitement that she was about to eat something that hadn't been dangling in their traps all afternoon.

Each turned to Dalton with chirpy introductions and polite nods. How to fit in? To seem a normal man? To behave as though he weren't about to piss himself in fear? He took a long gulp of his rum.

The cook shuffled round the table with her gravy pot and slopped a spoonful onto each slab of meat.

"Lumps again, Ellen," the stable-hand grinned. "Just the way I like it."

She whacked him on the knuckles with her serving spoon. "Got a nice pot of porridge on the stove you can have if you got a problem with my gravy. Plenty left now we only got two lags to feed."

Dalton snorted to himself. The convicts were eating gruel and here he was with a plate full of mutton. He picked up a slice of carrot and popped it in his mouth. Grace glared, gesturing to her knife and fork.

*For Christ's sake.* He grabbed the fork in his fist and stabbed the slab of meat, brought it whole to his lips and began to chew. At least with his mouth full he couldn't be expected to speak. The stable-hand snorted with laughter, but Grace's eyes were black.

"This is ever so good," she said, slicing off a miniscule piece of mutton. Wasn't she a little social butterfly with her manners and breathy compliments. A few nights ago, Dalton had watched her drop a piece of smoked meat in the mud, wipe it on her front and swallow it whole.

The cook grinned at Grace. "Nice to have some appreciation. Can tell you're a city girl." She pointed a fat finger at the stable-hand. "Better manners than this country hick here. London, you said?"

And then Grace was off. A great torrent of jabber about Stepney and blue houses and a sideshow with a mermaid. Dalton refilled his rum.

The stable-hand, it seemed, had seen a sideshow too when he was a lad. Blathered on about conjoined twins while Grace giggled and fluttered her lashes like something had flown into her eye.

Dalton despised the Grace of civilisation. All flirty eyes and exaggerated hand gestures. Sickening. Did she learn this performance from the toff emporium of Mr James Harris? Wondered if a little of her London charm might earn her an extra sliver of mutton? He liked her better when she smelled of river muck.

He lay awake that night, squeezed onto a sleeping pallet beside the stable hand. So close, Dalton could feel the heat of his body. Would have thought himself back at Macquarie Harbour if it were gruel on the stable hand's breath and not roast meat. Head swimming from the rum, he took his coat and blanket and carried them out to the barn.

He came into the house before dawn. He would sneak back to the servants' quarters and no one would know he'd spent the night with the animals.

A fine layer of frost lay over the land. They'd be up and about soon, these farmers. Dalton would have a master again. He felt an old tension return to his shoulders.

The back door opened into the kitchen. He took a match from the box above the range and lit a candle, carrying it into the parlour.

Here it was. The life he could have chosen.

A government man with a velvet armchair. Wasn't that just the best thing you ever bloody well heard?

*These fucking colonists*, he thought. Trying to turn this godforsaken prison into a civilised land.

*Don't you know the things that have happened out there?*

On the other side of this island, men were pulled from the triangle and sent to the logging stations with their shoes full of their own blood. Here, these bastards sat in velvet chairs and lay jewels upon their mantles. Could none of them feel the darkness in the forest? Or sense the ghosts hiding in the shadows? Could none of them see the monsters this system had created?

He held the candle up to the stone features of the sculpture on the mantle. He thought of his wooden carvings. Imagined them staring across the empty hut, creepers growing up the wall and swallowing them whole. Above the statue was an enormous gilded mirror. Dalton lifted the candle and, for the first time in more than a decade, looked into his own eyes.

God Almighty, who was this man? His skin was brown and weathered, his beard wiry. A permanent scowl creased the bridge of his nose. He brought a hand to his chin to make sure it was really him.

The last time he'd seen his reflection, he was a young man of twenty-three. An insignificant lag. He'd never seen Macquarie Harbour. Never met Robert Greenhill or Alexander Pearce or wretched Tom Bodenham. Had never considered the lengths he'd go to in order to ensure his own survival.

Once, he'd been vaguely handsome. There'd been women— flings, games, Maggies and Sallies. Never love. But now: such darkness in his eyes. He felt like all the horrors of his life were etched into his face. What had these colonists seen when he'd sat amongst them at the dinner table?

He turned his shoulders, checking those telltale scars were hidden beneath his coat. White streaks showed above his neck cloth. He wished he hadn't cut his hair. Wished he'd let himself hide.


After breakfast, Dalton traipsed out to the farm with Edward Porter and the two remaining convict workers; short stocky men with scowls and hunched shoulders. One was Dalton's age with a shock of orange hair on his head and chin. The other was older, greyer. Sunken and weary.

Frost crunched beneath their boots. There were fences to rebuild and their arms were loaded with axes and saws. The redhead looked over his shoulder and gave Dalton a twisted half-smile.

"All this is ours," Edward announced. "Right up to the creek."

*Yes mate,* thought Dalton, *you told me that already.*

The four of them got to work in the wood yard, sawing and planing tree trunks into fence posts. Dalton let himself get lost in the physicality of it, the way he used to do hauling pines at Sarah Island. Feel the burn in his arms instead of the ache in his chest. Don't think further than the next swing of the axe.

They'd not been at it a half-hour, when Edward wiped his brow with his shirtsleeve and wandered across the wood yard. Following his lead, the redheaded convict released the saw and let it rest in the log.

"Keep at it, Howell," shot Edward. "You got a whole forest to get through after that one." He nodded at Dalton. "Why you still got that coat on, bog-trotter?"

Dalton kept his eyes on the log. "There's ice in the air."

"Ice in the air. You're pouring sweat, you mad bugger."

Dalton tried to lose himself in the rhythm of the plane against the wood. *Shah. Shah.*

"Take it off. I'm hot at the sight of you."

Dalton looked over his shoulder at Edward. "I'm not one of your convict slaves."

Edward cleared his throat and spat into the grass. He leant against the barn and watched the men work.

Dalton snorted. "Lazy fucking narrow-back."

Howell grinned.

"You say something?" Edward demanded.

"No, sir. Not a word." He lost himself in the beat of it. *Shah, shah, shah.*

# XVIII

Hobart Town Gazette
Friday 25th June 1824

*'The Learned Gentlemen then proceeded to detail certain confessions made by the prisoner, [Alexander Pearce], before ... Lieutenant Cutherbertson— commandant at Macquarie Harbour— and to the Rev Robert Knopwood. Confessions which, although in some respects inconsistent, would yet, when coupled with all the facts, merit the most serious attention.'*

The bastards hired them. Called Dalton and Grace into the parlour on Friday morning and said they'd have them on at half rates, three shillings a week. Three shillings.

*Did you do the sums, Grace?*

Four years or more of sweeping the floor until she got two tickets back to London. Good thing she'd lost Violet, or she'd have had to earn enough for three.

They stood side by side in the Porters' parlour. Grace was gushing with curtseys and thank yous, pretending Dalton wasn't there.

He'd proved himself good with a saw. Convinced the Porters to hire him and made that Edward look like a right pansy in the process. He'd thought she'd have been pleased with him.

He followed her into the kitchen. Brought his muddy boots

from the doorstep and sat at the table. He slid his feet into them slowly, not taking his eyes off her. She had a faraway look about her. "I thought you'd be happy," he said.

"I am happy."

"You don't seem it." He followed her gaze. Through the window he saw the Porters' two daughters rolling a hoop across the lawn.

Grace went to the cupboard for the broom.

"You miss your girls," said Dalton.

She attacked the floor with violent, noisy scrapes. The broom shot out and collected his ankle. "Don't you got work to do?"

Dalton snatched the broom.

"Alexander—"

"Speak to me," he said. "Please."

She sighed. "They know you're sleeping in the barn. People are talking. Porter's only kept you on because he ain't going to find no-one else who'll work as cheap." She folded her arms. "Why are you out there?"

"I don't want people around me."

"You've had me around you for months."

"But these people... They're not like you."

Grace took the broom. "Please, just come inside. Try to fit in. Whatever you've come to believe, you belong in here, not out with the animals."

Dalton bent to lace his boots.

"Alexander? Will you try? Please?"

He nodded.

Grace smiled faintly. "Thank you."

A week, and then a rifle shot in the cold morning. Bill Porter stood on the edge of the cattle paddock with the gun in his hand. Beside him, Edward peered into the scrub. They stalked back towards the wood yard where the convict workers hovered, watching with disinterested eyes. Dalton stood beside them with his arms folded.

Mrs Porter stepped onto the porch and squinted. "Catch them, Bill?"

Porter spat in the grass. "Fucking animals ran off like dogs. You—" He held the rifle out to Dalton. "You a good shot?"

Dalton nodded.

Porter tossed him the gun and powder. "Couple of blacks come out of the bush and nicked my boots. Go find them. Take Howell with you."

Dalton slid a ball into the chamber. The click was loud in the cold morning. He wove through the cattle paddock and out into the thin blue-grey scrub on the fringe of the plains.

Howell trotted behind him. "We going to shoot these bastards then?"

"Why would I want to do that?" Dalton looked down. No flattened foliage here. If there truly had been blacks at the farm, they'd not come this way. He kept walking anyway.

Howell began to whistle. A tuneless thing with two flat notes. *Tuu, haa.* "Heard a story once. They say some bolters got themselves lost in these woods."

*Tuu, haa.*

Dalton felt something twist inside him.

"Done some real bad things. Inhuman things." Howell stomped through the scrub. "You heard those stories too?"

Dalton shook his head. Began to walk faster.

"I think you have." Howell combed two fingers through his rust-coloured beard. "Porter'll find you out, you know. Sooner or later."

Dalton kept his eyes down. "Don't know what you're talking about."

"Aye, you do. A man stumbles out of the bush half-dead, you tend to remember him."

And Dalton realised it sickly. He'd seen that bushel of orange hair before. Seen this man in a cattle duffing ring on the Fat Doe River. Howell smiled, like he'd seen the flicker of recognition in Dalton's eyes. He stopped walking.

"A silent man. A man that don't speak because he don't want no one to know his secrets." He laughed long and low. "Can't imagine the Porters would take it too well to find they'd hired a bolter. Especially one with a horror story behind him."

Dalton stared him down. "I'm no bolter."

Howell grinned. "I seen you come out of the bush, mate. Convict slops hanging off your shoulders. That canary yellow they dish out at Macquarie Harbour. I gave you my coat and a double ration of salted pork. Half carried you to the fire. You'd be dead if it weren't for me." He stepped close and held a grimy finger inches from Dalton's nose. "You, Mr Dalton, are the only one of those bolters never properly accounted for. You left our ring the day before we raided Bothwell. Ran into the bush. We all knew why you'd disappeared. We knew what you'd done. Did you really think us too foolish to put the pieces together?"

Dalton ran his hand along the shaft of the rifle. "You've got the wrong man."

"Have I now?" Howell chuckled and clapped him on the back. "I'll have to beg your pardon then."

That night, laughter rose from the house. A party. The man of the house Bill's birthday.

Dalton paced across the barn.

*We all knew what you'd done.*
*You, Mr Dalton...*
There was no anonymity in this land of new beginnings.

He stumbled into the night and peered through the steamy window into the parlour. Guests were crammed around a blazing fire. There was Bill Porter, his bald head shining like a melon, roaring with laughter at what Dalton was sure was one of his own jokes. People were clustered around him, hands full of rum and cigars. Strangers, workers, faces Dalton recognised from the farm beside Annie and Jack's. Grace was hovering by the hearth, watching the Porters' girls toss knucklebones on the rug.

Dalton felt disconnected from the world on the other side of the glass. A world he'd stopped being a part of the night Tom Bodenham had died.

"Let's do this." Greenhill whispering in Pearce's ear. A sound Dalton had never been able to forget.

They'd been walking for sixteen days. Macquarie Harbour lay behind them and who knew what lay ahead. The last of the bread they'd eaten days ago. Dalton's steps were crooked with hunger. His vision was blurred, throat dry.

It wasn't supposed to be like this, was it. They were supposed to have reached the mainland by now in that cursed boat. He ought to have been drinking ale with some beautiful lass in Kilkenny.

Instead, his stomach was bloated and leeches crawled inside his boots. He didn't have the strength to stop them. The man Greenhill chose to sacrifice wouldn't have the strength to stop him either.

"Tonight," said Greenhill. Dalton was crouched behind a monstrous pine tree. He didn't mean to hide. He was just too weak to stand.

"I can't." Pearce. *Yes, you can.* "Who then?" Pearce asked.

Greenhill whispered: "Dalton. Dalton, the flogger."

*So that's your justice then, Greenhill? I take the whip to your back once under orders and you'll cut out my heart?*

Did he know Dalton was there? Did he want the flogger to see death coming?

Dalton thought of trying to run, turning his back and tearing into the bush. But if he moved, the twigs beneath him would crackle. Ferns would sigh and birds would scatter. Greenhill would see him.

The axe dangled by Greenhill's side, bumping against his calf. Pearce stood opposite, but Greenhill's eyes looked past him, past Dalton. Thoughtful, hateful eyes. Was he tied up on the triangle at Sarah Island, while Dalton heaved fifty strokes of the cat into his spine? Couldn't he hear the overseer beside them, spitting and cursing?

*Put your bloody back into it, Dalton, or you'll be next.*

Greenhill's eyes panned across the bush and for a moment Dalton was sure he had been seen.

The night before, he'd sat with Ned Brown and Kennerly, hidden from the others. They'd talked of running. Talked of leaving Greenhill to his nightmarish plans. They'd argued on it.

Kennerly and Brown wanted to go back to the harbour. Face the commandant and his floggers. But there was no going back for Dalton. That hopeless existence at Macquarie Harbour, that wasn't life. He'd rather be dead. Easier to say such a thing, though, than face the reality of it. *I'd rather die*, a man could say with all the certainty in the world. But when death was staring him in the face, well that was a whole other story.

Greenhill and Pearce; they turned and spoke. A month from now they'd be circling each other in the night, fighting to be the last man alive.

Dalton stayed where he was, not daring to make the bush crackle or the birds scatter. He stayed as the sun sank, trying to keep his eyes on Greenhill and Pearce as they wove through the purple forest. And suddenly: the crack of iron to bone, hanging on the cold air. Men shouted and cursed at Greenhill.

*English dog.*

Silence fell over them.

Bodenham. He was only a boy. The youngest of them all. Why him? Did his legs not move as quickly as the rest? Had he cursed at Greenhill under his breath? Looked at him the wrong way over the supper tables one night? Or had he been singled out for his Scottish blood, Pearce reluctant to have the death of a fellow Irishman on his hands?

Had the poor bastard any idea of what was coming? Was there time for thought when he saw Greenhill's axe come towards him? Did his poor, sorry life play out before his eyes? Did he see the stained bulkheads of the convict ship and the blood splattered triangle on Sarah Island? Or was it just fear and hunger and then eternal darkness?

Afterwards, Dalton went to the creek. Tried to purge himself of all he'd swallowed. Fingers down his throat, retching into the stream. But his body clung to those precious scraps of meat. He splashed his face. The water was icy but he was hot with sweat and fear. Feverish. His slops were thick with dirt and hanging off one shoulder.

He heard a whisper: "That you, Dalton?"

He stumbled, terrified. Freezing water filled his boots. "Get the fuck away from me."

Bodenham would keep the men going for a few days at most. And they'd all stood on the top of that ridge and seen the endless miles of nothing. Someone would be next. If Greenhill had his way, Dalton wouldn't survive the second swing of the axe.

But this was Bill Kennerly, eyes glowing in the light of the moon. Another man behind him. Ned Brown. Last night, they'd talked themselves out of leaving. Convinced themselves there'd be no bloodshed. They were messmates. Brothers in arms. Surely not even Greenhill could go through with such a thing.

But now there was one man less among them. Kennerly squeezed Dalton's shoulders like he was trying to stop his humanity escaping.

"You're going back then?" asked Dalton. "Back to the harbour?"

"Going anywhere but here. I'd rather die than have this on my conscience. Thought there were nowhere on this earth worse than Sarah Island, but we're all wrong sometimes, aye?"

In every moving shape in the darkness, Dalton saw the arc of Greenhill's axe. In every sound he heard the choke of Bodenham's last breath.

"Kennerly." The footsteps paused. "I'm coming with you."

At daybreak, Brown and Kennerly turned west; back towards Sarah Island. Both men had refused to eat the night before. They'd be on the edge of starvation by the time they reached the harbour. Both would be dead by week's end.

Dalton turned east. Scratched out a life on the edge of survival.

He sank against the outside wall of the house, sweat trickling down his back. What a fool he'd been to think he could erase himself from history. A horror story like theirs would never die. It would be told around campfires for a hundred years or more. Spoken of over market counters, across bars pooled with beer. Told by children hiding under the bedclothes and trying to work themselves into nightmares. No one had forgotten. Eleven years and Howell had known his face at first sight. Had known his story, his name, his crime.

The kitchen door flew open and noise spilled into the yard. A sea of heads and voices. Among them were Edward and the stable-hand with the men Dalton recognised as Annie's neighbours. Two of Edward's younger brothers raced into the wood yard with a cricket bat and ball. Dalton tried to disappear into the shadows.

"What you doing out here, bog-trotter?" drawled Edward. "Our company not good enough for you?"

The faces came towards him. He stepped back. Felt the wall of the house hard against his spine.

"Leave him alone." Grace pushed past Edward. "Are you all right?"

Dalton nodded.

Edward slung an arm around Grace's shoulder. "I want to tell you a story, Miss Ashwell."

She glanced sideways at Dalton. "What is it?"

"You'll like this one, I'll warrant." Edward gulped his beer, a trickle escaping out the side of his mouth. "This is the story of Michael Howe, the bolter."

"I ain't interested." She unhooked herself from Edward's arm.

"He lived in the bush for six years like a savage. They caught him at the river just north of Bothwell. Cut off his head and sent it back to Hobart Town." He grinned. "Governor wanted proof he was dead, see. They can be right bastards, them bolters. Dangerous, too."

Grace snorted. "Fine story." She pulled Dalton away from Edward and the others. "Come on. You'll have a drink at least." She led him into the house and poured a glass of brandy from the bottle on the table, pressing it into his hand. "Something's happened," she said. "What?"

What if Howell were to tell her? What if she knew?

"Nothing's happened." He took a gulp and carried his glass back out to the yard. And then a rough hand was on his shoulder, yanking his arm backwards. The glass flew, its contents spilling across the grass.

"That's my pa's brandy," said Edward. "Better it go to waste than be drunk by the likes of you."

Dalton raised his fist. Grace's hand shot out and snatched his wrist.

"Bugger off, Edward," she snapped. "You're pissed as a bloody sailor."

Edward laughed and waved his empty measure at Dalton. "You catch those savages then? Second time this month they've come in and nicked our boots."

"Why would the blacks want your boots?" Grace demanded.

"As if I know how their savage brains work. They're right devils, those black Irish." He gave a liquored-up snort. "That's what we call them round here, you know. The black Irish."

Grace's hand tensed around Dalton's wrist. She glared until Edward gave up and stumbled out to the wood yard to join in the cricket match. She let her hand fall. "He's just trying to stir you up. Don't give him what he wants."

"Stay away from him. He's a bastard."

"Course he is. But his pa is paying us and we was lucky to get any work at all." Her eyes followed the children as they raced after the ball.

"Those kids," said Dalton. "It's not good for you to be around them."

Grace looked at her feet. "I'm fine," she said, though the drink in her blood sent a tremor through her voice. "Porter's kids ain't nothing like Violet."

"Let's leave," he said suddenly.

Grace sighed. "Don't be mad. Just tell me what's happened. Is it Edward? Does he know something?"

Dalton shook his head. "These people are just scum."

"That they may be, but they're the only way I got of making a life for Nora."

"The candlesticks on the mantle. They're worth a fortune."

Grace glared at him. "No. We ain't thieves." She sighed wearily. "You said you'd try and fit in, Alexander. This don't seem like trying to me."

Grace left the house with a list of medicines to fetch from the apothecary. The wind was icy but the sky a vibrant blue. Her boots crunched on the path, her hair whipping around her cheeks. The days were growing longer and the morning frosts beginning to melt in great bursts of sun. She was craving the spring. Rebirth. A reminder it was possible to start again.

She pulled her cloak tightly around her, savouring the stillness of the walk down the hill into town. After three months in the wilderness, the constant bustle of the house was exhausting. In the two weeks she'd been with the Porters, she'd worked harder than she ever had. Harder even than those first few months with Charlotte Harris when she'd been desperate to prove herself indispensable. She'd been exhausted at the end of every day then too, but it was a mental exhaustion— remembering all the quirks and etiquette of the wealthy. With the Porters, it was purely physical. As the only housemaid, her list of tasks seemed unending— fifteen-hour days of scrubbing, blacking and sweeping. Mostly, she welcomed the busyness, the aches in her body every night. It kept her from counting how many months and years she would need to scrub, black and sweep until she had enough to return to England. Kept her from focusing on all she had lost.

She bought the medicines for Mrs Porter and walked back down the sludge of the high street. Suddenly a little girl darted across the road, blonde plaits streaming out behind her. Grace stopped breathing. She dropped the parcel, the bottles thudding at her feet.

Violet.

# XIX

Grace leapt over the bottles and ran. "Violet!"

The girl disappeared around the corner. Grace tore down the side street, slipping, stumbling through the mud.

*There, at the bottom of the street.* Blonde hair. Brown dress, white pinny.

Violet darted out from between two warehouses and into the filthy grog shop at the end of the alley. Grace rattled the door. Pounded on the window. An older woman with a long nose and narrow eyes poked her head out the door. She reeked of tobacco.

"Ain't nothing for sale today. Coppers are on the prowl. They heard my whisky comes from something other than an honest source. Told 'em they're wrong of course. This is a fine law-abiding establishment. But I'm shutting up til I can get rid of it anyway."

"Did you see a little girl?" Grace asked breathlessly. "In a brown dress?"

"Ain't seen no one."

"She came in here." Grace tried to elbow her way through the door. "Let me in. Please."

"No chance, missy. You could be working for them coppers for all I know."

"I ain't working for no-one. I saw my Violet come in here! Let me through!"

"You're mistaken." The woman threw her weight against the door and it slammed, narrowly missing Grace's fingers.

She pounded on the glass but the woman had disappeared.

Grace's heart pounded. Was Violet truly alive? Was this woman hiding her? She didn't know whether to cry with happiness or grief.

She crossed the alley and peered up at the tavern. The narrow building was nestled between two small cottages; one with broken windows that looked to be abandoned. Grace slunk down the lane at the side of the building. She rattled the back door. Locked.

The barmaid threw open the door. "Get the hell out of here," she hissed. "We ain't got your girl. Now bugger off before I get my pistol."

Grace hurried back down the alley and hid between two crooked huts, keeping her eyes glued to the tavern.

As it grew dark, handfuls of men sidled up to the front door, to be shooed away by the barmaid. Some drifted away quietly, others hurled abuse, but the doors remained locked. One man pulled a bottle from his coat pocket and held it up to his friends. They howled with delight and stumbled down the road, laughing and passing it between them. Grace held her breath as they passed. She pressed her back against the wall of the hut, trying to hide without losing her view of the tavern.

One of the men caught her eye and grinned, revealing a gap where his front teeth had been. "And here I thought my night was ruined." He dug into his pocket and held out a sixpence.

"I'm sorry," Grace said tensely. "You're mistaken."

"Am I? Ain't that a shame." He pressed his arm against the wall to block her path. He stank of piss and cheap booze. Grace's heart began to race. She tried to duck beneath his arm. He snatched her wrist and dragged her back sharply, digging a hand inside her cloak. Her knee flew into his groin. The man grunted in pain and Grace shoved her way past, stumbling in the mud. She scrambled to her feet and ran.

Footsteps crunched behind her. Curses and drunken laughter. She kept sprinting towards the lamps of the high street. A rough hand snatched her arm.

"Grace."

She stumbled into Alexander's chest and gulped down her breath. She looked over her shoulder. The men caught sight of her with Alexander and dispersed back down the alley.

"What are you doing here?" she asked breathlessly.

Alexander stared after the men, his eyes black. "I've been looking for you. Mrs Porter said you never came back from town. That's a bad street. Don't go down there again."

"I saw her. I saw Violet."

"What?"

"She's in the tavern. The barmaid has her, I'm sure of it. She's hiding her."

Alexander paused. "Why would she do that?"

"How should I know?"

He took her arm. "Come on now, let's go back to the Porters'."

"Are you mad? I ain't going nowhere! I have to find her!"

He hesitated. "It wasn't her. How could it be?"

"I don't know! But it was!"

Alexander held her shoulders. "Listen to me. Whoever you saw, it wasn't Violet. I'm sure of it."

"How do you know that?"

He dropped his hands and sighed. "Because it doesn't make any sense for her to be here."

"I know what I saw." She wiped her muddy hands on her skirt began to walk towards the alley.

"You need to sleep."

"How could I sleep? Violet is out there. That awful woman's got her. I got to go back and keep watch."

"Then I'll come with you," said Alexander. "You shouldn't be down there alone."

They sat with their backs against a cottage fence, eyes on the darkened tavern. The lamps on the main street did little to light the shadows. Dalton blinked hard to fight off a wave of exhaustion. Beside him, Grace was sitting up on her knees, eyes alert, squinting through the darkness.

He had to tell her the truth about the girl. Owed her the truth. But he couldn't stand to think what it would do to her. There was a fragile peace between them he couldn't bear to overturn.

He knew she needed his innocence. Needed the image of an easy death for Violet. No violence, no suffering. Just a dream-filled sleep, surrounded by coloured birds and a glittering river. An end for Violet which would make her sorrow a little easier to carry.

He didn't want Grace to crawl through her days drowning in guilt and regret. There was too much life in her for that. He couldn't bear to watch her fade into the same darkness he woke to each morning. Her pain made him ache. He'd forgotten he was capable of empathy. He felt agonisingly human. A part of him longed for that wordless void he had existed in for the last decade.

When the sky began to lighten, he said: "She's not coming out. Even if she's in there, we'll not find her from here."

Grace stood and whacked at the mud caked to her skirt. "Then we've got to break in."

"We can't do that. You'll lose your job. You don't want that, aye?" He clambered to his feet. "We'll come back tonight when the tavern is open. If she's here, we'll find her then." He caught a flicker of hope in her eyes and hated himself for it. He put a gentle hand to her back. "Come on now. Let's go back to the Porters'."

The moment supper finished, Grace grabbed her cloak and charged from the house. Her eyes were red-rimmed with sleeplessness. Her food had gone untouched.

They traipsed into town without speaking. Laughter and yellow light from the grog shop spilled onto the road.

Dalton followed Grace inside. The air was thick and smoky. A fiddler played in the corner, accompanied by laughter and the clink and thud of glasses. Red-lipped women with breasts spilling from cinched corsets sashayed across the room. Dalton looked away, both aroused and oddly intimidated. His every sense felt heightened, overloaded. He fought the urge to run back to the empty street. Instead, he shoved his way towards the bar. He needed a drink.

Grace gripped his arm tightly as though she knew he was contemplating escape. "I've got to get into the rooms above the tavern." She narrowed her eyes at the barmaid. "We'll wait by the counter until that witch is out of the way."

At the bar sat Howell, watching the working girls with interest. Dalton cursed under his breath.

Grace glanced at him. "What?"

"Howell. Porter's government man."

"So what? He's nothing. Ain't even supposed to be here. We ought to report him."

Howell turned, his face breaking into a grin. He slid off his stool and ambled towards them. "Well now. The silent man."

"Leave us be," said Dalton.

Howell clapped him on the back. "No need to be like that. Let's all be civil and have a drink, shall we?"

The barmaid glared as Grace approached. "You again. Thought I told you to bugger off."

Dalton slammed a coin onto the counter. "We're paying customers." The woman eyed him warily before sliding the money into her apron pocket and handing over two glasses of ale. Dalton took a long gulp. Weak and watery. He longed for the numbing effect of Porter's brandy.

Three young men joined them at the bar. They wore holey trousers and stained shirts. Their hands and nails were grimy. "Got good news for you, Howell," said one. He opened the package in his fist to reveal a woolly cloud of tobacco. "New crop's ready for sale."

Howell grinned. "Brilliant. I bet my mate here would like a sample."

The man shoved the tobacco under Dalton's nose. "Fresh picked. Best in the colony. We'll do you a good deal."

Dalton turned away.

Howell gulped his ale. "It's good stuff. Billy over there brought the seeds all the way from Africa. We been growing it out by the creek. Selling it to the toffs. It's made us rich men."

Dalton snorted. "Shame you've not got the freedom to use it."

"That it is." Howell clapped him on the back. "But you see, silent man, I'm inspired by you. You ought to be swinging. And yet here you are, swanning around this bar with a pretty girl on your arm and Porter's money in your pocket. You make me think a life sentence may not always be as long as it seems."

Dalton kept his eyes averted. Howell thumped his arm and nodded towards a blond man on the opposite side of the tavern.

"That there's Jim Berry," he told Dalton. "Serving his sentence in the bloody police force."

Berry was tall and thin with trousers that reached his ankles. He'd adopted an odd lean against the table while one of the working girls played with the buttons on his coat.

"Happening all the time out here. People started whinging about the bushrangers. Asked them down in Hobart to send us more police. Instead we got Jim Berry." Howell nudged Grace, who was doing her best to ignore the men. "D'you ever hear such a thing, missy? Police force full of bloody lags."

Grace gave Howell a fleeting glance, then turned back to watch the door behind the counter.

Howell laughed. "What you reckon, Mr Dalton? Ever fancy yourself as a copper?"

A shout and clatter of glasses rose from the men at the back of the room. The barmaid cursed and shuffled out from behind the counter. Seizing her chance, Grace leapt from her stool and darted through the door behind the bar. Dalton chased her up a creaking timber staircase to a dim, low-ceilinged hallway.

"Violet!" She rattled and thumped on each of the doors. The steps thudded and Howell appeared behind them.

"What in hell is she doing?" Behind Howell stood one of the working girls from the bar. She was tall and broad shouldered, her curves accentuated by a tight bodice and dirty blue dress. Yellow hair was piled on top of her head, loose pieces clinging to her cheeks and neck. She looked to Grace and Dalton with creased, flinty eyes. "What do you want?"

"My little girl, Violet. Where is she?"

Howell clamped a hand around the top of Grace's arm. "I'll get rid of her, Maryann. The little dishclout can't hold her drink."

"Let go of her," hissed Dalton.

The woman snorted. "Too late for you to start being helpful, Daniel Howell." She turned to Grace. "Only girl in there is Emma. My daughter."

"You're lying. Open the door."

Maryann sighed and pulled a key from inside her bodice. Grace pushed her way into the room. Maryann stepped back to allow Dalton and Howell inside.

The bedsit smelled of tobacco and bodies. A lamp hissed on a crooked table. Blankets were strewn across the mattress in the centre, a crib pushed against one wall.

A little girl was asleep on a pallet by the hearth, her blonde hair in two messy plaits. A rag doll lay at her side. Her face was unmistakably Howell's.

Maryann folded her arms. "That who you saw?"

Grace stared at the girl for a long time. Her eyes glistened. Finally, she cleared her throat. "I'm sorry. I thought she were someone else."

Grace walked back to the Porters' house in silence. She sat on her bed and hugged her knees, without bothering to remove her cloak or boots. The loss of Violet felt raw.

She reached beneath her mattress and pulled out her pouch of money. Six shillings. Wouldn't get her back to Hobart Town, let alone London. She piled the coins into a stack on the mattress. They shimmered in the glow of her lamp.

She missed her girls so desperately. Longed to hold them to her, one little head pressed into each of her shoulders. She'd never hold them both that way again. Violet was lost forever and each day she felt Nora slipping further away too. Even if by miracle she made it back London, where could she go? And to what future? No man would have a barren woman for a wife. Was she to leave Nora in the hands of her gin-soaked mother while she went out at dawn each morning to work in the factories? Sell her body like the mother of Howell's daughter?

She'd trawled through the same arguments with herself when Harris's child was growing inside her. They'd led her back to the blue house. Without Harris, she had nothing. But the blue house was gone. Her relationship with Harris had rotted and crumbled. How was it possible, she wondered, to have such love for the twins and such hatred for their father?

She'd heard love and hate were two sides of the same coin. Never understood such a thing until James Harris. She'd loved him with a passion that went deeper than her desire for the good life. She had drawn close to him for his wealth and the security it offered, but she knew that even if he were the poorest man on earth, she'd have followed him to the slums and been happy just to wake up beside him.

Once, however fleetingly, he'd loved her too. She was sure of it. If he truly were a poor man they might have been together for real, without the critical eyes of society. It had been a thrill at first; waiting until the house was silent to sneak into his bedroom.

Curtseying by day, undressing him by night. But she'd learned quickly that being in love made you want to share. She longed to tell the world she fell asleep with James Harris's lips in her hair. But she would never have what Charlotte had had: that freedom to walk on his arm, to welcome him home with a kiss.

She'd believed Harris had hated the secrecy as much as she had. Believed he longed for the relative freedom Van

Diemen's Land would bring. But with the thrill of the secret ripped away, she saw their relationship for what it truly was. Master and concubine. She'd been no more than a toy to warm the cold sheets left by Charlotte's death.

A knock at the door made her start.

"Grace?"

"Go away, Alexander. What if someone sees you here? What will they think?"

"I don't care."

"Well I do care!" She waited for his footsteps to disappear down the hall. Instead he opened the door and sat beside her on the bed.

"Go away," she said, not looking at him. And then: "What do you want?"

"I'm worried for you."

Grace stared at her coin stack. "You must think me a right fool."

"You're not a fool. You're grieving. And you think her death was your fault." Alexander's voice was husky. "But it wasn't."

"Of course it was. I ought to have been taking better care of her."

He turned to face her. "I'm sorry about your girl, Grace. Truly. I'm sorry."

She lurched suddenly and threw her arms around him. He froze for a moment, taken aback. Then he wrapped his arms around her tightly, pulling her into him.

"Once, Nora, she got out of bed in the night and tried to go out into the street." Her voice was muffled against his neck. "Sleepwalking, you see. I thought, maybe that's what Violet done. Maybe she were sleepwalking and got herself lost."

"Aye. Perhaps."

"She's gone, isn't she."

Alexander nodded.

Grace sat back and wiped her eyes. "I wanted to believe it was her. I wanted to believe so badly."

Alexander glanced at the pile of coins.

"Six shillings," she said bitterly. "I worked myself to the ground and all I got is six shillings. I'll never get back to London without Harris. I never realised how much I relied on him. He stopped paying me when we come here. Said we were as good as man and wife now. 'We share everything,' he told me. Took all my money and put it in his bank account. A hundred pounds I saved, working for him and the girls. And he took every bit of it back. I thought I'd have everything once we were together. I thought I'd never go hungry or cold or wanting again." She swung a hand at the piles and sent silver skimming across the room. "I gave up everything I knew to come out here. Because I were such a fool to think he and I could make a life together." She laughed coldly. "Why am I telling you this?"

"Because there's no one else."

"You're right," said Grace. "There ain't no one else."

Alexander nudged one of the coins with his toe. "What I said about going back to London," he mumbled. "I meant it."

"London?" she repeated. "You? Alexander, I can see how hard this place is for you. How will you survive in a place like London?"

"It's here I can't survive," he said. "Not for much longer." He shifted suddenly and faced her. His grey eyes glowed with determination. "I can't live in this haunted forest. I can't live carrying the dead. Carrying the guilt. And neither can you." He grabbed her hand and squeezed. "We've got to leave this place It's the only way I can forget who I am and what I've done. I was a man once, Grace. I want to be again."

She had never heard so many words come out of his mouth

at once before. She reached down and ran her fingers over the tasselled ends of his belt.

"Aye," she said. "You were once, weren't you."

She had been the one to plant these ideas of escape in his head. How could she deny him a chance to start again?

She began to gather the coins. "Six shillings," she said. "That's three shillings more than I had a week ago. Six shillings more than I had last month. We work hard. Harder than we ever worked before. Get Porter to put us up to full wages." She sat up on her knees, her heart speeding with fresh enthusiasm. "This is possible, Alexander. It is." She pressed a coin into his palm. "Are you afraid?" she asked. "To go?"

He pocketed the coin. "Aye. But I'm more afraid to stay."

# XX

Dalton trudged to the top of the hill with Edward and Howell to rebuild the fences on the western side of the farm. He walked in silence, buzzing with nervous energy. He kept one hand in his pocket, wrapped around Grace's coin.

They needed money. Grace might have convinced herself they could earn enough to get back to London, but he had no such illusions. They had to get away from this place as quickly as possible. Before Howell sought to turn him in. Before Grace was strangled by her grief.

Bronze candlesticks at the back of the Porters' mantle. How much would such a thing fetch?

He looked out across the plains. At the bottom of the hill, he could see the tiny figures of Annie and Jack in their vegetable garden. Far behind, the twisted tree he'd buried their weapons beneath.

"Bog-trotter," called Edward. "You listening to me? I said, you take this corner."

Dalton nodded.

"*Yes sir*," said Edward. "Open your mouth, you useless bastard." He followed Dalton's gaze. Narrowed his eyes at Annie and Jack. "Bloody unnatural. That savage living like one of us." He raised an imaginary rifle and pulled the trigger. "Only his pa's white blood saving him from what we all want to do." He lowered his hands and began to pace, watching the men work.

Dalton clenched his teeth. He focused on the sound his hammer made as he drove the stakes into the earth. *Thud, thud.* He imagined sailing out of this place and leaving Edward Porter to fix his own damn fences.

"What the fuck is this?" Edward snorted. He kicked at the stake Howell was hammering. "Crooked as shit. Do it again."

Howell grimaced. He yanked out the stake and re-hammered it. Again, Edward kicked it to the ground. A light flickered behind Howell's eyes. He swung the hammer, narrowly missing Edward's stomach. Edward charged, head down, into Howell's middle.

Dalton felt his blood heat. He felt an urge to hold Edward's arms and let Howell punch the life out of him. Instead, he grabbed Howell by the hair and pulled him away.

"He's not worth it," he hissed.

Howell whirled around and grabbed a fistful of Dalton's coat. It slid from his shoulders, his shirt tearing with a screech. Edward climbed to his feet and wiped a trickle of blood from his nose with the back of his hand. He looked at Dalton and laughed throatily.

"Free settler, you say? Only the worst of the worst got scars like that."

Dalton tugged the torn shirt back towards his neck. "Your da got scars like that then?"

Edward stepped towards him. Flushed cheeks with that miserable fluff on his chin. All up in Dalton's face, youthful fuck. "Where's your paperwork? Show me your pardon. How we to know you ain't just a bolter?"

"Because bolters don't survive out here."

Edward took a step back, like he'd seen madness in Dalton's eyes. "That's right." A little of the cockiness gone from his voice. "They made it that way. All sea and mountains. The scum that get sent to Macquarie Harbour don't got no chance of ever getting out."

"Aye," said Dalton. "So I'm no bolter then, am I."

Edward wiped his nose again, leaving a smear of blood across one cheek. Finally he turned away from Dalton and glared at Howell.

"You," he said. "If you were dreaming of a pardon, you'd better bloody think again."

They carted Daniel Howell out for a good flogging that afternoon, lining the rest of the household up to watch. A bank of clouds had blown in and fine drizzle was falling.

Edward stood in front of the barn, bullwhip in hand.

Bill Porter marched Howell out from his quarters, a thick hand at the top of the convict's arm. Howell wore nothing but frayed blue trousers and a look of hatred.

"You got no right to flog your own workers, Porter," he spat. "You think I don't know that? I'll have the governor onto you."

Porter laughed. "The governor ain't listening to a piece of shit like you, Howell." He nodded at Edward. "Come on, son. Show this animal who's in charge."

Howell stepped close to his overseer. "You look at me like I ain't worth the time of day. But you got convict blood same as I do. The *hated stain* they call it. The scourge of this colony. You heard that before, I'll warrant. Sure you've come across some gentry who won't come near you. They'll see your criminal blood a mile off. Wouldn't share a shit bucket with an emancipist and his family."

Porter tensed his jaw. Chose silence.

Howell grinned. "I'm right, aren't I."

Porter shoved him against the wall of the barn. He glared at Edward, colour rising in his cheeks. "Do it, boy."

Edward brought the whip down with a loud crack. A line of

crimson appeared on Howell's back. Dalton glanced at Grace. She stared at her feet, wincing with each snap of the lash.

Dalton realised Edward was watching him. His eyes were cold, looking past Howell as he brought down the whip.

*Bolter,* said those unblinking eyes. *You'll be next.*


Dalton saw his reflection as he walked into the parlour. A cursed thing, he thought, to look into your own eyes at the very moment the crime is committed. For how could you ever hope to pin the blame on another?

He took the candlesticks. Two of them; long and thin. Angels were woven around the bases, their tiny bronze hands reaching skyward.

Dalton shoved them into his pockets. He hurried through the dark house and out into the barn. He placed the candlesticks in the pack with his old clothes.

He'd wake Grace, dig up the weapons. And by dawn this place would be nothing but a bad memory.

"What have you there, silent man?"

He turned. Howell stood in the doorway, a grin plastered across his face.

"Go to hell," said Dalton.

Howell snatched the pack and pulled out the candlesticks. He chuckled. "Funding an escape?"

Dalton said nothing. Howell tossed the pack back in the hay, keeping the candlesticks in his fist.

"You're right to do it. Edward Porter knows what you are. You really think a rat like that's going to keep quiet? The little prick's probably rounding up the police as we speak."

Dalton made a grab for the candlesticks. Howell darted out of reach. Spiderwebs of blood darkened the back of his shirt.

"Edward knows too much," he said. "But then again, so do

I."

Dalton clenched his teeth. "What do you want?"

Howell smiled. "Here's how it is. I'm going to run. And you're going to come with me. You know the bush. You know how to survive out there."

Dalton snorted.

"You think I'm joking?"

"A gun," said Dalton blackly. "Smoking pot. Rope for traps. Take those things from Porter and leave me the hell alone. I'm not going anywhere with you."

"Traps? Do I look like a hunter? No mate, I ain't going into that forest on my own. Heard some real awful shit can happen when the food runs out." He looked at Dalton pointedly.

"All the more reason to go alone."

Howell waved the candlesticks in front of Dalton's face. "I could open my mouth right now and have Porter out here. Not sure he'd take it too well to discover you've pinched these. Plenty more I could tell him about you too." Howell glanced over his shoulder at the black plains. "Even you couldn't make it far enough in this darkness without the police finding you."

Dalton stood, breathing heavily through his nose. "Grace comes with us."

"No. She'll slow us down."

"I'll not go without her."

Howell chuckled. "A man like you should know better than to grow attached to someone. A life on the run will always be a lonely one. You'll go. Because if you don't, you'll swing."

Dalton clenched his jaw. "I told you, I'll not go without her."

"Then you'll die with a rope around your neck."

Dalton paced across the barn with his hands behind his head. It wasn't the thought of death he cared about. He'd already lived far longer than he was supposed to. Death would come to everyone. But to stand upon the gallows and have the world know his crimes? To have Grace know his crimes? It was this he couldn't bear.

He rubbed his eyes. "When?" he asked finally.

"What do we need?"

"I told you. Pots and knives. Rope. Gun."

Howell grinned. "You can get us them things, can't you? You're a resourceful man."

Dalton thought of the rifle buried beneath the tree. He hated the thought of leaving Grace here without it. Hated more the idea of going back into the bush with no way to hunt.

Howell clapped him on the shoulder. "You'll get them tonight or I'll tell the world your whole grisly story. We leave at dawn."

# XXI

Hobart Town Gazette
Friday 6th August 1824

*'It was insisted upon that everyone should partake of Bodenham's remains, lest, in the event of their ultimate success to obtain their liberty, any of them might consider himself innocent of his death and give evidence against the rest.'*

"We go north," said Howell. They trudged out of Porter's back paddock with the first threads of sunlight. "I got means out of this place." He jangled the pouch of coins in his pocket. "Tobacco money. You get me the hell off this island, Dalton. But we go up through the wilds, you hear. Disappear into the bush like you and your mates done. Don't want no-one seeing us."

"Aye," said Dalton. "Through the wilds." He began to walk northwest, away from the settled districts. Through the wilds and north would lead them to snow drenched mountains, impenetrable forests. Over the bones of murdered bolters.

Starting again, it was all an illusion. How could he build a new life when he'd ruined this one so completely?

Perhaps it was best this way. Even if he and Grace ever

made it to London, Violet's ghost would always haunt the space between them.

They stopped at the edge of the river. Mist hung over the water. Howell looked up at the snow-flecked peaks that rose above the cloud. "The rest of your gang still out there somewhere? Living off the land like savages?"

"No," said Dalton. "They're dead."

"It's really true then. What Alexander Pearce said you done."

"Aye," Dalton said finally. "It's true." He took off his clothes and tied them to the end of the rifle, his fingers tight around Grace's coin. He stepped into the water. His chest tightened at the cold.

"They hanged him, you know," said Howell from the bank. "Pearce. Years ago."

Dalton turned in surprise. "Pearce? Hanged?"

"Aye. He escaped the harbour again. Killed the man he bolted with. They found him on the edge of the King River with his mate's liver in his pockets."

Dalton let his feet sink into the muck on the bottom of the river. So he was the last survivor.

*You hear that, Greenhill?*

It had been Daniel Howell who had relayed the story to him so many years ago, Dalton realised, grimacing at the irony. Pearce had made it to Hobart Town and news of the bolters was travelling into the highlands. Howell leaned close to the fire, his red hair brightened by the flames, a bottle of stolen whisky in his fist. "Heard the story of what these men done? Can't bring myself to believe a word of it."

He waved the bottle at Dalton, who was lying on his side, too weak from hunger to lift his head. "What d'you reckon, silent man? This Pearce fellow talking shit?"

Dalton had smiled into the darkness that night, glad to hear Pearce had taken the axe to Greenhill. The terror had been paralysing when there had still been eight of them left. How black those final nights must have been for the last two survivors.

Alone in a lightless forest, each wanting the other dead. Each afraid to close his eyes.

Greenhill had succumbed to sleep first. One swing of the axe and he had become a victim of his own depraved plan. Dalton was satisfied. Pearce would be back in Macquarie Harbour with his back in ribbons, but Robert Greenhill would forever haunt that cursed forest.

Howell stepped into the water and swore at the cold. "And you, Mr Dalton, Pearce told them in Hobart they'd killed you first. At Macquarie Harbour, he claimed you'd gotten lost in the bush. Either way, no one knows you're alive." He grinned. "Except me."

The alleyway was still in the early morning. The windows of the tavern were dark; stray cannikins lying half-buried in the mud. And there was little Emma, crouched beside a puddle, floating leaves across its murky surface. She wore a short-sleeved tunic, her pantalettes sodden with mud. Gooseflesh dappled her arms. Close up, she looked nothing like Violet. Emma's face was much wider, her hair darker. She couldn't have been more than three or four. *What tricks the desperate mind could play*, Grace thought dully.

"Emma? Is your mama about?"

The girl looked up. She moved her lips from side to side, as though debating whether to trust Grace. "She's sleeping."

Wind tunnelled through the alley. Grace slid off her shawl and bundled it around the girl's shoulders. She held out her hand. "Come on. Let's go and see her." Emma's fingers were cold and muddy. Grace squeezed them tightly. How she'd missed the feel of a child's hand in hers. She'd been with Violet and Nora since they were born. Had lifted them from Charlotte's chest when her arms grew limp and her eyes glassy. Grace had been both mother and father to the girls until Harris could bring himself to look at them. Another child's hand in hers felt like a betrayal.

She let Emma lead her down the narrow lane at the side of the tavern and into the hallway of the lodging rooms. Grace knocked softly.

Maryann opened the door. Her blonde hair hung tangled down her back; grey threads at her temples. Her eyes were underlined with shadow. She tugged a tatty pink shawl over her nightshift. "I see you're still hunting down my daughter."

Emma slipped past them and ran into the room. She plucked the rag doll from her sleeping pallet and sat up on her knees, eying the women curiously.

"Emma's father," said Grace. "Howell. Is he here?"

A baby in a crib by the door let out a sudden wail. Maryann ushered Grace inside and grunted as she fished the baby from the cradle. "Daniel? You think he'd come here? Give me a scrap of help? Only time I see him is when he sneaks out for a drink. The children don't even know who he is."

"He's gone," said Grace. "I work at the Porters' with him. He ran away in the night."

Maryann pursed her lips. She snatched a glass from the table and flung it across the room. It exploded against the wall and made the baby screech harder. Emma looked up with wide eyes.

"Bastard," hissed Maryann.

Grace chewed her thumbnail. "He didn't say nothing to you?"

Maryann shook her head. The baby grizzled and pawed at her neck. She dumped him on Emma's sleeping pallet and pressed a sliver of bread into his pudgy fist. "Are you sure?" she asked Grace finally.

She nodded. "He left with Alexander."

"The man you were with. The one with the wild eyes."

"You ain't got no idea where they've gone? Or why?"

Maryann sighed. "Daniel's a no-hoper. Got caught duffing cattle a few years back but earned himself a ticket of leave. Only had six months til his sentence were up. We talked about making a go of it. Land of our own and all. Few sheep or something. Anything so I don't have to do this no more. Then the stupid scab knocked out his overseer. Now he's a lifer. He thought of bolting before. I thought I'd talked him out of it. Don't know what I was thinking pinning my hopes on him. So, no, I got no idea where they are. But I sure ain't surprised."

Hatred for Howell simmered beneath Grace's skin. He'd taken Alexander from her. Left his children without a second thought. "All right," she said finally. "Thank you." She turned to leave.

"You find your girl, then?" asked Maryann.

Grace avoided her eyes. "Violet disappeared in the bush a few months ago. When I saw Emma, I just wanted to believe…"

"How does someone just disappear?"

Grace hesitated, taken aback by Maryann's bluntness. "She got up in the night, I suppose. Got herself lost."

"She got up in the night? Wandered into the bush on her own? Is that really what you believe?"

Grace wrapped her arms around herself. "Perhaps."

"And this Alexander. Was he there?"

"Why?" she demanded.

Maryann shrugged.

"He didn't kill her," said Grace, surprising herself with the intensity of her voice.

"You said it. Not me."

She swallowed heavily. "I trust Alexander."

"Well. I trusted Daniel too. And look where that got me."

"Why would he kill Violet?" The words fell out scratchy and half-formed. She'd convinced herself of Alexander's innocence. How deep had this doubt been hiding?

Maryann shrugged with infuriating nonchalance. "Perhaps he wanted you all to himself."

Heat washed over her. "No." She felt her carefully cultivated ignorance about to topple. "No, that ain't true." The baby let out a long, high wail. Grace felt the muscles in her neck tighten. She had to leave. Now. She hurried towards the door.

"You looking for a reason for him to disappear?" said Maryann. "Perhaps he was afraid you were going to find him out."

Grace felt anger flare inside her. She shoved Maryann against the wall. "Shut your damn mouth! You ain't got no idea what you're talking about!"

Maryann pushed her away. "Get your bloody hands off me. And stay away from my daughter."

They trudged into the hills until Dalton's eyes were straining in the twilight. He dropped the pack. "Get us some kindling. Lay a fire."

"Here? You reckon we're far enough away from the settlement? They'll not see the smoke?"

Dalton sat. "Can't go any further in the dark. Ground's too steep."

With a thin flame licking the wood, Howell lay back on his elbows and stretched out his legs. He pulled a loaf from the pack and broke off two large pieces. Dalton took the bread and tore the first chunk in half.

"Too much. The food has to last."

Howell chewed slowly. He took one of the candlesticks from the pack and traced a finger over the face of the sculpted angel. "What's it feel like, then? To do such a thing?"

Dalton felt his breath coming thick and fast.

*You want to know how it feels?*

*This is how it feels.*

Thomas Bodenham was just twenty years old. Arrived at Macquarie Harbour a few months before Dalton. The harbour was not a place where men bonded, but Dalton and Bodenham had shared words over the supper tables many a night. They'd shared their desperation for liberty, shared excitement when they'd fled the harbour. The first night of their escape, they'd talked about the women they'd met in Hobart Town. Two young men with dreams of freedom.

This is how it feels, Daniel Howell, to steal a friend's life for your own survival.

Self-hatred. Revulsion. Terrified by the knowledge that you'll be forever haunted. Afraid to look into the shadows in case there are dead men lurking there. You hide yourself away from the world in the hope that the solitude might steal your memories. But you know that what you've done is buried so deep within you that you'll go back there every time the sun goes down.

"Would you do it again?" asked Howell. "If you had to?"

*Never.*

Dalton chewed the bread slowly. He knew the land now. How many edible plants must they have passed in those sixteen days after they had left the harbour? How much wattle seed that could be ground into flour? How many men would still be alive if Dalton had known then the things he did now?

"Stop talking about it," he mumbled.

Howell chuckled. "You understand my fascination, mate, surely."

Dalton stared through the trees to the scattered stars. He wondered if Howell knew how to read the sky. Could he tell they were walking in circles?

He lay awake long after Howell began to snore. The crescent moon hung directly above his head. Midnight. He took Grace's shilling from his pocket. He had to get back to her before whatever fragile trust she had in him was shattered forever. Before she drew her own conclusions about his disappearance. Her own conclusions about the girl.

Dalton looked across at Howell. He stood and reached for the gun. Howell moved suddenly and snatched the rifle before Dalton could get a hand to it.

"Don't you try, silent man. You're getting me out of this place."

"Give me my gun."

Howell rolled over, back to Dalton, clutching the rifle to his body. "No, mate. I need a little security."

It said plenty about the village of Hamilton, thought Grace, that there were countless grog shops and no church. She and God had never seen eye-to-eye, but she felt the need to cram into the inn with the rest of the villagers each Sunday and listen to the reverend spout the dangers of a liquored-up life. It gave her a sense of belonging, she realised. A fragile sense of community to which she could try and belong.

Maryann was waiting outside for her when she left the service that morning. The baby was dangling from her hip and she had a hand clamped around Emma's wrist. She was dressed in a threadbare cloak and the low-cut blue dress she'd obviously been wearing the night before. The lampblack intended for her eyelids had made its way across one cheek.

Grace walked faster. "If you've come to convince me of Alexander's guilt, I ain't interested."

"I ain't come to convince you of anything." Maryann tossed Grace her shawl. "Thought you might want this back."

"Thank you." Grace slowed her pace slightly and let Maryann walk beside her. Emma ran ahead, leaping over puddles and enormous piles of horse dung. Two older women shuffled past them, whispering and shooting black glares.

Maryann grabbed Grace's arm. "This way." She guided her off the main street and down the track towards the creek. She snorted. "Bloody toffs looking at me like I ain't worth the time of day. Think they know I seen more of their husbands than they have?"

"They know," said Grace. "That's why they're looking at you like you ain't worth the time of day."

Maryann chuckled humourlessly.

Grace watched Emma swing her rag doll in her fist. It was threadbare and misshapen like Violet's Rosie had been.

Rosie was the obstacle in Grace's sleepwalking theory. The doll, like Violet, was gone without a trace. Had she carried it in her sleep? They'd searched for weeks. Every inch of the land, she was sure of it. There had been no Rosie.

Images came to her fleetingly: hands flinging the doll into the river. Into the fire. Whose ashes lay in the fireplace outside Alexander's hut? She forced the thoughts away.

"Daniel left me some money," said Maryann. "Some of what he'd made from that tobacco crop. Found it last night behind the flour pot." She heaved the baby onto her other hip and sighed. "I know we're better off without him. Just wish he'd said goodbye." She touched Grace's elbow. "Listen. I know you don't want to think nothing bad about your Alexander. I went through the same with Daniel. But it got to a point that I couldn't deny it no more."

How could she manage anything but denial? *There's no one else*, Alexander had said. And he was right. She had no one else, so how could she ever think about those dead bolters, or the glassy eyes of the murdered marines? How could she believe Violet's death had been anything but an accident?

She sucked in her breath. "The man I love struck me, then threw me in the madhouse when I tried to leave him."

"Christ," said Maryann. "I thought I were a bad judge of character."

"I left my family on the other side of the world to come out here and make a life with him. Now I have nothing. Alexander is the only person I can trust."

"Alexander left you," said Maryann. She gripped Grace's shoulder with her free hand. "Look. I ain't trying to make trouble. You've been through hell, I can see that. And we're all afraid of being alone. Especially in this place. It's natural to want to cling to someone. But sometimes you got to open your eyes. Or else what happened to your Violet might just happen to you." Maryann tried to catch her glance. "Don't you owe it to her to admit to yourself what really happened?"

Grace swallowed hard. "I don't know what really happened." She looked up to see Emma tottering down the muddy bank into the creek. Grace's heart shot into her throat. She raced towards the water. "Emma! Get out of there!"

Maryann planted a hand on her hip. "Leave her. She's just playing."

Grace splashed into the water and swung Emma into her arms. The girl screeched in shock and kicked against her. Maryann sat the baby on the bank and yanked Emma out of Grace's grip. The doll tumbled to the grass.

"What the hell d'you think you're doing? You've bloody terrified her!"

Grace gulped down her breath. "How could you let her out there? She could have drowned!"

"Drowned?" Maryann set Emma down and rubbed her back. "She weren't in an inch of water! You're off your bloody head, you are!"

"We got a problem here?"

"Oh look," drawled Maryann. "If it ain't Jim Berry, world's crookedest bloody police lag."

He strode towards them, chest puffed out like he'd swallowed a cat. Grace pulled her shawl tightly around her shoulders. Her hands were shaking violently.

"Bugger off, Berry," Maryann hissed. "This ain't got nothing to do with you."

"You watch your mouth, Maryann Fairlie."

She unhooked Emma's arms from around her waist. "Why? What you going to do?"

"Could think of plenty nice things to do to a woman like you." Chuckling, Berry stepped close and slid a hand inside her cloak. Maryann yanked away and punched him hard in the nose. Blood spurted down the front of his uniform. He snatched her wrists and wrestled her to the ground. Howls from Emma and the baby.

"Let go of me!" shrieked Maryann, kicking under him. "She's the one you want! The loony won't leave my bloody kids alone!"

Grace stood with her spine pressed against the trunk of a tree. The children sprawled on the grass, red-faced and screaming. A second policeman came running towards the creek. Berry yanked Maryann to her feet and wrenched her arms behind her back.

"Hand her over, Berry," said the sergeant. He grabbed hold of Maryann's arm and led her back towards the town. Berry wiped his nose with the back of his hand. He pulled the children from the mud and tucked one under each arm.

Grace watched blankly as they left, the children's cries disappearing beneath the sigh of the creek. She sank to her knees, wet skirts tangling around her legs. Beside her, Emma's doll lay face down in the grass. Grace picked it up and held it to her chest. Tried to slow her speeding heart.

Again, the river.

Howell stopped walking. "You bastard. You've led us back to Hamilton." He wrenched an arm around Dalton's neck and threw him backwards. Arms flying, stumbling, hands in the mud. They scrambled for the weapons. Howell came away with the rifle. Dalton, the axe.

Howell raised the gun. "Think I won't tell anyone who you are?"

"Just try. You're a bolter now too. Open your mouth and you'll be on the scaffold beside me."

Howell paused, breathing heavily through his nose. Dalton swung the axe into the barrel of the gun. Howell's shot flew across the river. Head down, Dalton charged, knocking Howell onto his back. His money pouch spilled into the mud. Dalton threw a wild fist to the side of Howell's head. His cheek split, blood spurting down his face. Dalton punched again, leaving Howell on the edge of consciousness. He grabbed the rifle and rummaged in his pack for the powder and shot. Rammed in the ball. He snatched the money pouch and ran without looking back.

He tore across the plains, past Annie's cottage and over the bridge. Up the hill towards the Porters'. He threw open the kitchen door and charged inside, the rifle in his hand.

The cook swallowed a shriek. She pressed a hand to her heart. "You. What do you want?"

"Where's Grace?"

"She's not here."

"You're lying."

The cook narrowed her eyes. "I never lie. Mrs Porter sent her packing. Her and that dollymop Maryann Fairlie caused a right scene at the creek this morning."

"What?" Dalton gulped down his breath. "Where'd she go?"

"Couldn't tell you. But you'd best leave too. Mr Porter'll have your head if he catches you here."


He found her sitting at the edge of the creek. Her hands were clasped in her lap and she wore her tattered tartan cloak, the hood pulled up over her choppy curls.

She turned as he approached. "You came back."

"Aye. Of course." He sat beside her. A dirty rag doll lay in her lap. Dalton took the shilling from his pocket and held it out to her. Grace looked at it, but kept her hands tightly clasped. He placed it between them. "Howell knew who I was. He recognised me from the cattle ring. Said he'd turn me in if I didn't help him get away. But I couldn't go without you."

Grace said nothing.

"The Porters let you go?"

She nodded.

"What happened?"

She didn't look at him. "Emma... Maryann's daughter. She ran off and jumped in the river... the creek. I was afraid she'd drown. I jumped in there after her and Maryann went mad. Started screaming at me. She punched that police lag when he came to see what was going on." She sniffed. "Mrs Porter heard about it. Said she didn't want no-one working for her who spent their time with easy women like Maryann." She stared into the water. "Thing is, I don't know why I behaved the way I did. When I saw Emma in the creek, it was like something else took a hold of me. Like something else was making me act. You ever feel that way?"

Dalton nodded faintly. He'd felt that way more times than he could remember. "You think that's what happened to Violet? You think she fell in the river?"

Grace looked at her hands. "You tell me what happened to Violet."

Dalton's stomach tightened.

Finally, she turned to face him. "Am I to believe she just wandered out into the bush on her own? How could she just disappear? How could there be no trace of her?"

Dalton watched the brown water bubble over the rocks. He pulled Howell's pouch from his coat pocket and tossed it into Grace's lap. "Here. Enough for passage to London. And more."

She frowned, opening the pouch. "Where did you get all this?"

"It doesn't matter."

"You stole it? From who?"

"I stole it for you. For us. So we can forget this place."

Grace sucked in her breath and placed the pouch on the ground.

Dalton slid it into his pocket. "We'll go back to Hobart Town. Get Nora. And then we'll be on the first ship back to London. No more Harris. No more asylum. That's what you want, aye?" He put a hand to her shoulder, forcing her to face him. "Grace? Isn't that what you want?" He glimpsed Howell's blood on his knuckles and pulled away. "Would you bloody well speak to me?"

She laughed thinly. "Silence is a real bastard, ain't it."

"She won't go, Dalton. Not with an animal like you."

They turned at the sound of Howell's voice. Grace's eyes fixed on the blood snaking down his cheek. She stood hurriedly, the rag doll tumbling into the water.

Dalton leapt up, clutching the rifle. "Leave us be," he said darkly.

Howell glared. "Give me my fucking money."

Dalton felt Grace's eyes on him.

"Give him the money, Alexander," she said.

He stood motionless, his hand tight around the gun.

Finally, Howell took a step towards Grace. "Ask him about the man they killed."

She looked at Dalton. "What is he talking about?"

Sickness rose in his throat. He reached into his pocket, clasped his fingers over the pouch and held it out to Howell.

*No.*

He couldn't do it. The money was his ticket out of this place. His ticket to give Grace what she longed for. He shoved the pouch back in his pocket and raised the gun. "Get away from us."

Howell laughed. "You won't shoot me here. You'd hang in a second." He turned to Grace. "Ask him about Tom Bodenham. Ask him what they did to the body."

Dalton stared down the barrel of the rifle. Anything to avoid Grace's eyes. His finger on the trigger. Howell in his line of sight.

"Don't, Alexander. Please." Her voice was husky.

He squeezed the trigger. His warning shot flew over Howell's shoulder.

Howell glared, then laughed coldly. Ran back along the creek and disappeared.

# XXII

Confession of Alexander Pearce
As recounted to Lieutenant John Cutherbertson, commandant
of Macquarie Harbour
1824

*"'I'll warrant you," said Greenhill, "I will eat the first part myself, but you must all lend a hand that we may be equally guilty of the crime."'*

Alexander lowered the gun. "We need to leave." He handed Grace the axe.

"Where are we going?"

He began to walk. His silence told her everything. Back to the forest. To the mountains, the rivers. Back to his world.

They trudged past cattle, past rickety fences, out into the open plains. Grace felt a great weight pressing down on her. She couldn't do this again. Couldn't climb mountains or sleep beneath snow and stars. A pink sky stretched endlessly above her, the plains beneath her feet vast and open. What was she but a speck amongst this desolation? If she were to part ways with Alexander, the emptiness could swallow her and who on this earth would ever know? Her heart thumped at her vulnerability. And so she kept up with his steady footsteps, inching their way towards the foothills.

She said nothing. To speak would mean facing questions

she couldn't bear to ask, facing truths she couldn't accept.

They crossed the river, communicating in sparse, wordless gestures: *go, stop, this way*. Grace stumbled out of the water and stood with her arms across her chest, her wet shift tangled around her legs. She crouched, feeling horribly exposed. Alexander tossed her the pack and she hurriedly pulled out her dress and petticoats.

Her clothes clinging to her wet skin, she stood on the bank and felt her bare feet sink into the mud. Alexander's back was to her as he buttoned his trousers. Giving her the privacy she craved or needing to hide from her scrutiny?

The foothills rose, then dipped into a slight valley. Night was approaching, the shrieking of the birds fading into stillness. Grace could hear her heart thumping in her ears. She sucked in her breath. There had to be an end to this uncertainty. Suddenly not knowing seemed the most frightening thing of all.

She stopped walking. "Tell me what happened out here. Tell me the truth."

Alexander paused several paces in front of her. She watched his shoulders sink, his head droop. He'd been fighting these questions too, she realised. Fighting to keep the answers inside. He threw down the pack and sat with his knees drawn up. He stared at the earth and shook his head slowly.

Grace stood over him. "Yes," she said.

He hung his head with resignation. His words were low and slow; speaking to the ground as if hoping the earth might swallow his confession. "We'd not eaten in more than a week. There was nothing out there. No animals, no berries, not even a fly. We were at the end of the earth." He covered his eyes. "Greenhill, he'd heard this story of some sailors who had gotten lost at sea. Sacrificed one of their own so the others could survive."

Grace's stomach tightened. *Stop, I can't hear this.* But she couldn't form the words.

"Greenhill wanted it to be me, but in the end they chose Tom Bodenham. Greenhill took to him with the axe we'd been using to cut the pines. Hung his body from a tree and let the blood run out of him. We cut off his head and hacked him up like he was a pig. Put his liver to the fire and shared it among ourselves. Greenhill said it was the only way we'd survive."

Grace bit down on her lip until she tasted blood. She wanted the story she'd concocted the night the marines were killed. Wanted Alexander to have killed those seven men. A simple murder; it was easier to conceive. Easier to give a self-righteous sigh and push away. And the murder of a government man? Weren't they all sent to Macquarie Harbour in the hope they'd die off anyway? But this, this pushed against the boundaries of what it meant to be human.

She stared into the purple sky, trying to cling to the last threads of light. "I don't believe you."

"Yes you do. You don't want to, but you do."

For a long time, neither of them spoke.

"I ran," Alexander said finally. "Before anyone else was killed."

"Stop," Grace mumbled. But his confession seemed to have opened something up inside him. Something he couldn't close down. A need to tell the whole story.

"The soldiers caught Pearce," he said. "He told them everything. After Bodenham, it was Mather. He was praying, Grace. They killed him while he was praying."

And Grace thought not of Mather, but of Alexander raising the rifle as she and Violet hunted for flowers.

Alexander said: "Travers, he was next." And she thought of poison mushrooms mixed with her tea. The thud of soldiers' bodies as they rolled into their graves.

"Greenhill and Pearce, they were the last. Both knew they had to kill the other to survive. Afraid to leave the other's sight." He leapt up suddenly and grabbed her cloak. "Imagine it. Being too afraid to sleep in case you never woke up."

"Stop!" she cried. "I can't hear no more! Not when I'm trapped with you in this cursed forest again!"

He pressed his hot palms against her cheeks. "I've got the money. We'll get out of the forest. We'll get back to London." He pushed back her hood and dug his hands into her hair. "It's all right, my Grace. You're safe here. It's better this way. Just the two of us. Without the Porters or Howell or Maryann's little girl."

"Just the two of us?" she repeated. "The two of us without Violet? Alexander?" Her voice grew louder. "The two of us without Violet?"

He stood, breathing heavily, his hands still hard against her cheeks. "Yes," he said finally.

Grace heard a cry from deep in her throat. She stumbled, fighting off a wild sweep of dizziness.

Only two sets of footprints.

The proof had been there since the beginning. She imagined Alexander lifting Violet from her bed. Carrying her into the bush. And then…

With day-to-day tasks, it had been easier to block everything out. Bake the bread and convince herself Violet had just gotten lost in the dark. Wash the clothes, tell herself she'd slipped and fallen. But she couldn't hide from the truth any longer. Shy little Violet, who wouldn't venture as far as the kitchen without her nurse by her side. Timid Violet who wouldn't sleep in the dark unless she were pressed against Grace or Nora. Little Violet who would never, ever have left that hut on her own accord.

Alexander held up a hand, backing away from her. "Let me speak."

"Let you speak?" Her voice was barely more than a whisper. "She was just a little girl." Grace stared at him and saw the beast he had been when she had stumbled to his hut. She had fought with herself then. Trusting the wild man in the woods had seemed a gamble she had had no choice but to take. If only she had taken Violet and kept walking. *If only.* She felt all the compassion she had once felt for him washing away in a flood of hatred. And an odd sense of inevitability.

She lurched for the weapons. Alexander grabbed the rifle before she could get a hand on it. Her wild swing of the axe clipped the side of his head. He stumbled, collapsed at her feet. She grabbed the gun.

"Animal," she spat.

He hovered on the edge of consciousness, waiting to die. Waiting for the shot. But nothing.

*Animal.* And then silence. He tried to move, but felt a great weight on his chest. Darkness behind his eyes.

*An animal? Of course I am.*
*Even dogs don't eat their own kind.*
*Imagine it.*
*Imagine the smell of wood smoke. Eucalyptus. Boiling meat. Hear the pot bubbling, the fire crackling, devils snorting in dams of spilled blood.*

*No man speaks. They all know that when this pot is done boiling they'll stop being men. Become beasts.*

*Imagine you are sitting around that fire, surrounded by men you have come to despise. Imagine hating these men so much you wish you had chosen the hell of Macquarie Harbour over their company. Can you hear the men breathe? There is one man less than the night before. You are watching when someone dips a stick into the pot and brings out the slab of meat. It is passed around. Grey. Tough. Each man pulls off a portion. Passes it on.*

*Who is the first to put it on their tongue? The first to swallow it down? And where do these bolters go from here? They can never be normal men again now. Not after this.*

*One day, my Grace, you'll see it was better for you to be freed of your Violet. You'll see everything I did was for you. How could I let anything come between us, mo shíorghra? How could I let anything take you away from me when you are the only thing that makes me human?*

# PART THREE

# HOBART TOWN

# XXIII

Bathurst Free Press
Wednesday 28th January 1857
Derived from the Hobart Town Gazette, 1824

*'When the first horror was over, a consultation followed. Some would have died rather than live by cannibalism; but it was fiercely contended ... that all might share the guilt.'*

Dalton felt a sharp kick in the shoulder. He opened his eyes. Grace was standing over him, gripping the rifle. His wrists and ankles were bound with his bootlaces. He squinted in the pale dawn. There was a coldness to her. Like she was made of stone.

Dalton sat, his head pounding. He lifted his bound wrists and touched a swelling above his ear.

"The gun is loaded," said Grace.

He nodded slowly.

"Take me to Violet. Show me what you done with her."

He hesitated.

"Of course. Silence. Silence is easy, ain't it? Silence and lies."

Dalton glanced at the rifle. "You mean to kill me, Grace?"

"Take me to Violet."

He nodded. "Let me stand."

Grace reached into the pack and pulled out his whittling knife. She sliced the laces at his wrists and ankles. Dalton stood slowly. A wave of nausea swept over him as he bent to thread the remains of the laces back through his boots.

"Where is she?" Grace asked.

"At the top of the escarpment. Near the police grave. Back over the mountains."

Tears escaped down her cheeks and she brushed them away furiously. "Take me."

Dalton reached for the axe. Grace cocked the trigger.

"We need it to get through the bush," he told her. "Cut ourselves a path. You know that."

She took a step back, allowing him to take the axe.

"We'll not get over the mountains without food," he said. "We need to hunt."

"We'll go back towards the settlements. There are kangaroos." She shoved him in the shoulder with the gun. "Walk."

They paced up the gradual incline of the plains. The river lay ahead.

Dalton stopped. A few hours earlier he had watched Grace climb from the water and pull on her dress. That blue dress of Annie's, he was sure of it. Now her skirts were brown, her petticoats dry. Her hair, her skin, dry, like she'd been brought across in a boat.

"Grace? Where have you been?"

She dug the gun into his spine. "Move."

Dalton turned. She'd never trust him again. What did he care if she pulled the trigger?

"I been to the police," she said finally.

Panic shot through him. "Police?" And he realised they were all around him. Men hidden in the dip of the earth, waiting for her to deliver him into their clutches. He looked into her eyes and ran.

Marines swooped like a flock of red birds. Grace crouched, pressed her eyes against her knees. Couldn't bring herself to watch.

The night before, she had walked into the Hamilton police station.

*Government man*, she had said. And *bolter*. Eyes lit up and guns were loaded. And then, the worst of them.

*Cannibal.*

And that was it. The police had Alexander pegged for the murder of Grace's girl, for those four words were all the evidence in the world.

"My girl, Violet Harris," she said. "And two British marines."

Soldiers were brought in from the surrounding settlements.

"Miss Ashwell," they said. "Where can we find the bodies?"

Five days walk. By the Styx River. An unmarked grave at the water's edge, beneath the pine tree covered with rings of moss.

And: "Miss Ashwell, where can we find Alexander Dalton?"

"I will lead you," she said. "Follow me."

The police reported back. Disappeared into the bush like a ghost. Men sent after him, they said. Heading towards the river, looking for the graves.

Grace sat at the constable's desk. She felt hot and breathless. Surely any second she'd be discovered as a runaway. They'd throw her into the police wagon and back to New Norfolk she'd go. "Can I leave?"

The constable peered over his glasses. "You may. We'll let you know if we find anything. You'd best stay nearby. You work for Bill Porter, you said?"

"Aye," she lied. "For Bill Porter."

The sun was dull and low. Grace hooked closed her cloak and trudged down the middle of the road. She crossed the bridge to the farmland, traipsing through the wet grass to Annie and Jack's cottage.

Annie was sitting in a chair beside her vegetable patch with a pipe in her hand. She wore black riding boots over a pair of mud-splattered drawers, her skirts hitched up above her knees. Her pale hair hung in pieces over her face. She puffed a cloud of smoke at Grace.

"Heard you and your friend been causing a stir."

"He ain't no friend of mine." She felt the loss of Alexander as though he had died. In a way, he had. Of course, the Alexander she had known — the one who had helped her hunt for Violet and had pledged to take her back to London — had only ever been an illusion; cobbled together by her own desperation. Hatred bubbled inside her.

"You'll be wanting somewhere to stay, I suppose."

Grace sniffed. "I ain't got nowhere else to go. I'm sorry. I don't know what to do. I—"

Annie breathed out a long line of smoke. "Well. There's a bed here, though I can't guarantee it's a safe one."

"What's happened?"

"Nothing." Annie stood and ushered her inside. "Come on, girl. You look as though you need a drink." She kicked off her boots and poured two glasses of whisky. Handed one to Grace. "Drink up. Bed's yours for as long as need it."

Grace tried for a smile of thanks but tears spilled down her cheeks.

"Stop that," Annie said sharply. "What good did weeping ever do anyone?"

Grace pushed away her tears. She ached for her mother. "I trusted him," she coughed. "We'd made plans to get home."

Annie gripped Grace's shoulders with surprising ferocity. "This new world is a tough place. A woman's got to make her own life. Can't be relying on no man if we're to survive out here. 'Specially not a wild one like that Alexander."

Grace nodded and gulped her whisky. She knew Annie was right. This was no place for the woman in silk she'd once dreamt of being. And it was no place to trust men who kept secrets. Because the secrets woven into this land were horrifying. "He wasn't the man I thought he was. He was a beast."

"He loved you," said Annie. "Beast or no. I could tell. What's he done that's got you speaking of him like this?"

"Love," Grace spat. "A man like that don't know love. Not anymore. I doubt he ever did." She tried to continue, but her throat tightened and the tears threatened to return.

Annie emptied her glass. "You'll tell me in your own time, aye?"

Jack opened the door, arms loaded with hoes and rakes. He dropped the tools beside the hearth. "Don't want nothing left out there," he said. "Those bastards'll take whatever they can get their hands on." He squeezed Annie's shoulder. "Any trouble here?"

She shook her head and smiled wryly at Grace. "Just her."

"What's happened?" Grace asked again.

"The Porters had some cattle killed," Jack said darkly.

"Bodies gutted in the paddock and the flesh cut out. Blaming us, of course. They've been trying to get their own back." He nodded at the windows. The glass had been broken, Grace realised. Been patched with rags and nails.

"Howell," she said.

"What?"

"The cattle. It was Howell, Porter's government man. I'm sure of it. He's run away. Needed the food."

Annie refilled her glass. "Porter knows it weren't us. We've got our own bloody cattle. He just wants someone to blame. Makes him feel powerful." She snorted. "Helps him forget he's nought but a lag."

"Why don't you leave?" asked Grace. "Find somewhere new and start again."

"You know what this land is like." Annie lifted her head to look through the window, but the murky rags blocked her view. "It's no place to be roaming without nowhere to go."

The path from the river to the traps had been taken over by ferns. A wallaby carcass dangled from the rope, besieged by flies. Had been there for weeks, Dalton assumed. He hacked at the rope and flung the meat into the bush. Reset the trap and paced slowly towards his hut.

Was he mad to have returned?

He had run west from Hamilton. Crossed rivers and climbed mountains until he was sure the marines hadn't followed. On the fourth night he lay awake until light began to filter through the trees. He sat and untied the pouch containing Howell's money, stacking the coins into silver columns. At the top of the pile he sat the shilling Grace had given him. The money would get him off this island and out of the haunted forest. But it would put oceans between he and Grace.

Dalton had heard Pearce had tried to hang himself while wandering alone in these woods. *Now where's the sense in that?*, Dalton had thought. After he'd gotten through the rest of the group. After taking the axe to Greenhill before Greenhill had taken the axe to him. For Pearce to take his own life after using so many men to ensure his survival, it hardly seemed a fair thing.

Dalton saw it now, fleetingly, the attraction of ending it all. Ending the pain in his legs, his chest, his heart. But he was the last man standing. His will to survive had always been stronger than his will to die, even when he had felt there'd been little left to live for.

He swallowed the end of the bread. The last of the food, but he knew this land now. Knew its secrets. He tucked the coins into the pouch and shoved it into his pocket. He grabbed the axe.

*How are you going to hunt with that?*

The voice in his head was Greenhill's.

*There's only one kind of animal you can hunt with an axe.*

"Go to hell," Dalton said aloud. He looked about him. The highest mountains were capped with snow. The Derwent glittered in the pink light. He knew the voice in his head was right. A man couldn't hunt with an axe. Cross the peaks and he would find his hut, his traps. An easier life, surely, than rummaging for berries and digging tubers with his bare hands. Dare he go back? It had been weeks since he'd killed the marines.

He began to walk, silencing Greenhill's voice with his own rhythmic footsteps.

He stood in the clearing, shards of his woodpile beneath his feet. The roof of the hut lay on the ground to his left, the splintered table to his right. The walls hacked at, the door torn off. His boots crunched over the dried ferns of the sleeping pallets. Flour was scattered everywhere. The locker upturned and empty. Cannikins gone. Shelf torn from the wall. The life he had spent eleven years building from nothing had been obliterated. Axed and pissed on. All that was left standing were the two stools.

He sat on one, because he could think of nothing better to do. He nudged a pile of dried ferns with his toe. Beneath it, a sprig of black hair— his beard.

Wooden faces peered up at him from beneath the fallen shelf. Frozen expressions, still eyes. None of them seemed surprised to see him. Grace's was the only one he had carved from life. He slid it into his pocket. He longed for her then like he'd longed for nothing else. Longed to hear her lullabies and see her skirts hung about the hut and hell, how he longed to speak to another living person. He couldn't go back to silence. He'd wandered through the bush, Gaelic rolling off his tongue. Sometimes to himself, sometimes to the invisible men.

He needed her there to answer back. To say: *you're being a right fool, Alexander, there ain't no one there but your own shadow.*

He hacked at the broken table until it was kindling, then lay it in the clearing where his fire pit had once been. Green shoots were pushing through the blackened earth. He lit the fire and stared, mesmerised, at the flames.

The forest crackled and he glanced over his shoulder in a vain burst of hope. The phantom men had appeared from nowhere, so why not Grace? This was a forest full of mystery, after all.

He ran his fingers over the carving in his pocket. Then, one by one, he gathered the wooden men from the ruins of his hut. Tossed them into the flames.

Bodenham, the first to die.

Kennerly and Brown, whose last view of Earth was the grey shroud of Macquarie Harbour.

Mather, Travers, sacrificed in vain.

Pearce, hanged for his crimes in Hobart Town.

Greenhill. *Burn in hell.*

He watched the figures until they were ash. If only he could burn Alexander Dalton away like this too. See the man he used to be disappear in a puff of smoke. He'd tried hard, but the past had found him. The past would always find him.

He couldn't bear for Grace to live the same way. He wanted her to have London. She'd never leave with him, of course. Not now. But he'd stolen the money from Howell so she might see home again. He pulled the pouch from his pocket. After all he'd done, perhaps this might go some way to helping him sleep at night.

Where to find her? She'd go for the girl; of this he was certain. Would return to Hobart Town, fleetingly at least. Perhaps he'd find her there, perhaps not. Perhaps he'd threaten that bastard Harris into giving him some clue.

*Yes.* He felt determined. A strange sensation after existing in a void for so many years.

He stood. The light was beginning to fade and the fire had burned itself out. His stomach groaned loudly. Tonight he would eat, rest. In the morning he would go and find London for Grace.

He trudged towards the traps. Flattened ferns. Were they human footprints in the mud? He froze.

Voices. The slosh of shovels.

He took a step backwards, seeking out the patches of moss

so he might not make a sound. Another step. Another. He brushed past a tree fern and the leaves sighed noisily. The voices fell silent. The digging stopped. Dalton
began to run. He heard footsteps after him. A rifle exploded into the sky. He kept running. And then from in front of him, the sly bastards, two police officers burst from the bush, thrusting their rifles at his chest.

# XXIV

Dalton stood on the edge of the grave, hands tied in front of him. He watched two officers dig, searching for the dead by lantern light. Their sergeant stood at Dalton's side, a rifle swinging against his hip.

No-one spoke. Above their heads, an owl cooed rhythmically. The river sighed beneath the hiss of the shovels. An acrid stench rose suddenly from the wet soil and the officers recoiled. They hauled the mud-caked bodies from the earth. Their features were sunken and twisted. One of the men reached into the grave and pulled out a dirty bundle. Grace's shawl.

The sergeant pressed a hand to his nose. "Where's the girl?"

Dalton said nothing.

"Tell us where she is."

"And make your job easier? Why would I do that?"

"So we can bloody well get out of here."

"And you can have me on the scaffold?"

The sergeant sighed. "What did you do with her?"

"Nothing."

The constables hauled themselves from the hole. Their legs were caked in mud.

"You told Grace Ashwell you buried the girl by the marines' grave."

"Aye, well. Now I'm telling you I didn't." He smiled at the sergeant. "You can choose to believe me or not. But the night will only get darker. I'm sure none of us want to be out here on the graves of murdered men."

The police sat around the fire they had built a few yards from the grave. Close, they huddled; the orange glow of the flames flickering on their cheeks. Clinging to the light. The exhumed bodies lay on the grave's edge, covered in old grey blankets. Dalton sat a foot away, hands bound. He felt the thickness of the dark. The bush seemed restless.

The police passed around a loaf and canteen of water. One of the constables handed Dalton a scrap of bread.

"Ought to let you starve," spat the sergeant. "Save the hangman the trouble."

Dalton brought his bound hands to his lips. "You're hoping I'll tell you where the girl is." He chewed slowly. A throaty screech rose from the bushes and the constable flinched.

"Let's go, sir," he said. "This bog-jumping scab ain't going to tell us a thing."

"Can't go anywhere in this darkness," said the sergeant. "We'll stay here the night."

The constable glanced over his shoulder at the bodies by the water's edge.

Dalton caught his eye and smiled slightly. "The Styx River. The boundary between the living and the dead."

"I don't believe in ghosts," the constable said edgily.

"Nor do I. But this forest; it makes you see things that aren't there."

"Shut your mouth." The constable shuffled closer to the fire. After a moment, he looked back at Dalton. "What do you mean, things that ain't there?"

Dalton rolled onto his side and closed his eyes. "Dead men," he said. "Little girls."

At dawn, the sergeant roused them, yanking Dalton to his feet. Fine rain was falling and the mountains lay hidden behind a thick bank of cloud.

"You need to untie me," said Dalton. "I can't climb without my hands."

"You can and you will."

"Where will I go? I got two men behind me with guns up my arse. If you don't untie me, it'll take us far longer to get over the mountains."

The sergeant scratched his beard. "Do it. Keep the guns on him at all times."

Up they went, into the foothills, into the mountains. The black rock was streaked with snow. Clouds hung in silver threads. At the top of the ridge, the wind howled and stung Dalton's ears. The ground twisted and dropped away into a dramatic downward slope. Peaks Dalton had navigated in the past. Terrain he knew. The marines were forced to lower their guns and climb with their hands.

Dalton took his chance. He hurled himself down the incline, his back scraping against the rocks. A shout from the police. Bullets whizzed above his head. He ran until sweat poured down his back. The foliage grew thicker. Vast banks of fern he could hide between. He lay on his back, breathing hard, hidden in a sea of glistening green.

Grace woke abruptly at a slam of the front door. She could see the faint glow of candlelight flickering in the kitchen.

"Jesus, Jack," Annie said loudly. "What happened to your face?"

A chuckle. "Edward Porter thought to shoot his mouth off

at me. He'll not be trying that again." His words were brassy with drink.

"Bloody fool."

Grace heard heavy footsteps.

"So what? I'm just supposed to take it?"

"You can't go round swinging your fists!" cried Annie. "The Porters are too powerful. They've got those crooked coppers on their side. They'll have you strung up if you don't bloody watch yourself."

Grace sat suddenly at a flare of orange light. She pushed aside the curtain. Behind the house, a great wall of flame was tearing through the wheat field. She charged into the kitchen, tugging on her boots.

"They're burning your crops," she said breathlessly. Jack's eyes flashed. He snatched the rifle and charged into the paddock, firing wildly into the flickering light.

"Water," said Grace. "From the creek."

Annie shook her head. "It's too late."

They watched in silence as the flames roared through the wheat and lit the night with plumes of orange smoke. The fire crackled and faded, leaving a field of glowing ash and the earthy smell of burning.

Annie marched inside and sat at the table. Her cheeks were flushed and smeared with soot.

Jack pressed a hand against the back of her neck. In the lamplight, Grace could see a faint swelling beneath his eye.

"We've got to leave, Annie," he said. "I'm sorry. I know we're giving them what they want, but our pride's not worth risking our lives for."

Grace hovered by the hearth, feeling an intruder.

"Our pride?" Annie repeated. "What about our farm? Our house?"

"Our farm that's burnt to ash? Our house full of broken

glass?"

Annie rubbed her eyes with resignation. "Where will we go?"

"Hobart Town," Grace said suddenly.

They turned to her. "What?" said Jack.

"Take me to Hobart Town. I've got to get my Nora away from her father." She grabbed Annie's wrist as her thoughts began to take shape. "He's a wealthy man. Keeps a hundred pounds or more in the house. He don't trust the bank manager because he went to school with him in London and caught him cheating on his finals. So he always keeps a stash at home. Get me to Hobart Town and I'll bring you that money. I'll take what I need to get back to England and you can have the rest. Go somewhere you'll be safe."

"Fine plan," said Jack. "But we've no horses. How are we to get to Hobart Town?"

Annie began to laugh. She popped the lid from the whisky bottle and filled three cannikins. "I'm sure the Porters have some damn fine horses."


The river murmured and sighed. Grace knelt on the bank, the damp earth soaking through her skirts. The hush of the water calmed her a little. She needed Nora. And, yes, she needed to show Harris he wouldn't get away with locking her up like an animal. But she also needed this stillness. Needed to accept that Violet was gone.

She knew it now, deep within herself. There was to be no more searching, or hoping. The time for miracles had passed.

Her fingers tightened around the stalks of the flowers in her fist. Pink powder-puffs of sunshine wattle that had erupted over the tree behind Annie's vegetable garden. The first of the spring. Violet would have liked the pink. She would have twisted it into her hair, poked a stem behind Grace's ear.

She tossed the rosy globes into the water, one-by-one. Hoped with all her heart Violet was in Heaven with her mother, not haunting the forest with a gang of dead convicts. Deep, breathtaking pain welled inside her. Violet's body was out there. Hidden in the forest among those blood-covered soldiers. Grace felt a desperate need to see her, even for a second. To hold her and say *I'm sorry*. To beg forgiveness for her terrible judgement, her most costly of mistakes.

She let her tears fall. A release. It was almost a relief to stop hoping. A relief to take a step towards acceptance.

She hugged her knees. What was she becoming? *We ain't thieves*, she'd told Alexander. And yet, when night fell, she would follow Annie and Jack up the hill and raid the Porters' stables. Ride to Hobart Town and steal from the man she'd loved. Take his daughter to the other side of the world.

*What dreadful things we are capable of*, she thought. *What lengths we will go to for survival.*

"Grace!"

She turned to see Annie trudging towards the river. Grace wiped her eyes hurriedly.

"Get back to the house and pack your things. We're to leave at dusk."

Grace stood and flung the last of the flowers into the river. They swirled in the current. Disappeared below the surface.

Dalton found the house by following Grace's stories. Tales she'd told by the fire in the clearing.

A house on the edge of the settlement. Northwest. Stone fence. A tunnel of trees.

He'd tried four other farms and found nothing but old men and earth-stained convicts. But this one, this yellow monstrosity with the forest at its edges, this was it. He felt sure of it.

Two looming storeys, stables, shacks for his convict slaves. A patchwork of neat paddocks stretched out into the haze. Who did this toff think he was, claiming so much of this land for his own?

Dalton waited out the daylight behind the stables. Come the dark, he'd go looking. Put Howell's money in Grace's hands and send her home.

They rose from the valley and looked down on the river as it widened and poured into the sea. The lights of Hobart Town opened out before them.

Grace shifted in the saddle. "The northwest of the settlement," she said. "You can reach Harris's house without going through town."

They turned onto a narrow dirt path that snaked through the farmland. Jack held a lamp out in front of them and the three stolen horses paced in its orange glow. Lamps flickered in the windows of the sparsely spread properties.

"Which house is it?" asked Jack.

Grace hesitated. The darkness was disorienting. The land felt strange and foreign. "Keep going," she said. And the path disappeared into a sea of black scrub.

Jack halted his horse. "We must have passed it."

Grace tried to sift through her memories. Had they made a wrong turn? No, this forest was familiar. It fringed Harris's land. That thick bank of gums with their branches twisted around each other. A tunnel of trees. They'd kept away from it in those first weeks, wary of its alien shadows and tangled arms. Violet had been afraid of it. *Monsters in there*, Nora had said.

Grace pointed to a faint glimmer in the blackness. "It's that one. That's Harris's house. Where the tunnel of trees comes out. That's where Nora is."

They paced down the narrow track and followed an off-shooting path to a low stone fence. The house rose square and symmetrical at the front of the property, lit by a flickering lamp above the front porch. A long, straight path led to the door. The house looked nothing like Grace remembered. But was that surprising? The last time she'd been here, she'd been dizzy with laudanum and had been frantic to get the girls out before Harris came home. She climbed from the horse and stared up at the lightless windows. "I'll bring you the money. Wait outside."

Jack slid from his horse and handed the reins to Annie. "I'd best come with you. In case there's trouble."

Annie pulled a pistol from her belt and handed it to Grace. "Take this. Just in case."

Hesitantly, Grace wrapped her hand around the gun. She slid it into the waistband of her skirt and led Jack around the enormous sandstone walls. Two storeys of black windows stared down at them. Grace trailed her fingers along the wall to keep her bearings in the dark. She rattled the kitchen door. Locked. She tried the windows. One was open a crack. She clambered through into the dark kitchen. Jack hauled himself over the windowsill.

Up the stairs. Grace held her breath. Her eyes adjusting to the dark, she opened the first door. An enormous curtained bed stood in the centre of the room, a washstand and dressing table against one wall. Grace crept towards the bed. Harris lay asleep on his side, his nightshirt open across his chest. A twist of fair hair lay across his forehead. Grace felt a startling urge to reach out and touch it. Nora was curled up against his stomach. Grace's throat tightened. Frozen, she stared at them both; Harris's breath making Nora's hair flutter with each exhalation. She touched Nora's cheek, then let her hand drift until it found Harris's chin. His skin was warm. She could feel the beginnings of a beard. Her heart lurched with buried love.

For a fleeting moment, she was sitting beside him on the piano bench, their knees pressed together as she picked out each chord. She was strutting through the blue house in silk petticoats, falling asleep cocooned in his arms. Then: the creak and thud of her cell door, icy water, straps at her wrists. *Yes*, she thought, *wash the good memories away.*

"Hurry now." Jack's voice made her start. "Grab the girl and let's get out of here."

Grace slid a hand beneath Nora's sleeping body. The bed creaked. Harris opened his eyes and his breath left him.

"Gracie."

# XXV

"Gracie," Harris said again, his voice stronger. Deciding perhaps, that she was more than a dream. He leapt from the bed. "My God, Gracie, I was so afraid you—"

Grace stumbled backwards, clattering into the dressing table. Jack stepped between them.

"Who in hell are you?" Harris's eyes flashed.

Jack raised his pistol. "Give her the girl."

"What?" Harris sought out her eyes. "Grace?"

Her heart thudded. She gripped the corner of the table. Knocked over a bottle of scent. Hers, she realised. She had kept it on her nightstand in the corner of her attic room.

"The girl," said Jack.

Harris glared at him. "You'll have to kill me first."

"I'd never hurt her," said Grace. "You know that. Give her to me."

Jack cocked the trigger.

Harris clenched his jaw. He scooped Nora from the bed and placed her in Grace's arms, gripping her wrist in desperation. "What are you doing?" he whispered.

Grace turned away. She was shocked at Nora's size. She was far heavier than Violet had been. Taller perhaps? Her legs seemed far longer. Was such a thing possible?

"Your money." Jack's voice sounded distant.

Harris glared, but pulled open the drawer of his nightstand without a word.

Jack looked over his shoulder at Grace. "Take the girl. Get on the horse and wait for me down the road. I'll see he doesn't follow us."

"Don't hurt him. Please." The words fell out of her mouth on their own accord.

"I'll not hurt him if he does as I say."

Grace nodded tensely. She held Harris's glance for a moment, then rushed down the stairs.

The darkness was thick. Grace felt her way through the entrance hall and out into the night. Annie's lantern flickered faintly at the edge of the property, surrounded by a pool of black.

She clutched Nora and set out towards the horses.

She was grabbed suddenly from behind. A hand was clamped over her mouth to muffle her scream.

"Don't say a word." Alexander's voice was close to her ear. "I'm not here to hurt you."

Her fear gave way to hatred. She slid a hand inside her cloak. "I've a gun in my hand," she hissed. "Let go of me or I'll shoot you in the stomach."

He released his grip. Grace pulled the pistol from her skirt and held it out in front of her. She could see little of Alexander's face. Just shadows and glowing eyes.

"How did you find me?"

"A tunnel of trees beside the northwestern farms. One end leads to the forest. The other to Harris's land." His glance fell to the sleeping girl slung across Grace's shoulder.

"Don't you even bloody look at her," she spat.

Alexander raised his palm. "Don't shoot. I've just come to give you this." He held the coin pouch out to her. "Use it to get home."

"I ain't taking nothing from you."

She heard Jack's footsteps behind her. "Grace!" he whispered. "Come on. Now."

"Get out of my way," she hissed at Alexander. "I got to go."

"No. Wait." He held the pouch close to the end of the pistol. "Take it."

She tried to push past him. Faint voices and hooves. The light vanished. Jack and Annie had gone, Grace realised sickly. Taken Harris's money and left her alone with these men. She stumbled back into the entrance hall, needing the security of the house over the open land.

"Please," said Alexander, following her inside. "Let me do this one decent thing." He tossed the pouch towards her. It clattered noisily on the floorboards.

"And help you clear your conscience? Never." She kicked it away. Stray coins shot across the floor. "You ought to be out there with those dead men, spending every minute thinking about the things you've done. Thinking about what a monster you are." She shook her head. "No. Why should you get to live when Violet don't?" Her voice began to rise. "I wish you'd died when you were supposed to. I wish those men had killed you and torn you to pieces like you did to Bodenham." Her fist tightened around the gun, her arm aching under Nora's weight.

Alexander met her eyes. "Are you going to shoot me to my face?"

"Why shouldn't I? Did you look into Violet's eyes when you killed her? Did you see her face when you tossed her in the river?" Her finger trembled on the trigger. "Tell me, Alexander. Did you?"

"Gracie, put the gun down."

She whirled around. She hadn't realised Harris was behind her. He set his candle on the side table, his eyes darting between Grace and Alexander. He lifted Nora from Grace's arms and laid her gently on the chaise. Grace swallowed hard. She had to tell him. In spite of all he'd done, he needed to know what had happened to his daughter.

"He killed Violet, James." A tremor in her voice. "She's gone. I wanted to believe she'd just run into the forest and gotten lost, but he... I... He took Violet in the night and he killed her." She looked at Harris, not moving her aim from Alexander's chest. His face was unreadable. "James? Did you hear what I said? Violet is gone."

She saw a tremble in his jaw. He stared blackly at Alexander. "Whoever the hell you are," he said, "get out of my house this instant."

"What?" Grace demanded. "You want to let him go? The man who killed your daughter?"

Harris didn't look at her. "Go!" He pushed Grace's arm, shoving the gun aside. Alexander ran. She yanked free of Harris's grip and snapped the trigger.

# XXVI

She fired again. This time, the hollow snap of an empty barrel. The front door slammed. Harris snatched the pistol and tossed it across the room. He grabbed her tightly.

"Let go of me!" Grace thrashed against him. "How could you let him escape?" She turned in Harris's arms to face him. His cheeks were flushed in the candlelight. Hair hung over one brown eye. She could feel heat rising from his body.

"Why did you let him escape, James?" Her voice wavered, terrified of the answer.

On the breeze came the glassy twitter of wind chimes. A sound from the blue house. A sound from the past.

And suddenly she was breathing the smoky London air. Cold stung the tip of her nose.

Two girls in matching blue coats, fur trims, high collars. Quilted bonnets over their ears. Nora clung to Grace's left hand, Violet to her right.

The river was high and hungry. Tents were lined up at the water's edge; stripes of red, white, gold. Strings of tiny lanterns glittered against the midday gloom. People shoved their way along the riverfront, laughing, talking all at once. Inside the tents were bearded ladies, tattooed men, two girls joined at the hip.

Violet tugged Grace's gloved fingers. "My head hurts," she said. "I want to go home."

"We've not seen the mermaid lady yet," said Nora. Violet's cloudy eyes brightened. And so Grace let Nora lead them into the last tent. The mermaid was a young woman with legs fused like a tail. She wore a dress of silver and blue. Grace felt sorry for her, but the woman's smile reached her eyes. Her hair was long and golden, flowing loose over her bare shoulders. The girls stared, entranced.

Harris clutched her cheeks in his hot palms. "Grace, you need to listen to me."

But she was not listening. She was in the sideshow booth beside the mermaid. Opposite her sat the bear man; covered in hair from head to toe. Grace stared into the wildness of his brown fur and searched out his eyes. He stared back. Perhaps a smile. Impossible to tell.

She turned suddenly. The girls were gone. She felt hot with dread. So unlike them to run away. She shoved aside the flap of the tent and raced into the crowd. People were queuing at the ticket booth, others huddled at the river's edge, waiting for a waterman. Grace glimpsed the two blue coats several yards ahead of her. They were swept up in the sea of people elbowing their way toward the pier.

"Violet!" she called. "Nora!"

One of the girls slipped through the crowd towards Grace. Her face was stained with tears.

"The bear man," she was sobbing. "I don't like the bear man."

Grace grabbed a fistful of the blue coat before the crowd could swallow her again.

A shriek. People crammed onto the pier. Grace shoved her way through. Women were screaming, waving at the filthy brown river. The waterman tore off his coat and dived beneath the surface, searching for the second blue coat, the second fur trim. The girl left on the riverbank was screaming and crying, pulling on Grace's skirts, hysterical. Grace realised she didn't even know which one had fallen. She pushed back the bonnet of the child at her skirts. She had Nora. The river had Violet.

Grace felt her legs give way beneath her. Harris dropped to the floor beside her and clutched her hands. "Gracie, this man, he didn't kill Violet. Violet died eighteen months ago at the sideshow at Bankside."

She opened her mouth to speak. Couldn't form the words. "No," she managed finally. "You're lying."

But then she was home in Covent Garden, she and Harris screaming at each other, breathless with grief.

*What were you doing taking her out? What in hell were you thinking?*

And, God, she was curled up in Harris's bed, her head pounding when she heard the police come to the door, telling him his daughter's body had been found at Saint Katharine docks at the low tide.

Her breath began to race. Cold sweat prickled her skin and she thought for moment she'd be sick. She leapt to her feet and raced upstairs to the girls' room. Ribbons hung from the ceiling like threads of cloud. The walls were draped in fabric; the breeze making them ripple like sea. Dolls peered out of the darkness with unblinking eyes.

One bed.

The room asymmetrical, incomplete. Grace threw open the wardrobe. One coat. One pair of boots. One quilted bonnet.

"Where are her things? Where are Violet's things?" She felt Harris's hands around the tops of her arms. "She was here," she managed. "In the forest. And here in Hobart Town. I held her hand as we walked down the gangway. I put both of them to sleep at the end of our bed in the lodging house." Her voice began to rise. "I was up all night with her those first few weeks because she was afraid of the forest."

Harris nodded. "She's been with you since the voyage, hasn't she? That's when you began to see her again." He pushed her damp curls off her forehead. "Doctor Barnes, he says she came back to you because you feel responsible for her death. He says you let yourself believe she was real because it was the only way you could cope with losing her."

"No." Grace shook her head. "No, no, no. That ain't what happened. He killed her. He's a monster. He's done such terrible things. Inhuman things."

Harris squeezed her hands. "We buried her at Saint Mary's beside her mother. It rained that day. I know you remember it. The day we left London, Nora didn't want to go without Violet. You told her they were twin sisters and they would always carry a part of each other with them."

"No. I never said that." She remembered that morning with such clarity. Buttoning Nora into her dress, tying her bootlaces. She remembered the clatter of hooves on stone, the rotten smell of the river. Nora on one side of her in the carriage to the docks, her forehead pressed against the glass. "Goodbye blue house," she was saying. "Goodbye market, goodbye church..."

*Where was Violet?*

Grace tried to sift through her memories. "Violet was sitting next to you in the coach." But she could hear the waver in her voice. Felt the solidity of her world dissolve to nothing.

*No Grace, I never saw the girl. I'm sorry. I saw you sitting on my chopping log singing to the empty night and I saw you curl around your cloak as though it were her body, but I never saw your Violet.*

*I can imagine the way you'd look at me. Don't be like that. Perhaps I ought to have told you from the start; that you lost her that day because she was never really there. That your mind let her go because you were finally ready.*

*But who am I to bring your madness to the light? Would you have believed a word that had come from me? The man who sees his murdered mates when he looks behind the shadows? The man who builds an extra stool to convince himself he won't die alone?*

# XXVII

Hobart Town Gazette
Friday 25th June 1824

*'The circumstances which were understood to have accompanied the ... crime had long been considered with extreme horror. Reports had associated the prisoner with cannibals; and ... our eyes glanced in fearfulness at the being who stood before a retributive judge, laden with the weight of human blood and believed to have banqueted on human flesh! We heard His Majesty's Attorney General ... entreat the jury to dismiss from their minds all previous impressions against the prisoner; as however justly their hearts must execrate the fell enormities imputed to him, they should duteously judge him, not by rumours, but by indubitable evidence.'*

Grace lay on her back, staring at the dancing ribbons. Left to right, left to right. The coloured walls moved like sea.

Her thoughts were slow and cloying. She felt Harris's hands in her hair and at once she was back in the blue house, curled up in his arms and tasting his breath. And from Covent Garden to the wild snarls of the Derwent Valley. She felt the wind in her ears, rain on her skin. Saw curls of smoke twirl upwards, disappearing into a silver black sky.

The thought yanked her back to reality.

She had pulled the trigger.

She leapt to her feet and rushed dizzily down the staircase. She heard Harris behind her, calling her name. She snatched the candle from the hallstand. At her feet sat Howell's money pouch. The pistol lay in the corner of the room.

Heart thumping, she held the candle up to the wall, running her hand across the surface and searching for a bullet hole. Nothing.

A sound of horror came from her throat. At her feet: a splatter of blood. Sickness rising, she followed the ruby trail out the door. Across the porch. And then nothing. She stumbled down the path and stood at the edge of the stone fence. The land opened out before her, orange in the dawn. She walked towards the silhouetted trees.

"Alexander?" Her voice sounded out of place among the jagged birdsong. She crouched at the edge of the forest, hiding her eyes against her knees.

She'd needed to escape her guilt. Pin the blame on another. And who better than a man who had done the unthinkable?

Her accusation had been all too easy to believe.

Guilty of murdering a girl he had never even seen.

She felt Harris's hand on her shoulder. "Come inside, Gracie, please. You need to rest."

She shook her head. "I got to find him."

"No. Nora's gone long enough without you. You've got to be there when she wakes."

Nora clutched Grace's hand and launched into a whirlwind tour of the house. A bedroom full of rainbow ribbons. Dining room with an enormous pine table. Two guest bedrooms with canopied beds, Harris's study, kitchen and laundry. A sitting room with textured gold wallpaper that glittered in the morning sun. He'd transplanted the luxury of their life in London. Built walls against the wilderness.

Grace peered through the sitting room window. The edge of the forest was visible, but it felt distant. A land on the other side of the glass.

"Papa said we can get a piano. So we can sing our songs again." Nora pulled her from room to room, her bare feet pattering on the floorboards. "It's much bigger than the blue house. And much prettier too. Don't you think?" She grinned. She was every inch her sister. Every inch that little white face that had appeared between the reeds of the river. But older, Grace realised. Her baby blonde hair beginning to darken. A front tooth missing. The Violet of her visions had been frozen in time; the fragile four-year-old she'd been when she had died. But here was Nora, almost six and a half, long-legged and tanned. Cheeks flushed with sea air.

Grace smoothed Nora's flyaway hair and kissed her forehead. "Yes, mopsy," she said. "It's much prettier."

That morning, she'd opened the wardrobe and found her neatly pressed dresses hanging beside Harris's waistcoats and shirts. On the clothes, she could still smell the smoke and rose air of the blue house. Here was everything she'd brought from London, waiting patiently for her return. A belief she'd come home.

Nora led her through the kitchen where a teenaged girl in an apron and mop cap was slicing ham for breakfast. She bobbed a curtsey and eyed Grace curiously.

"This is the cellar," Nora announced, heaving against a heavy door beside the range. "Papa built it to store the wheat. There's ghosts and monsters in there."

Grace steered her away from the door. "Don't go looking for ghosts and monsters, mopsy."

"Nora knows she's not allowed down there, doesn't she?" Harris's voice boomed into the kitchen.

Nora huffed dramatically. "Yes Papa."

He herded her out of the kitchen. "Why don't we show Nanny Grace the farm instead?"

They walked past lush green paddocks dotted with sheep, past the wheat growing in neat arrows. Magpies carolled above their heads. The farm smelled of damp earth and animals. And there, behind it all, was the clean eucalyptus scent of the bush.

Harris reached tentatively for Grace's hand. "The crop is growing well. Better than I could have hoped in its first year."

"You're a farmer," she said. "Just like you said you'd be."

Harris smiled. "It helped to keep my mind off things," he admitted. "Losing yourself in physical work helps you forget yourself a while."

Nora clambered onto the paddock fence and leant over to touch one of the sheep. Grace waited for Harris to scold her— *that's not the way young ladies behave*—but instead he smiled faintly. He had grown a little rough around the edges, she noticed. Marching about unshaven, his hair curling past his collar, rolled-up sleeves and no coat or hat. The thought made her smile.

"I was so afraid you'd never see all this." Harris stopped walking. "Gracie, I know I haven't always treated you right and I'm sorry for it. More than you could know."

Grace watched Nora edge her way along the fence. For a long time, she said nothing. "You're ashamed of me," she said finally. "The Wintermans..."

"Ashamed? No, Gracie." He turned her to face him. "You weren't well. I didn't want those people judging you... I..." He pressed his lips against hers. "I love you. And as soon as you're ready, I'm going to make you my wife for real."

Grace felt her thoughts knock together. Unravelling. Untangling. She let Harris hold her. Felt her desire for him creep towards the surface.

"I shouldn't have taken Violet out that day," she said. "She was complaining her head hurt. I took my eyes off them for a second. They never ran away before."

Harris turned to face her. There was kindness in his eyes. Sadness. "It wasn't your fault. It was a terrible accident. That's all. Please, Gracie, you have to believe that."

She couldn't look at him. "I'm so sorry, James. For Violet. For running away. For bringing those men here. I'm so sorry for everything."

He said nothing, just combed his fingers through her hair, caressing her jagged curls with the same tenderness he had when they'd reached her waist.

"Violet is dead," she said after a moment.

"Yes."

"She drowned in the river. In London."

Harris nodded.

"Violet never came to Hobart Town with us."

"No. It was just the three of us."

"She was with me, James. She was so real. I could see her, hear her. I carried her on my back. Plaited her hair." How could she trust her eyes now? Her ears? Her hands? She ran her fingers over the smooth fence posts. Over the fabric of her skirt. Over the coarse skin on Harris's knuckles. There was solidity to everything. It wasn't enough. How was she to know where reality ended and dreaming began?

Harris pressed his forehead against hers. "I was a fool to leave so soon after her death. I know that now. I just thought it would be the best thing for all of us."

She'd felt his hot breath against her skin like this, those terrible sleepless nights after Violet had died. Nights when he would climb to her attic room and slide into her bed. He'd said barely a word about his daughter, the way he had never spoken of Charlotte. But that one night, his blood hot with brandy and his cheeks wet with tears, he'd pulled her towards him.

*I don't blame you,* he'd said. And: *I love you, Grace.*

"She came back to you on the ship, didn't she?" he asked. "That's when you began to see her again."

*Yes. On the ship.*

They'd been at sea, how long? Perhaps a fortnight, but already the days had begun to blur. After three days confined below decks, the sea had calmed enough for them to venture out. Grace held Nora's hand as they climbed the ladder from their cabin to the deck. They stood in the sunlight, letting sea spray arch over their heads.

Nora gripped the gunwale, giggling and shrieking. Grace felt numb.

She had not let herself feel anything. Violet's death, Harris's impulsive proposal, a voyage away from all she knew. Blocking it out was the only way she could survive. This ship, this eternal sea, the *great adventure* Harris wouldn't stop speaking of; it was all an illusion. A dream from which she'd one day surely wake.

Nora turned to Grace, her cheeks glittering. "I'm all wet, Nanny Grace!"

They'd been sweltering in the same clothes since London; much of their luggage packed into the hold. Grace had kept them clean as best she could, sponging their salty clothes each evening and draping them over the bunks to dry. She took Nora into their cabin and pulled out the small trunk they had stowed beneath the bunk. She found Nora's fresh dress and helped her out of her wet clothes. Grace took her back onto deck with Harris and returned to the cabin to find her own dry things.

She rifled through the chest. A clean shirt and coat. Petticoat and drawers. And then, a flash of pink silk. Grace

pushed the clothes aside curiously, peering at the unknown item. Whatever it was, Harris must have packed it himself.
She lifted out the rose-coloured bundle. A pink shawl that had belonged to Charlotte. Wrapped inside was Violet's rag doll.

Grace stared at the doll. It peered back at her with its one bewildered eye, its hair still in the lob-sided plait Violet had made the morning of the sideshow. Grace felt a great surge of grief well up inside her. She hadn't known Harris was even aware of the doll's existence.

In that chest was everything he was unable to say. All the sorrow he was unable to express. Grace saw then that Van Diemen's Land wasn't about adventure. It was about escape. A journey to the other side of the world in hope it might dull the pain of so much loss. Fifteen hundred acres so Harris might never again walk among the ghosts of his wife and daughter.

All her fault. The girls were her responsibility and she had failed them. Failed Charlotte and Nora and Harris. Most of all, she had failed Violet. The guilt was an unbearable, physical weight. She couldn't think, couldn't speak. Just took the doll to her bunk and stayed there until she slept. In the morning, the girls came to find her. Two of them, hand in hand.

*Get up, Nanny Grace. Come and see the mermaids.*

Grace looked back at the house. The sandstone glowed gold in the sun. Each brick was flecked with the marks of the government man who had moulded it. Arrows, patterned scoring. A signature design for each convict so their labours might always be remembered.

She'd been convinced she'd visited this house. Convinced she'd crept inside and plucked Violet from her bed. But of course, it could never have been. When last she had been on this land, they had been living in a tent amongst nothing but foundations. Harris had taken her to New Norfolk so their life might not be built on illusions.

"Tell me about the journey," Alexander had said one night as they sat by the fire in the clearing. "From the asylum back to Hobart Town to get the girl. How did you find your way in the dark? Why did no one see you?"

"I don't want to talk about it."

She had lain awake that night and tried to sift through her memories. Days and nights of hills and mountains and tangled trees. She didn't want to talk about the journey, she realised, because she remembered nothing of it.

*Castor oil and laudanum*, she had told herself. *That's why I don't remember.*

But now she saw the truth. She remembered nothing of the journey because it had never happened. She had run from the asylum straight into the forest and passed out from the drugs. When she had woken, Violet had been sleeping beside her.

*Is that really what happened, Grace?*

She'd taken Alexander's words as an accusation. But now she saw with clarity. He'd just been trying to blow away the smoke in front of her eyes.

# XXVIII

She searched the city. Futile, she knew, but how could she just stand still and hope?

Harris walked beside her as she charged out of the farmland and down Campbell Street. Horses pulled coaches up the hill, sprays of brown earth flying from beneath their hooves. Outside the penitentiary, a gang of workers were being led into the city, arms laden with shovels and picks. Chains clattered around their ankles. They turned to watch Grace as she passed. She crossed the road and hurried away.

She wove through the streets towards the battery, calling Alexander's name. Stopped at the bottom of the hill and looked out over the harbour. The sea glittered in the morning light. Whaling ships dotted the anchorage and people swarmed the wharf. Carts rolled between the docks and the markets. Rhythmic hammering came from the convicts building the warehouses in Salamanca Place.

Hobart Town felt different. Pulsing and vibrant as though a cloud Grace hadn't been aware of had suddenly been lifted. Around her were sailors, convicts, soldiers. The city was noisy and smelled of the sea.

How vivid her memories of this place were; her boots crunching on the cobbles, Violet's hand in hers. But there was a new haziness to these recollections, as though Violet knew she didn't belong in the memories. As though she knew Grace had walked unaccompanied down the gangway of the *Duckenfield*. Slept alone on that bed of ferns. Whispered bedtime stories to empty shadows.

Grace followed the docks, squinting in the sun. A great ship lay at anchor off Hunter Island.

*Enchantress*, the signs at the ticket office announced. *Hobart Town to London.*

*Imminent departure.*


They walked wearily back to the house. Lost in her thoughts, Grace barely noticed the silence until Harris said: "Police."

She stopped walking. Her chest tightened.

Harris strode up the front path. The two officers slid from their horses and looped the reins around the posts of the verandah.

"Good afternoon, sir," said one. "We're looking for Grace Ashwell."

"I have told Doctor Barnes I do not wish to return my wife to the asylum at this time," said Harris. "Thank you for your concern, gentlemen, but it's unnecessary. She's recovering well." He glanced over his shoulder at her. "Go inside, Gracie. Everything's all right."

"I'm afraid we need to speak to her regarding another matter," said the sergeant. "The murder of two British marines and the escape of the convict Alexander Dalton." He turned to Grace. "A word, Miss Ashwell, if you please."

"This is mistake, surely," said Harris. "A murder?"

"Is there somewhere we can speak in private?" asked the sergeant.

Grace's heart pounded. "Of course. In the dining room—" She led the men inside and looked about her, flustered. "Where's the dining room, James?"

Harris took her arm, holding her back. "You'll not speak to her anywhere! My wife was not long ago a patient at New

Norfolk asylum. She is no state to be interrogated by you!"

"Indeed. An escapee of New Norfolk, I believe."

"It's all right, James," said Grace. "I want to speak to them. It's all a mistake, ain't it? Like you said. Best to be cleared up nice and quick. Now please, where's the dining room?"

Harris led them resignedly down the hall. "I insist you let me stay with her. She is not of sound mind. She cannot be held responsible for her actions."

"Very well." The sergeant gestured to the chairs around the dining table. "Sit. Please."

Grace strode up to him. "The things I said to the police in Hamilton, they were all lies. I didn't know what I was saying. I— He never did any of them, I swear it. I—"

The sergeant cleared his throat and Grace fell silent. He nodded to the chair. "Sit, Miss Ashwell. You'll speak when spoken to."

She sat stiffly. "It's Mrs Harris." She reached beneath the table for Harris's hand. "You don't need to be here," she murmured.

"Of course I do."

Grace said nothing. She felt hot and sick, her skin damp beneath her bodice. She looked back at the officers.

"The Richmond Police apprehended a couple for bushranging yesterday on the road to Launceston," the sergeant began. "They gave us your name in exchange for a lesser sentence. Told us about your time in the Hamilton settlement and said you knew how to find Alexander Dalton."

Grace felt a flush of anger. "They're lying."

"You sent the police after Dalton, did you not? You witnessed him kill two British marines. And you had reason to believe him responsible for the disappearance of Violet Harris."

"I was wrong. He didn't have nothing to do with that, you understand me?" She shook Harris's wrist. "Tell them, James. Tell them what happened to Violet."

"She's telling the truth." Harris's voice was husky. "My daughter died in England a year and a half ago."

The sergeant gave him a fleeting glance. "My sympathies." He walked slowly towards Grace. "Six days ago, members of the Clyde Field Police unearthed the bodies of two marines on the south bank of the Styx River. They were following the directions you provided them with on the twelfth of September this year."

Heat flooded her. With the marines' bodies found, Alexander was as good as hanged.

"These same policemen then apprehended Dalton, but he escaped into the bush."

Grace felt the sergeant's eyes on her, but refused to look at him. She kept her eyes fixed on the garish floral walls. What god-awful taste in wallpaper James Harris had, she thought dully. "The man you caught," she said, "the one you think is Alexander Dalton, he never killed no-one. He was just a free settler who liked his own space. I heard of them bolters from blasted Molly Finton at the asylum. She told me about the convict, Alexander Dalton, who disappeared in the bush all those years ago. But I'm telling you, the man I were with in Hamilton, that weren't him. The madness in me made a monster of an innocent man."

The policemen exchanged glances. Grace felt her story tangling. She drew in her breath. "They found a shawl buried with the marines. Grey wool with a hole in one corner."

The sergeant nodded.

"That's my shawl. The marines that got killed were sent to find me and put me back in the asylum."

*She cannot be held responsible for her actions.*

She looked the sergeant in the eye. "I was the one that killed them. I weren't of sound mind."

"What?" demanded Harris. "*What?*"

The sergeant chuckled. "One of the marines died from a blow to the head," he said. "An attack like that was not delivered by a woman your size. It was delivered by a man with military training, like Alexander Dalton."

"Let me speak to her." Harris pulled her to her feet. "I told you she's not fit to be interviewed."

"Mr Harris—"

"James," Grace hissed. "Please."

The sergeant stood, blocking the door. "It may also interest you to know we found traces of dirt inside the nose and mouth of one of the victims. He was still alive when he was buried. Were you aware of that?"

Grace's stomach turned. She remembered the heat of the blood soaking through the shawl. Remembered the dull thuds as the bodies rolled into their graves.

"Alexander Dalton is one of the most troublesome convicts we've had in this colony, Mrs Harris. If you ask me, you're lucky to have come away from this ordeal with your life. Are you aware of the horrific crime Dalton and his fellow escapees committed eleven years ago?"

Grace said nothing.

"I don't know what in God's name would possess you to protect him like this, but I can assure you that if you stand before a jury and claim to have murdered these soldiers, there's not a man in the colony who will believe you. Perhaps you were not of sound mind when these men were killed, but your husband's decision not to return you to New Norfolk suggests to me that you now are. Therefore you will be held fully accountable for any statements you make today." He hovered over her. "Perjury in a double murder trial will get you a sentence at the Female Factory if you're lucky. The hangman if you're not. Although there's always the chance the judge may see a lifetime of incarceration at New Norfolk as the most suitable sentence."

Grace clenched her jaw. The sergeant stepped aside and let Harris pull her into the hallway.

"This is who you're so desperate to find?" he hissed. "This is who was in my home?" He stood close, his voice low and taut. "You told me you'd been in Hamilton with the couple that brought you to Hobart Town. And now I hear you've been out in the wilderness with this madman? And that men have been murdered?"

She turned away from his furious eyes. "I knew what you'd think if I told you."

"What I'd think? Grace, I've no idea what to think. Why in God's name are you protecting this animal?"

"He saved my life, James. Several times over. And I sent the police after him for Violet's murder."

"He deserves to be hanged!"

"I can't just turn him in after all he did for me!"

"It's too late. You've already turned him in. And if he truly killed these soldiers, you were right to do it. Lying for him now can't save him. It will only bring you both down."

Tears spilled suddenly down Grace's cheeks. "It can save him. It can. If I'm found guilty of these murders, I can't be punished."

"The only thing they're going to find you guilty of is perjury. Nora and I have just got you back. Are we to lose you again because you hold yourself responsible for the actions of some degraded convict? If this is what you believe is right, then I fear I've brought you home too soon. Perhaps I ought to send you back to New Norfolk."

"No." She wiped away her tears with the back of her hand. "I carry Violet's death with me every minute. I couldn't bear to carry Alexander's as well. I can use this madness to save him. Let a little good come from all that's happened."

For a moment, Harris said nothing. He stood close, his breath fast and hot against her nose. "I understand," he said, his anger fading slightly. "Truly. But you won't escape your guilt this way. You'll escape it by being a good mother to Nora. By letting us finally start our life out here. Don't we deserve that? After all we've been through?"

She looked up at him. His face had narrowed; the lines around his eyes become more pronounced. Threads of grey had appeared at his temples. Hobart Town had been nothing of the fresh start he had hoped it would be; anyone could see that by looking at his face.

Grace blinked away a fresh rush of tears. "I've got to try and save him."

"No." Harris's voice hardened. "You don't. A man like this ought to be shot on sight. Your duty is not to him. It's to Nora and I." He gripped her shoulders. "I love you, Grace. Nora loves you. I don't want to have to put you back in the asylum. But I won't hesitate to do what I think is best for you. And what's best for my daughter."

Grace swallowed hard. She nodded. *Understood.*

She wiped her eyes and walked back into the dining room. Sat at the table opposite the policemen.

"I hope your husband has talked a little sense into you," said the sergeant. He leant across the table. "Who killed the marines, Mrs Harris?"

She stared into her clasped hands. "He did. Alexander Dalton."

"Would you be willing to state this in a court of law?"

"Yes."

"Good." The sergeant folded his arms across his thick chest. "Now, where can we find him?"

How to find a man who'd hidden from the world for more than a decade? She'd been looking in the wrong place, she saw that now. She'd have to bury herself in that tunnel of trees she'd once been afraid of. Enter the forest on the fringe of Harris's land. Return to the wilds where she'd found him the first time.

"You can't," Grace told the sergeant. "He's too good at hiding."

# XXIX

*They've been walking for sixteen days. Macquarie Harbour lies behind them and who knows what lies ahead. The last of the bread they'd eaten days ago. Dalton's steps are crooked with hunger. His vision is blurred, his throat dry.*

*"Dalton," Greenhill whispers. "Dalton, the flogger."*

*What if it were to end here? What if he is the sacrifice? There would be no guilt, no hiding. A better end, surely.*

*Dalton stands, looking Greenhill in the eye. "Do it," he says.*

*The axe comes towards him slowly. Why so slow? What's wrong with time?*

*No. If it ends here, he will never climb the mountains and see the valleys unfold below him. Never stand beneath an electric black and gold sky. He will never feel Grace's heart thud beneath his fingertips, or hold her in the night. And Dalton realises he'd go through all that guilt and hiding a hundred times over so he might know how it feels to come back to life.*

*He lurches away from Greenhill's axe. Feels a shock of pain as the blade clips his shoulder.*

Dalton heard himself cry out. The pain at the top of his arm, it was different now. Sharper, hotter.

And the light. That was different too. Flickering lamplight, not purple dusk.

*Grace.* Why was Grace here? There was blood on her cheek. What was she doing amongst all this carnage? He couldn't make sense of it. He reached out, sure she'd vanish if he touched her. Her skin was hot beneath his fingers.

"I told him to kill me," he said. "But then I thought of you."

"You're delirious," she said. "Try not to move. I got the ball out. Lie still and let me sew it up." She crouched over his shoulder, needle in hand. She frowned in concentration, lamplight flickering on her cheeks.

Dalton swallowed a grunt of pain. He felt lines of blood run across his bare chest. "Greenhill. He was here. But you made him leave." Relief washed over him. The men were in their graves. And the blood on his hands belonged only to him.

Grace cut the thread carefully. She rinsed her hands from a canteen of water and wrapped a length of cloth around his upper arm. Her cheeks were pale. "I watched the doctor stitch a cut on Violet's head once," she said. "I done the best I can." She dampened a second cloth and wiped it across Dalton's chest.

He tried to sit. She held a hand against his other shoulder.

"Stay down. I think I made it worse."

Dalton grabbed a fistful of her chemise and drew her towards him until her face was inches from his.

She swallowed hard. "Violet... I let her drown... in London. I know you... I don't understand, Alexander. Why let me believe you killed her?"

"You found out what we did to Bodenham. You were going to leave me. But I knew you'd stay if you thought I could show you where Violet was buried."

She sat. "Christ. Do you have any idea of the trouble—"

Dalton said to the sky: "And I thought you'd stop blaming yourself if you believed I was responsible."

Grace closed her eyes. "Alexander..."

"I don't want you to carry that guilt every day," he said. "It will destroy you."

"So you thought you'd carry it for me?" She shuffled on the earth and lay beside him. "That was really bloody stupid."

"Aye," said Dalton. "I know."

"But it was also very kind." She turned her head to face him. "Can you ever forgive me?"

He smiled. She'd searched for him. She knew what he'd done to Bodenham and still she'd come. Trying to fix her own mistakes, yes, but the fact she cared enough to ask his forgiveness brought him a step closer to his own absolution. He touched the coil of hair that hung across her cheek. She flinched and pulled the coin pouch from her bag.

"The *Enchantress* leaves tomorrow for London. You need to be on it. The police will find you here. You got to go, you understand me?"

"Come with me. You and the girl. Like we planned."

She looked away. "You're better off without me, Alexander. Look at all I've done to you. You're lying here in pain. The police know you're alive. They want you on the scaffold."

"It was my fault. All of it."

Grace said nothing. She busied herself wrapping the scissors and tweezers in the remains of his shirt. "I'm not going back to London," she said finally. "I'm sorry."

Dalton felt suddenly cold. Sick. "Is it because of him? Harris? That bastard who locked you up?"

"He was right to do it!" she cried. "You know that! You knew that all along! And you let me go on planning my miserable revenge! Did you never think to tell me the truth?"

"Tell you?" He laughed coldly. "In what world would you have believed such a thing from a madman like me?"

"You're no madman," she mumbled.

Dalton sat, dizziness coursing through him. Pain radiated down his arm, across his chest. It seared through his head, tangling his thoughts. "Christ," he hissed. "What in hell have you done to me?" He clenched his teeth. "You trying to finish the job?"

"I'm sorry. I'm sorry. I knew I couldn't get help. I—" She fumbled in her bag and pulled out a bottle. "Drink this. It'll help a little." She held the flask to his lips and drizzled brandy down his throat. He felt warmth rise in his chest. The pain remained hot and sharp. Grace pressed a hunk of bread into his hand. "Eat. You're weak."

He chewed slowly, not taking his eyes off her. "He know you're here then? Creeping around the bush at night?"

She looked away. "Of course not."

"So you'll give up home for a man you speak to in lies."

"I've told him no lies." She picked at the blood beneath her fingernails. "He's sleeping."

Dalton glared at her. "He lays a hand on you. He takes away your chance to be a mother. All those things you said he's done. Were they real?"

"Yes. But I know he'd never set out to hurt me. And I know he'd never hurt his girls. Violet weren't even there!" She sighed. "He's no angel. But I'm not neither. And, Alexander, you of all people should know the value of forgiveness."

"Forgiveness? I'd kill him for what he did to you. I'd make him suffer like he made you suffer. And then I'd kill him."

Grace swallowed hard. "You don't mean that. I know you don't. You wouldn't do that to me." She met his eyes challengingly, waiting for his anger to fade. Or perhaps explode. "Why do you despise a man who wants nothing but the best for me?"

For a moment, Dalton didn't answer. Finally, he said: "I hate him because you love him."

Grace let out her breath. "Well. At least now we're getting somewhere." She stood and brushed the leaves from her skirt. Held out her hand. "Stand up."

"What?"

"You can't stay out here. Not in this state. I'm bringing you back to the house. And tomorrow I'm going to take you to the harbour. See you get on that ship."

Dalton began to laugh, slowly, without humour. "You want to take me back to your house? You want to lead me straight to him?" He stood slowly, shakily. "As you wish, my Grace."

Her jaw tightened. She slid his battered coat over his shoulders. "I can't leave you here. Not after all you've done for me." She picked up the lantern and the shadows shifted. "Please don't make me regret it."

Grace shouldered open the door of the cellar and helped Alexander down the stairs. She left him sitting up against the wall and hurried through the dark house, gathering up food and blankets. She returned with her arms full and lit a candle. In the orange light, she could see blood splashed across her skirt. She pulled off her soiled clothing and tossed it beside Alexander's bloodied shirt. She crouched at his side in her petticoats. "I've brought you food and water. A little brandy. You need anything else?"

Alexander said nothing.

Grace tensed at his silence. She wrapped the blanket around his shoulders. "I need to trust you. Please. If you truly care for me, you'll stay down here and not let no one see you."

"He'd never forgive you for keeping me here."

"No." Grace stood. "He would never forgive me."

She climbed the stairs, heart thumping. Glanced back over her shoulder. "There's good in you, Alexander. I know it. Please don't let the darkness win."

She pulled the cellar door closed. Stupidity, she knew. But how could she leave him at the mercy of the forest?

She crept up the staircase, her neck and shoulders aching with tension. Nora's bedroom door hung open, the ribbons motionless in the still night. A girl sat in the middle of the room, clutching a rag doll to her chest. Grace tiptoed towards her.

The scarred forehead.

Grace's breath left her. "Violet?"

The girl turned and smiled. "Yes, Nanny Grace?"

Grace's eyes overflowed with sudden tears. "I thought you were dead. The sideshow…"

"I liked the sideshow," said Violet.

Tears dripped from Grace's chin. She knelt on the rug, afraid to touch Violet in case she vanished forever. "You disappeared. Why did you disappear, angel? Was it because of Alexander? Did he scare you?"

"I thought you wanted me to leave. You said you wouldn't carry me anymore."

Grace stifled a sob and pulled Violet into her. Clung tightly in case she should ever slide away from her again.

"Grace?" Harris's voice in the doorway made her start. "What are you doing?"

"Violet," she whispered. "Violet, angel, it's Papa."

Harris knelt beside them.

"James, it's Violet. See?"

Harris sucked in his breath. He lifted the lamp to the little face on Grace's shoulder. Now she was sleeping. Now the scar on her forehead was gone.

"It's Nora, Grace. You know that. Violet is gone." A tremor in his voice. He lifted his daughter from Grace's arms and laid her back on the bed. Grace stayed on the floor, staring at the rug.

She had seen that scar. Heard that little voice.

She felt suddenly cold. She wiped her eyes with the back of her hand. "Yes," she said, forcing a steadiness into her voice. "Nora. Of course." She heard the clunk and groan of the New Norfolk water pipes. She stumbled to her feet. "I was dreaming, that's all. I was sleepwalking or something. James... I—"

Harris kissed her forehead with unnerving kindness. "I dream of her sometimes too."

But he wouldn't look her in the eyes.

# XXX

The cellar door creaked as it opened. Dalton squinted. A silhouetted figure stood at the top of the stairs. A girl.

"Are you a ghost?" She gripped the bannister and edged towards him. "I told them there was ghosts down here! And monsters."

"Aren't you afraid of ghosts?" asked Dalton.

She shook her head. "I'm not afraid of anything." She peered at him with wide blue eyes, a spellbound smile in the corner of her lips. A messy blonde plait hung down her back, loose pieces clinging to her cheeks.

So this was the face Grace had seen in the river. The face that haunted her. It was like looking into her mind.

"Is it morning?" he asked.

The girl nodded.

"Where's Grace? Tell her to come and see me."

Nora shook her head. "I'm not supposed to be down here. And besides, she can't."

"Why not?"

"Because she's going away again."

Dalton stood, clutching at the wall to keep his balance. Pain shot through his shoulder and made his stomach turn. "Away where?"

"To the place."

Dalton felt his breathing quicken. "Why?"

Nora shrugged. "Papa said."

He reached into the pocket of his coat and handed her the carving of Grace. She peered at it curiously.

"Do you like it?"

She nodded.

He took it back and slid it inside his pocket. "I'll make you one of your sister."

"My sister is in Heaven," she said.

"I need you to bring me some things. A piece of wood. And a knife. Can you do that?"

A nod.

"Good." Dalton stepped towards her and she shuffled backwards. "Go on now. Quickly. Before someone catches you here."

"I'm sorry, Gracie," said Harris, pacing across the parlour. "Believe me, this is as hard for me as it is for you."

Grace sat on the couch and chewed her thumbnail. "I doubt that."

Harris knelt in front of her. "This is for the best. You know that as well as I do. I wanted you home with me so badly I refused to see you were still unwell." He brought her hand to his lips and kissed it. She pulled away quickly before he saw the bloodstains from the previous night she'd not managed to remove.

"Violet is gone," she said. "I know that. Please don't send me back to that place."

Harris sat beside her on the couch and sighed. "You can't spend your life seeing ghosts. Please, Grace. Just go and get your things."

The maid was dragging a trunk out of the bedroom. She

smiled awkwardly at Grace and bobbed a curtsey. "You need help with anything, Mrs Harris?"

Grace shook her head stiffly.

"All right, ma'am." The trunk thudded as the girl dragged it down the stairs.

Grace opened the wardrobe and yanked two of Harris's clean shirts from their hangers. Waistcoat, scarf and a heavy woollen overcoat she hadn't seen him wear since London. Gloves, neck cloth, scissors. If she was to be locked back up, she'd at least make sure Alexander got away.

She ran downstairs with the clothes in her arms and tried to slip through the parlour.

Harris stood suddenly. "What are you doing with my clothes?"

She tried to edge past him. "I'm sorry, James. I'll explain everything, I swear it. Just not now. I can't."

He rubbed his eyes. "Go and get in the carriage." He took the bundle and placed it on the side table. Grace hid her hands hurriedly in the folds of her skirts. Harris frowned. He took her hand and turned it over in his. Faint brown blood was streaked across her palm.

Harris looked up slowly. "Grace?"

"Don't go with him."

She whirled around. Alexander walked slowly towards them, a kitchen knife in his fist. His greatcoat was buttoned loosely over his bare chest. "Come with me."

Harris face darkened. "Jessie!"

The maid hurried inside. Her eyes widened in shock at the sight of Alexander.

"Get my pistol," said Harris. "From my desk drawer."

Jessie thundered up the stairs. Grace took a step towards Alexander, holding out her hand for the knife. She stopped abruptly.

A girl in the corner of her eye.

She glanced out the window. Beside the chopping log sat Violet, Rosie in her lap, building a bed of leaves as she had done in the forest. Grace felt heat flood her.

The maid returned breathlessly and Harris snatched the gun. "Go for the police, Jessie. Now." He glared at Alexander. "Grace? You would risk your life for this monster?"

"He ain't no monster."

"The police sergeant told me about this dog, Grace. He's done more than kill those marines. He's done things no right-minded human would ever consider."

Grace stood protectively in front of Alexander.

Harris let out a humourless chuckle. "You know. You know what he's done and still you're trying to save him."

She met his eyes. "I'm still trying to save him. Because if he's hanged it will be my fault. And I ain't living with any more death on my conscience."

"How dare you think of this bastard's death in the same way as my daughter's! You'll be doing the world a service by seeing him hanged."

Anger bubbled inside her. "He saved my life. Ain't that worth nothing to you?"

"And what about the lives he's taken?"

"There's good in him. I know it. He's a decent man."

"A man? How can you see a scrap of humanity in a beast who's done what he has?"

Grace's voice began to rise. "How can we ever know we wouldn't have done the same? I know what damned, desperate things a person will do to survive. How do you know where you'd draw the line?"

Harris stared, his eyes on her like she was a stranger. Outside the window, Violet made the doll dance on her knees.

Grace looked away hurriedly. Perhaps New Norfolk was where she belonged, washing away this ghost girl in a flood of icy water.

Harris turned to Alexander. "Get out. You may have fooled my wife into thinking you're a decent man but I have no such illusions."

"She's not your wife."

Harris raised the gun.

Alexander smiled crookedly. "I'm just a wild animal you got to shoot, aren't I?"

"You expect anything less than to be shot like an animal after the things you've done? You don't deserve to be treated like a human."

"Grace treats me like a human."

"Grace is delusional. But she'll soon see you for the beast you are."

Alexander's eyes shifted. "Tell him he's wrong. Tell him, Grace."

"Don't shoot him, James," she said huskily. "He's leaving. He's going to get on that ship and leave before it's too late. Ain't that right, Alexander?"

Harris stood with the gun poised. "Against her better judgement, Grace seems to care for you greatly. Out of respect for her, I'm not going to shoot you like I ought to. But you leave my house this instant. Get on that ship and leave our lives."

"Grace?" said Alexander. "Is this what you want?"

"Give me the knife," she said. Alexander hesitated, then pressed it into her palm. She turned to Harris. "And the gun."

He didn't move.

"Please James. You told me you weren't going to shoot him." She held out her hand. Harris clenched his jaw, then passed her the pistol. "Thank you." She placed the weapons on the table. Nudged the pile of clothes towards Alexander. "Tidy yourself."

Alexander opened his mouth to speak, but said nothing. He slid off his coat and eased himself into the clean shirt, stifling a grunt of pain. He looped the neck cloth awkwardly with one hand. Grace stepped forward and tied it carefully at his throat. She took Harris's gold threaded waistcoat from the table and slid it over Alexander's shoulders. Buttoned it down his chest. She smelled brandy on his breath. The bush on his skin. She could feel Harris's eyes burning into the back of her. She picked up the scissors and trimmed Alexander's beard until it lay close against his chin. The scissors squeaked and clicked noisily in the silence. Black hair fluttered to the floor. Grace slid the gloves into the pocket of the clean greatcoat, along with a flask of brandy from the side table. She handed the coat to Alexander.

"You got to leave us now," she said. "Please." She stepped back, feeling Harris's hand circle her upper arm. Alexander hesitated. Then slowly, without a word, he turned and began to walk towards the door. Grace stared at him until he disappeared.

Harris stood silent for a moment. He began to pace, his boots clicking across the floorboards.

Grace leant her hot forehead against the window. She felt a deep ache for the loss of Alexander, for the loss of Harris that would surely come. She closed and opened her eyes, willing Violet to disappear. There she stayed on the grass beside the chopping block, blanketing the doll in leaves. Grace looked away.

Silence hung between them.

"I always considered my girls very lucky to have you as a

mother," Harris said finally. "I always believed they could do no better than to be raised by you. This defiance you have, this determination, I always thought it a positive trait. But I suppose we can see now where your loyalties lie." His voice began to rise. "For you to harbour that monster while my daughter slept upstairs!" He swung a wild arm across the table and sent a vase crashing to the floor.

Grace said nothing. How could she find any miserable justification?

Harris rubbed his eyes and looked back out the window. "Where's Nora?"

"Nora?"

He opened the window and shouted into the garden. That look on his face, Grace had seen it before. Seen that panic, that desperation, the day she'd come back from the sideshow. With the police and without Violet.

Rosie lay abandoned beside the chopping block, the leaves scattered by the swirling wind.

"She was right there," he said. "Playing with Violet's doll."

# XXXI

"Where is it?" the girl demanded.

"What?"

"The wooden doll of Violet. You said I could have it if I came with you and didn't make noise."

Dalton hesitated. He looked up as Grace approached, her yellow dress bright against the shadowy forest. She shoved aside the hungry undergrowth.

"Nora!" she cried. "Get here now!" She snatched the girl's wrist and glared at Dalton. "Stay away from her!"

"She came to me."

"Like hell she did."

"I had to see you."

"Christ, Alexander, the police are on their way here. Don't you understand that?"

"I can't go without you."

"Well you'd best find a way. You ain't a dead man no more. I've caused you nothing but trouble. You're far better off without me."

"No." He clutched at her collar. "You brought me back to life. I'm so grateful you found me. I thought I'd survived, but all I was doing was waiting to die." She was laced into an embroidered gown, her hair swept back neatly. Where was his Grace with muddy toes and smoked meat in her fist?

He yanked out the comb holding up her hair, trying to bring her back to him. Hair fluttered around her cheeks. He could see the faint scar on her chin, could feel her heart thudding beneath his fingers.

Her, with her messy curls and tartan cloak, she'd reminded him there was a scrap of humanity left inside him. Reminded him that even though he'd done things no one dared speak of, there was a part of him that was still a man. How could he give her up?

"You woke me," he said. "Without you, I'd still be lying in that hut grunting at the shadows."

"I tied the noose for you, Alexander! How do you think the marines found those bodies? Because I told them where to dig! I may have brought you back to life, but I did it in the worst possible way!"

"So you'll stay in this Godforsaken prison and let him lock you up? Never see London again?" He shook the money pouch in front of her face. "A way home, Grace. Today." She closed her eyes.

*Yes, my Grace. A way home.*

Distant voices. Movement in the bush. She turned suddenly.

"Christ," she hissed. "Harris will find us here. He has the gun. You got to leave, Alexander. This second. Get on that ship before it's too late."

She began to march through the bush, clutching Nora's hand. Dalton lurched after her and pulled her back to him. "Did you ever ask yourself why Violet left when she did?"

Grace let out her breath. Squeezed her eyes closed. "She left because I was ready." Her voice caught in her throat.

"She left because you were free of *him*!" Dalton hissed. "Because it was just you and I out there and the rest of the world fell away. You know I'll never judge you for what you did. But he'll wake every morning and at your face and remember how you let his daughter drown."

Grace's eyes flashed. "Damn you to hell." Her glance fell suddenly to the clearing. A glassy, vacant expression passed across her face. Dalton felt a smile in the corner of his lips.

*Well now...*

"You still see her."

"No." A tremble in her voice. "No. She's dead."

He followed Grace's line of sight. "Where is she? What is she doing?"

"Nothing. She ain't doing anything." She blinked back tears. He stood close to her.

"I see them too. The dead. In my hut. In the forest. I see Bodenham, who I used for my own survival. And I see Greenhill, the one who made us do it. They're a reminder of what we've done. I tried to take it away for you, but I know now that was foolish. It will always be inside you. Harris will never understand. But I do. We need each other, my Grace."

She glanced over her shoulder as the voices grew louder.

"Nora!" Harris was calling. "Nora, where are you my love?" And: "Show yourself Dalton, you dog."

He grabbed Grace's chin and turned her to face him. "You want to spend your life rotting amongst the lunatics? Have your senses washed away under those water pipes?"

A warning shot exploded into the sky. Grace clamped a hand over Nora's mouth. She glanced at Dalton. "Harris has the carriage ready. If we take it, we can get to the docks in time. But we got to go now."

Sullivan's Cove was bustling. Coaches crowded Davey Street and streams of passengers hauled trunks and duffel bags towards the docks. The sky had darkened.

Black clouds drooped over the harbour.

"Leave the carriage here," said Grace. "We've got to hurry."

She slid from the coach and lifted Nora out after her. Alexander climbed down from the box seat. In Harris's clothing, he could almost pass for a gentleman. Grace felt underdressed beside him in her dirt-streaked dress; her hair unpinned, no bonnet or cloak. She touched his elbow. "How do you feel?"

His cheeks were pale beneath his beard. "Tomorrow I'll wake and see something other than this cursed outpost of the world." He smiled faintly. "I've never felt better."

"There's a flask of brandy in your pocket," said Grace. "It'll ease the pain. But you got to wait til we're on the ship. You got to have your wits about you til then. You can't hold the stuff no more." Do you have the money?"

Alexander nodded.

"Go. Three tickets. I'll get the luggage." She hauled the trunk Jessie had packed out of the carriage. It thumped noisily against the cobbles. She gripped its handle with one hand and Nora with the other. Began to walk toward the checkpoint. The wind swirled and whipped her hair against her cheeks.

"Nanny Grace? What are we doing?"

She forced a smile. "We're having a great adventure, mopsy." She glanced edgily over her shoulder. No sign of Harris. How long until he found the carriage gone? Enough time for the ship to cast off her moorings and slide through the heads?

Alexander handed their tickets to the guard. Out before them stretched the rocky outcrop of Hunter Island where the ships lay at anchor. On the right of the island was a dark wooded whaling vessel with try pots lined up across the deck.

On the left, the bustling migrant ship *Enchantress*. And behind, fifteen thousand miles of ocean that would sweep them back to England.

Grace stepped onto the stone causeway that wove through the shallows towards the island. Water licked at the edge of the walkway, washing over her boots with each swell. She'd walked this narrow path, hemmed by sea, almost a year ago. Traipsing into Hobart Town with Harris and Nora. She'd been disoriented and scared. Now she saw things with clarity. Her fear replaced by determination.

They reached the tiny island and walked up the gangway of the migrant ship. The sailor at the gunwale heaved Grace's trunk onto the deck. People swarmed; sailors in white slops, passengers with bags slung across their shoulders. Laughter and nervous chatter. Shouted instructions to the crew.

Grace glanced sideways at Alexander. When had he last been among so many people? His shoulders were hunched, eyes at his feet. She touched his arm in a gesture of solidarity.

They were herded down a narrow staircase into the steerage passage. Men to the left. Women and children to the right.

"Go," Grace told Alexander. "Before Harris comes looking." Passengers pushed past them, chatting, laughing. "We'll find each other once we're at sea."

Alexander nodded. He turned and walked slowly down the passage.

"Nanny Grace?" Nora tugged her hand. "Are we going back to England?"

Grace's throat tightened. "No, mopsy. But Alexander is." She ushered Nora towards the staircase. "Quick now. We got to get off the ship." A woman with two children in her arms shoved past her. All these people would soon see London. They'd go to church at Saint Mary's. Buy fruit from Leadenhall. Walk down Maiden Lane and see the blue house filled with a new family. Grace felt an ache of longing. She pushed it away. She needed to look forward. Escape the past.

"Grace?"

She turned in dread at the sound of Alexander's voice.

"What are you doing?"

She stepped off the staircase. "I'm sorry," she coughed. "It was the only way."

Alexander's eyes darkened. "He's going to send you back to the asylum. He's going to put you under those water pipes until you scream."

"Perhaps. But perhaps that's what I need. I don't want to spend my life seeing the dead." She touched Alexander's cheek. "I'm sorry I lied to you. But you got the chance to start again. You got to take it."

He gave a faint nod. His fingers found hers and she squeezed gently. His hand moved up to her wrist. And then he was pushing her backwards, backwards until her spine was hard against the bulkhead. He forced an arm across her chest.

She tried to pull away. "Alexander, let go of me."

His grip tightened. Grace glanced over his shoulder. The passage was bustling. Cry out and men would come running. But so would the marines.

"Harris will have found the carriage gone," she hissed. "He knows about this voyage. He's going to come for Nora. And he's going to bring the police. You've got to let us go."

"I can't." His fingers clenched her wrist and she swallowed a cry of pain. "Without you there's just emptiness and death. But you keep those dead men away."

The ship groaned loudly. Shouted instructions to the crew filtered below deck.

"You were willing to take the blame for Violet. You were willing to make such a great sacrifice for me. Why are you doing this now? After so much selflessness?"

His lips were close to her ear. "Because selflessness brought me nothing but a bullet in the shoulder. It's not human nature to be selfless. You know that. We can try, but deep down, there's that animal need for self-preservation. That need to put ourselves first."

"Then put yourself first!" cried Grace. "Let me go and save your own bloody life!" The anchor groaned beneath her feet. A flurry of children raced back to the deck, trailed by their mothers.

Grace's breathing quickened. "Nora," she said. "You got to get off the ship. Run. Tell them you got to get off."

Nora began to cry.

"Go, Nora. Now."

She pulled Grace's skirt. "I want you to come too."

Grace met Alexander's eyes. She sucked in her breath and shoved against his injured shoulder. Alexander cried out, his arm falling from across her chest.

"Run, Nora. I'm right behind you." Grace looked back at Alexander. "I'm sorry. I'm so sorry." She backed away from him and ran up the staircase. Heard footsteps behind her. She kept running. Alexander chased her up the stairs. Across the deck. Back onto the island. Grace stopped at the bottom of the gangway and collided with the whalers who were loading supplies onto their ship. She fell to her knees, gasping for breath.

"I'm sorry," said Alexander. "I can't do this without you." Sweat glistened on his forehead. The shoulder of his coat was black with blood.

Grace climbed to her feet. "Hell," she said. "You bloody fool." She reached into his pocket and pulled out the flask of brandy. "Drink this. It will help the pain." She held it to his lips, a hand behind his head stopping him from pulling away.

A long drink. A big dose. She kept pouring it down his throat until he began to cough. She tossed aside the flask and gripped his arms. Began to walk, forcing him backwards. He stumbled dizzily.

"Do you really want to look at me every day and know I was wishing I were somewhere else?" She stepped onto the gangway, guiding him carefully. "Wishing I were with another man?" One step. Two steps. She looked into his eyes. "Let me go. Be the good man I know you can be." Another step and his boots thudded onto the deck. He stumbled to his knees and gripped the gunwale. Grace knelt on the gangway and clutched his head in her hands. Tears slid down her face. "There'll not a be a day I don't think of you." She held her lips against his bristly cheek. "Goodbye Alexander."

He looked up at her with cloudy eyes. Nodded slowly, defeatedly. "Goodbye, my Grace."

She turned and walked down the gangway, unable to look back. She grabbed Nora's hand and hurried towards the wharf.

And then the clattering of footsteps. Shouting voices. Marines poured onto the island and shoved Grace aside. Guns out, they charged up the gangway and onto the *Enchantress*.

Grace's legs gave way and she sunk to the ground, her dusty skirts pooling around her. Nora scrambled onto the wharf. Harris snatched her into his arms; clung to her in a desperate embrace. His face was lined and shadowed with weariness. He ran a hand through Nora's tangled blonde hair. Kissed the side of her head once, twice, three times. He looked over his daughter's shoulder at Grace.

*I'm sorry,* said his eyes. And: *what choice did I have?*

# XXXII

Grace packed her things. Took her earnings from Harris and hauled her rose-scented dresses to the Female Factory.

"You got experience with children, then?" the overseer asked, leaning back in her chair and wiping beads of sweat from her forehead.

Grace nodded. "Yes ma'am."

The overseer sniffed loudly. "You want to work in this hell hole, the job's yours." And like that, she became an attendant in the factory's overflowing nursery.

The building was hidden in a valley at the southern end of town. The women woke, worked and slept in the constant shadow of the mountain. The place was damp and grey. Immune to the approaching summer.

Here, there was no Violet. She wouldn't come to a place like this. Here, reality was clear and cold.

Separated too early from their convict mothers, the babies were sickly, weak and needy. The hours were endless and exhausting, but kept Grace's mind from dwelling on all it had lost. She felt needed, worthwhile, like she might do these wretched children some good and begin to atone for her mistakes.

She found Maryann Fairlie in the laundry.

"You." Maryann tossed the sheet she was scrubbing back into the tub and looked up and down at Grace's uniform. "You're here by choice? What's the matter with you?"

"Just want to be of use." Grace drew in her breath. "Are you all right? You and the children? Healthy?"

Maryann nodded faintly. "Daniel. Did they find him?"

Grace wound her finger around the corner of her apron. "Last I saw he was headed into the bush."

"Stupid scab," said Maryann. "Don't he know there's nothing out there? A man can't survive in that place. Not alone." A tremor in her voice. She plunged her arms back into the tub and began to scrub at the sheet with a new ferocity. Suds cascaded down her legs. Finally, she turned back to Grace. "And your Alexander?"

Grace looked down. "Alexander's gone."

"Well," Maryann said brassily. "If you ask me, it's good riddance to the both of them." But her eyes met Grace's in a moment of unspoken grief. She turned back to her washing. "I'm being assigned. Housekeeper to some toff in Campbell Town. Emma and her brother are being kept here at the factory. They'll be sent to the orphanage when they're old enough."

"I'm sorry," Grace mumbled.

Maryann put a soapy hand out and grabbed her wrist. "You'll take care of them, won't you? You'll make sure they're all right?"

"Of course."

"And you'll tell them about me? Only the good things. Don't tell them what I done to end up here. Just tell them I love them."

Grace nodded. "Every day."

She'd been at the factory a week when the overseer found her in the nursery. She took the baby from Grace's arms. "You got a visitor."

Harris was waiting outside the front gates. He wore a frock coat and silk scarf and looked very much the man who had plucked her from the mop fair so many years ago. Grace drew in her breath and stepped through the gates.

They stood without speaking for a long time, the silence loaded with regret and unspoken apologies. Finally, Harris cleared his throat.

"There's a piano at home, Gracie. I hoped you might like to play it."

She managed a faint smile. "Home, Sweet Home."

Harris took a step towards her and tucked a strand of hair beneath her cap. "What are you doing working in this dreadful place?"

"I need a purpose. Something to put my mind to."

The guard at the entrance eyed them curiously. Harris took her arm and led her away from the gates. He stepped close and touched her cheek. "Come home and put your mind to being my wife. To being Nora's mother."

"You want me around Nora?"

"She needs you. So do I." He smiled. "You're part of my great adventure. Come home with me now and I'll see you never need work another day in your life."

"I want to work," said Grace. "It's all I know. I can't just sit on my arse and watch the grass grow."

Harris grinned.

"I'm needed here in a way I ain't needed in that house. You got Jessie doing all the chores. Nora's off at school. And James, all those empty rooms you built, they'll never be filled with children."

Something passed over Harris's eyes. And in that second, Grace saw he too carried his own deep guilt and regret. He took her hand.

"Grace…" He swallowed hard, then met her eyes hopefully. "So perhaps you'll come back to the house with me tonight. And when you're due to work with these children, I'll have Samuel bring you back in the carriage. What do you say?"

# XXXIII

He'd seen the marines coming.

So the gallows would find him at last. With blurred vision, he watched Grace disappear down the path towards the docks. *A fitting end*, he thought. She who had brought him back to life would also bring about his death.

He crawled across the deck on his knees. Tried to stand, but the brandy she had poured down his throat tangled his thoughts and weakened his legs. The ship felt unfamiliar. Distorted.

Here came the marines; their footsteps like drums. Dalton's heart raced. He readied himself. The soldiers charged onto the ship on the other side of the island.

Dalton looked about him. And he understood.

This was no migrant ship. A face peered down at him; the brown, sea-hardened face of the whaling captain.

Grace had seen the marines coming too, he realised. Backed him up the whaler's gangway and given him the chance to disappear.

Dalton heard the marines shouting to the crew of the *Enchantress*. He dug into his pocket and pulled out Howell's pouch, still half full with coins. He tossed it at the whaling captain's feet.

"Hide me."

The whaler picked up the pouch and peered inside. He pulled Dalton to his feet and shoved him into the forecastle.

When the captain opened the hatch, they were at sea.

Dalton stepped out into the grey light. Hobart Town was disappearing. Fading into the shadow of the mountains and being pulled slowly over the horizon.

*New Zealand*, the whalers had told him. *Tahiti*. Strange names, foreign places.

The sky opened. Down fell great marbles of rain that made the deck slick and black. Thunder rolled and jagged light ripped through the clouds.

Dalton gripped the gunwale and turned his face to the sky. He closed his eyes. Imagined the feel of her hands on his cheeks, the blade of his whittling knife sliding through his beard. With each roll of the ship, the distance between them grew. He felt an ache deep inside him.

But then he opened his eyes. Van Diemen's Land had vanished behind a sea of cloud. Dalton felt a great weight dissolve from his chest. A heaviness that had been there so long he had ceased to be aware of it. He felt his breathing deepen. Felt the memories of seven dead men begin to lose their sharpness.

The haunted forest had released him.

Around him were men who knew nothing of his past. Ahead of him, an endless ocean on which Alexander Dalton and his crimes might finally be forgotten. A great wave of gratitude swept over him.

*So, my Grace,* he thought, *you couldn't save your Violet, but you have saved a man who had been beyond redemption.*

*Remember this. And find something close to absolution.*

# Historical Note

When Alexander Pearce was captured in 1823 and confessed to the murder and cannibalism of his fellow escapees, there were few in the colony who believed him. Pearce's confession was seen as an attempt to cover for his mates who most believed were living as bushrangers. Pearce was sent back to Macquarie Harbour where he escaped again, this time with young convict Thomas Cox. When they reached the Gordon River, Pearce discovered Cox was unable to swim and killed him with a swing of the axe. Pearce then gave himself up at the King River (near present-day Strahan) and was discovered to be carrying human flesh in his pocket. Pearce was taken back to Hobart Town for execution and his tales of cannibalism began to be taken seriously.

There are several inconsistencies in the confessions of Pearce, mostly concerning Alexander Dalton. In his first confession at Macquarie Harbour, Pearce claimed there had been four murder victims; Thomas Bodenham, John Mather, Matthew Travers and finally, Robert Greenhill, whom Pearce had killed single-handedly to avoid his own murder. According to Pearce, the remaining three escapees— William Kennerly, Ned Brown and Dalton— fled the group in fear for their lives with an intent to return to Macquarie Harbour.

Kennerly and Brown returned alone to the harbour and were either unable or unwilling to shed any light on why

Dalton was no longer with them. They died of starvation soon after arriving.

But in Pearce's confession to the Rev. Thomas Knopwood in Hobart Town, the details of the story had changed. It was Dalton, Pearce claimed, not Bodenham, who had been Greenhill's first victim, chosen as the sacrifice as he had been given the role of a flogger at Sarah Island.

What could have accounted for such glaring discrepancies in Pearce's confessions? Had the details been blurred by time and immense mental and physical stress? Or did Pearce feel the need to confess his involvement in a fifth murder before his impending execution? Either way, it seems impossible we will ever know the true fate of Alexander Dalton.

What we do know is that Dalton, a twenty-three-year-old soldier from Kilkenny, Ireland, was transported to Van Diemen's Land in 1820 after being sentenced at Gibraltar Court Martial. In this era, no records were kept of convicts' initial crimes (to avoid judgement in the colonies from overseers and fellow prisoners), but as Dalton received a sentence of fourteen years' transportation, we can surmise he committed a crime such as robbery, forgery or assault. Such crimes were often punishable by death, with many convicts — possibly including Dalton— having their sentence transmuted from hanging to transportation.

On his arrival in Van Diemen's Land, Dalton committed a series of misdemeanours, including perjuring against his fellow convict Michael Flannagan in 1822. It was for this crime that Dalton was sent to Sarah Island Penitentiary at

Macquarie Harbour, which would forever be known as one of Australia's most brutal penal settlements.

Grace, Harris and all other characters are purely fictitious.

# Acknowledgements

The biggest thank you to my brilliant sister Ally for all your help in writing this book. Thanks so much for your psychology expertise, advice, feedback and for trawling through possibly the worst first draft of all time!

To my editor, Heather Osborne, thank you so much- your help and feedback has been invaluable.

Huge thanks also to Julia Kolyanda for the fantastic map, Adrijus for the beautiful cover and Chloe Keegan, my Gaelic dictionary.

To Danny Ransley at the National Trust of Australia, thank you so much for your enthusiasm, knowledge and for taking me back to 1830s Hobart.

Finally, thank you as always to Davis for your endless support, advice and boy-reads. Sorry there was no shanking…

# About the Author

Johanna Craven is an Australian-born writer, pianist and film composer. She has lived in Melbourne and Los Angeles and is currently based in London. She loves ghost hunting, cooking (and eating) and playing the Celtic fiddle.

Johanna released her first novel *Music From Standing Waves* in 2015 before signing with Endeavour Press for her second book *The Devil and the Deep Blue Sea*.

Find out more at www.johannacraven.com.

CPSIA information can be obtained
at www.ICGtesting.com
Printed in the USA
BVHW080602240221
600896BV00002B/136